I0589874

Murder, She Blogged:
Just in Time

Doris Gaines Rapp

Huntington, Indiana

Copyright 2020 Doris Gaines Rapp

Daniel's House Publishing
Huntington, Indiana

Huntington, Indiana 46750
website: www.dorisgainesrapp.com

For information contact: Daniel's House Publishing at: danielshousepublishing@gmail.com

Doris Akers Lyrics, "Sweet, Sweet Spirit." Chapter 26. Copyright 1965, Manna Music Inc. Burbank, CA.

Cover design is stock imagery from @Dreamstime.com. Put in place by @Debi Lindhorst/The Type Galley.

Library of Congress Control Number: 2019918611

ISBN: **ISBN-13: 978-0-9988590-5-7**   (paperback)
ISBN: **ISBN-13: 978-0-9988590-7-1**   (eBook)

Dedication

Dedicated to all those who create programs and inventions for the betterment of others. Rarely do their stories appear on the news, or are lifted up in social media, newspapers and periodicals. They live quietly to be a blessing to their neighbors. The mystery and intrigue in this fictional story reveal the complicated society in which people live, and yet they still choose to "do good."

Acknowledgements

Thanks to my writers group, Soli Deo Gloria (to God be the glory) for their encouragement, positive suggestions, and willingness to share their faith in God.

Many thanks to Vicki Borgman for her time and creative energy in editing, *Just in Time.*

Debi Lindhorst at The Type Galley in Warren, Indiana can do all of the tech stuff I can't do. Thanks for rescuing me, Debi.

Many, many thanks to my readers who waited for the sequel to *News at Eleven.* I've heard other authors say how important their readers are. I agree totally. I write because I love to write. Finding people who enjoy reading what I've written is a second blessing.

Table of Contents

Character Introduction

We first met **Clisty**, **Jake**, **Becca** and all the other Indiana characters in a serialized novella written for **Glo Magazine** in 2015. The four installment cozy mystery short novel, expanded to *News at Eleven – A Novel*, became the prequel to the series, **Murder, She Blogged**. Book one in the series, *Just in Time*, is here for your enjoyment. You will enjoy reading the entire series as we release them. Happy reading.

Chapter 1
The End of the First

It's amazing how a well-planned life can suddenly turn upside down. All you thought you wanted lands on the bottom, while great new opportunities you never even considered end up on top demanding your attention. That may be okay for the adventurous, but Clisty Sinclair was not a thrill seeker or even a toe-in-the-water tester. She needed control over every small detail. Life was safer that way.

As Clisty sat in the courtroom, her mind wandered from the trial that only awaited the verdict, rambled here and there, and landed on a new tagline for her blog. She hadn't created the tag, but the few words given to her would change her life.

Christy's career in a Fort Wayne newsroom shot up so rapidly she sometimes felt like she couldn't hold on to the rocket. Now, the national office of the Bryson News Network offered her an unbelievable opportunity as a result of the amazing success of her blog, *Crime Beat*, an in-depth investigation of current crimes with write-in help from her followers. Some long days, she wrote her blog in the middle of the night. Regardless of her commitment to blog writing, she was always able to maintain her position as second chair of the 6 o'clock and 11 PM local newscasts. Her blog was so successful, the readers of *Crime Beat* actually helped find Faith Sterling. With 100,000 followers, many feedback messages came in. One reader responded to Clisty's post with information on Faith's actual location. It was from that clue that Clisty and her group traced the kidnapper to his home location. Faith was home now and Ezra Treadway's trial was finally over except for the jury's verdict.

The tagline the network sent her was only one of the distractors that flitted through her head late that afternoon. The new position also included the problem of relocating. If she accepted BNN's contract, she wouldn't live in Indiana anymore, just as Faith finally came home. The awesome opportunity was in New York City. Clisty's response was now required.

"Think it over, Clisty. Talk to your lawyer and people you trust. But, I'll have to have an answer. The deadline is immediately following the reading of Treadway's verdict." The phone conversation with the network CEO was warm but business-like. "If you choose to accept our offer, I want you to read the new tagline I sent you at the close of the 11 PM news and also place it at the end of the blog you'll post later this evening."

Clisty wasn't sure she liked the too-cute arrangement for something as important as a complete life change. It seemed like the network was making a game out of the profoundly sharp detour her career would take. If she used the tagline the network wrote for her, it would mean she accepted BNN's offer.

Truthfully, something else also demanded her mental and emotional attention. Sergeant Jake Davis was new to Clisty's world. He warmed her heart whenever she saw him. What would happen to their budding romance if she moved away?

After *Crime Beat* hit it big, creative ideas raced through her head. Clisty knew, creativity creates creativity. However, the Network's offer tied her artistic thoughts into knots. They were interested enough in her joining the flagship station in New York and producing her blog, the network offered the additional gem of publishing the true crime books she wrote. But, the move, six-hundred eighty-three miles away from all those she loved and those she was beginning to care for, was the grit that might tarnished the shine.

She slouched a little in her seat and sighed. She was only beginning to unwind from the grind she had been under in recent months. Clisty had researched, tracked, and traveled out of state to aid in the capture of Ezra Treadway. He was the man who broke into Clisty's home, snatched Faith, and tried to kidnap Clisty too, eighteen years before.

The network's biggest enticement was their offer of her own segment, *Stories from the Heartland*, on their national weekly TV program, the American News Magazine. She would travel around the country, interviewing and lifting up people who create programs and ideas to benefit others. Still, how could Clisty keep up with all that?

As Clisty shifted in her seat, she noticed everyone in the Allen County Superior Courtroom seemed as anxious and restless as she, waiting for the jury to come back. Faith sat beside her, wringing her hands in rapid twists. Clisty's eyes panned up and down her row. It was obvious others were holding their breath, too. She saw some observers sitting with their eyes closed and their hands folded in prayer. Others appeared to depend on luck, crossing as many fingers as they could. One man ahead of her had his head down, rocking back and forth in a near fetal position. Silence hung like a thick fog over everyone in the gallery. Clisty sat halfway back from the witness stand, behind the bar of the court, with a good view of everything.

When the side door burst open, the bailiff brought Treadway back in and sat him beside his attorney. Due to the defendant's uncontrolled outbursts during the trial, handcuffs dangled from his wrists.

All of Clisty's reflexes snapped to attention when he looked her way. She sat up rigidly. Feeling Faith's body tremble, she whispered, "Treadway can't get to you. He may have been able to drag you away when we were both young; now, you have many friends in this courtroom to help you if he tries anything today. They'll take him out or tie him down if he flips into another tantrum."

As the jury returned, all eyes turned to the judge as he asked the anticipated question. "Mr. Foreman, has the jury reached a verdict?"

"Yes, your honor," the foreman stated firmly. When the judge handed back the verdict form, the foreman read, "In the matter of the state of Indiana against Ezra Treadway for the kidnapping of a minor, Faith Sterling, and transporting that child into Illinois, the jury finds Ezra Treadway—guilty. In the matter of the attempted kidnapping of Clisty Sinclair, the jury finds Ezra Treadway—guilty."

When those in the courtroom heard the foreman announce the guilty verdicts, it wasn't just Clisty's exhale alone that filled the room. A sigh of relief rolled across the gallery like the cleansing breath for God.

"Thank goodness," Clisty sighed and threw her arm around Faith's shoulder.

Faith sobbed. "The nightmare is over. I'm finally home."

"After eighteen years of captivity," Clisty whispered, "it will take a while for the idea of freedom to soak in. We were only nine years old. I still have horrible dreams from that afternoon … and I was the one who got away."

Faith dabbed at her eyes with a tissue then squared her shoulders. "Knowing Ezra Treadway will serve many years in prison, will be my only satisfaction. Well …" she smiled softly, "I did find love with their son, Steven. He was so gentle and loving. Then our daughter, Pooky was born. Even though Steven died, his love saved my life while I was locked up in that horrible house all those years."

As authorities started to lead Ezra Treadway away, he turned and hissed at Clisty, "I shoulda taken you, too. I woulda taught you to keep your mouth shut." Treadway's attorney tried to tell him something but Treadway jerked away, turning his back on her. When the guards firmly guided him from the room, Treadway jerked around and glared at Clisty again. "I woulda broken you!"

Clisty stared confidently at Treadway until he was completely out of the courtroom. She turned back and whispered to Jake, "After eighteen years, he couldn't break Faith. Why does he think he 'coulda' broken me?"

"I would place my bet on you any day, tough lady." Jake smiled warmly as he put his hand on her shoulder.

Chapter 2
The Man in the Suit

A stranger in an expensive black cashmere suit, black shirt and matching silk tie sat on a bench in the hallway just outside the courtroom. When Clisty and Jake walked out after the verdict came down, Clisty saw the man. He looked out of place. She had never seen anyone hanging around the courthouse dressed like him.

"Miss Sinclair?" the man gestured to her. "May I speak with you?"

Clisty was usually comfortable talking to strangers, but she never stepped away from a safe group to do so. Treadway, the one stranger in her life who changed her interactions with the world, left her leery of those she didn't know ... or left her wiser. She still wasn't sure. Turning back to Jake, she patted his arm. "Excuse me, Jake. Please, wait for me right over there. I'll only be a minute."

The man stood as she walked toward him. "I'm Victor Rogers, Vice President of BNN, Miss Sinclair," the suit-man explained.

"From New York City?" Clisty gasped.

"Yes. Our CEO, Mr. Funderbird, knew your decision was due as soon as the verdict was in, so he asked me to fly out to help you make it."

Clisty automatically threw her hands to her hips. "Just how are you supposed to help me make a decision about my own career?"

Rogers reached into a rich leather pouch and removed a manila envelope. "Mr. Funderbird realized you were conflicted over a point in the contract. Naturally, the two Heartland elements are still there, your crime blog and the stories segment for your spot on TV… no changes. He did change a major piece, however. Hopefully, it will make it easier for you to decide. He asked me to hand-carry the updated version so you can respond tonight as planned. Be sure to have your attorney look it over. The boss will be happy to work through any small items with him or her." Rogers handed the envelope to Clisty then reached out his hand. "I have a plane to catch. I'll see you when you come to New York."

Clisty's head was swimming. The man flew all the way from BNN headquarters to meet with her for a few minutes. "Unbelievable. Thank you, Mr. Rogers."

As Rogers walked away, Jake came back to her side. Putting his hand on her shoulder, he watched the man hurry down the steps. "Are you okay, Babe? Who was that?"

"He's the Vice-President of BNN, Gunny," she said, still in a blur. "We seem to be in the fast lane today." Looking down, she checked her watch. "We'd better go. I have to write a post for my blog yet this afternoon. The feed from here at the courthouse we filmed a little while ago is my contribution to the 6 PM news. I'll be in the studio for the later broadcast."

"What are you going to write?" He sounded concerned and supportive at the same time.

She stared off in the direction Rogers had walked as if still in a trance. Finally, she whispered, "I have no idea."

Chapter 3
The Beginning of the Second

Treadway's verdict was in. Clisty's hour of decision had come. Now the question was, would Clisty accept BNN's offer or not?

Victor Rogers had brought the amended contract. With the emotional day she had, Clisty hadn't had a chance to read it. Rogers said Mr. Funderbird would work through any small adjustments with Clisty's attorney.

After they left the Court House, Jake checked in at his office at the Fort Wayne Police Department and Becca stopped off at the TV station. Then, they met up with Clisty at her apartment to wait while she posted to her blog. Dan Drummond, the senior newscaster would handle the 6 o'clock news on his own. It was the news at 11 and the tag line she chose, that would determine all their futures.

There at her kitchen island, Clisty opened her laptop. She'd have to have silence so she could concentrate. She brushed off Becca and Jake's presence in the room with a dismissive wave of her hand. "You two stay over there on the couch and don't talk."

Jake and Rebecca Landers, Clisty's friend and news producer, said nothing. Becca did smirk a little at Jake. "A little bossy aren't we?"

"Not even a whisper," Clisty quipped as she looked up from her computer. Smiling at her safe apartment, she relaxed.

The minimalist decor ... no frills, no tchotchkes ... was everywhere, except on the mantle. The prayer angel she had gotten at church the Christmas after she turned nine spread her wings over the room from her little spot on the

17

corner above the fireplace. That year, her grandmother had chosen Clisty's prayer angel from the angel tree at church and Clisty had gotten Grandma's. Every day during the New Year, she prayed for her grandmother and Grandma prayed for her. Clisty certainly needed prayers that year. That was the year Ezra Treadway changed all their lives. Clisty smiled at the ever-present, always consulted prayer angel, and inhaled the promise of prayers answered.

Clisty glanced at Jake on the sofa across from her spot in the kitchen. She watched him fold his arms, slouch down on the sofa, and close his eyes. He looked comfortable in so many ways.

Staring at her computer, she knew this was the most important post the Super Blogger of Fort Wayne would ever write. Admittedly, Jake and Becca also had an interest in what she would post. To make her decision, she had to be able to think clearly.

With Treadway's trial just ending, Clisty's mind kept drifting away from her blog and back to Faith Sterling. Amazingly, it was just months before that evening that Clisty found Faith. The evening she first spotted her childhood friend, Clisty was behind the camera at WFTW-TV.

Clisty had lifted up a citizen whose private channel call-in homework assistance program had expanded to include thousands of children in Allen County. In addition to Clisty's broadcast duties that evening, Rebecca had planned to interview her in recognition of Clisty's own success in growing her blog to 100,000 followers.

During her interview that evening, Becca had reached over and patted Clisty's arm. "Those who follow you regularly at www.crimebeat.blogsmith.com have found your true crime blog fascinating. How do you do it?"

There at her kitchen island, Clisty's mouth turned up at the corner. Mumbling to herself she wondered, *"That's my question. How am I going to do it?"*

While Clisty was being interview that evening at the TV studio, a breaking news alert flashed across the studio monitor. It was a request from the police department to show the viewing audience a photo of a woman they believed may be a witness to a bank robbery. As the picture burst across the broadcast video monitor, Clisty froze, staring at the screen. "It's her. I know it's her," she whispered in shock.

Clisty's blog was the tool she used to help law enforcement solve many crimes. That evening, after the interview, Clisty called on her many followers to help find Faith and identify her kidnapper.

● ● ● ● ●

Crime

Beat

Friends, Faith Sterling is back. She is the woman whose face appeared on the news this evening. Police identify her as a witness in the bank robbery at Fort Wayne Bank on the north side of the city. The police are seeking your help in locating her. We must let Faith know it's safe to come in out of the darkness. We must find her, learn where she's been, and discover who took her. Research my friends. If you recognize her from the picture posted on the news alert this evening on WFTW, please message me.

| Share |

Contact: <u>*clistysynclair@ebox.com*</u>

● ● ● ● ●

In the convoluted case of the man who held up the bank, it turned out the robber had a long time connection with the man who actually kidnapped Faith. A tip from a blog follower broke the case. The team: Clisty, Jake Davis, Rebecca, and their cameraman Griff, tracked Treadway into Illinois where the kidnapper held Faith all those years. After authorities captured Treadway, Clisty blogged regularly as the kidnapping case progressed.

One of her blog followers messaged her one night about halfway through the investigation. "Clisty, Jamie Ireland, my cousin, shared your blog with me. Remember her? Jamie graduated from high school with you. I wouldn't miss one of your posts. I even got my boss, the CEO of BNN here in New York interested. You're in the big-time now, Clisty."

When Clisty found out one of her blog followers was Bradley Funderbird, her whole career path took a detour she never knew was ahead of her.

The large envelope suit-man gave her still lay on the kitchen island screaming for her attention. She knew she had to read it. Maybe BNN had withdrawn their offer. That would be a huge contract adjustment. But, Rogers said both Heartland pieces were there. She glanced over at the two on the couch. They fixed their eyes on their electronic screens as they waited for the blog post to appear. She reached in the envelope and pulled out the few pages. Reading it, she saw not much had changed, but there was one point that made her smile. Now, what was she going to do?

If she accepted Funderbird's job offer, that evening would mark the end of her solo ride as the Super Blogger of Fort Wayne. If she said "yes" to the multi-faceted contract offer, Mr. Funderbird would read her blog and know her answer. If Clisty signed off with her usual words of "Thanks" or "You guys are great," that would mean the answer was "No."

Crime Beat is my blog, my baby, she argued silently in her head. *I created it, sought out advertisers, did my own research, and wrote every post. Do I really want to be under someone else's thumb?*

That one sentence, the tagline Funderbird sent— "This is Clisty Sinclair, with *Crime Beat from the Heartland*"—would announce the re-launch of her blog. The newly offered contract would put *Crime Beat* under the financial backing of BNN, with all of their marketing skills and tech support. That wasn't all. They had also offered Clisty her own segment on BNN's American News Magazine, the *Stories from the Heartland* segment. That was the reason for the tagline Mr. Funderbird asked her to add at the end of the blog she just wrote. Holding her breath, she clicked the "enter" key on her laptop.

Clisty sat there a few seconds longer, letting the last posting experience be hers alone, even though Jake and Becca were just feet away. She knew the tagline gave her more opportunities than she ever dreamed of. Becca too had cash in this lottery of life. She had agreed to link her future to Clisty's as her traveling producer for the national TV segment — if Clisty decided to accept the offer.

Clisty heard Jake whisper something to Becca. Thankfully, his tone was low enough Clisty didn't really hear what he said. It was her moment and she would savor it for the little bit of time remaining in her quiet, Indiana life.

Becca's e-tablet and Jake's cell phone screens lit up seconds later with Clisty's post. Becca jumped up from the "isolation couch" and danced around the room. Clisty watched her prayer angel rock a little on the mantle. Jake smiled, but was less excited. Clisty hoped he would brighten when he heard the details of the amended contract.

"You did it!" Becca yelled. "Accepting your contract will give us all promotions: you, me, and your favorite cameraman, Clint Griffin."

"Too bad Griff isn't here," Clisty sighed. "His wife wanted him home tonight."

"Great going, Clisty!" Jake sang out as he circled over to the island and grabbed her off the bar stool.

With her eyes avoiding Jake's, she whispered, "Are you sure you're okay with this opportunity?"

"How could I deny you what you have earned? It's just that—"

"The move?" Clisty's stomach growled loudly. "Sorry," she apologized as she doubled over in embarrassment. "That rumble reminds me, I had no lunch. I didn't have a chance to finish my small cup of potato rivel soup over at the Courtroom Grill before Treadway's verdict came in this afternoon." She groaned a little and tried to ignore the growls from her mid-section.

"I was just thinking," Becca said as she tried to pull herself together. "Rather than being the only celebrity super blogger in town, you will explode onto the national stage by tomorrow morning."

"Oorah!" Jake shouted. "I'm on your side one-hundred percent, Babe."

"Thanks Gunny," Clisty smiled. She paused and studied Jake a moment. "Will I still be able to call you Gunny when I want to?"

"Sure, why not?" he shrugged.

"You don't like to talk about combat and your injury. I wouldn't want to draw unnecessary attention to you."

Jake cupped Clisty's chin with his hand. "Don't worry about it. I can handle any questions that may come my way ... or not answer any if I don't want to."

"Good," she said as she smiled, then dropped the topic.

Jake threw his head to the side and looked at Clisty cautiously. "When do you have to move?"

"Are you excited?" Becca jumped in, matching her excitement with Clisty's.

Clisty was glad Becca had changed the subject. She had to think about how she was going to discuss the move. "Yes, I'm really excited. I am so relieved Mr. Funderbird finally amended that original offer." Clisty looped her arm through Jake's. "Funderbird actually listened to what I said." Her eyes sparkled with excitement.

"What?" Becca's mouth flew open. "An amended offer? What does that mean?"

"That man in the fancy pants?" Jake stopped with his finger waving. "Rogers. What did he want?"

"He brought the new offer."

"Oh, yeah, here we go," Becca grumbled with her shoulders in a slump. "It's falling apart."

"No, actually it's coming together." Clisty threw her arms around Jake and nearly shook with excitement. "Mr. Funderbird said, I can continue to use Fort Wayne as my home base. I'll travel to New York for the shows in which my segment will appear, but return home when it's over. Blogging, research, writing, and planning will all take place here at home. I'll have a network liaison in New York to handle our mail, field interview suggestions, and make our travel and all other arrangements." She looked sheepishly at Becca. "But, I still have something to stew about. How am I going to research and track down a Heartland hero story every few months for the American News Magazine? I'm exhausted right now after just one story."

"Yes, yes, yes," Becca screamed, then stopped. "Well," she raised her eyebrows with a twinkle, "I'm glad Miss Obsessive-compulsive still has something to worry about."

"It wasn't just research and capture that kept you chasing Treadway, Babe," Jake reminded her. "A long time ago, Treadway attacked you, too. He grabbed you and Faith both when he broke into your home that day. You had to track that evil man down while carrying the weight of eighteen years of nightmares. That would exhaust anyone."

Clisty stole a look at Becca who was bending to pick up pillows strewn around the room. With Becca's gaze diverted, Clisty seized the precious moment and secretly buried her head in Jake's chest. "Is a whole new life really beginning, Gunny?" she whispered as she cuddled closer.

"It would seem so." Jake's soft breath warmed her neck. "The main question would be, is 'beginning' okay with you?"

In joy and confusion, Clisty admitted. "Oh yes," she softly gasped, then added, "I guess."

"You do look tired," Becca observed with a furrowed brow. "Are you going to take a nap before the 11 o'clock news, or have some supper?"

"Clisty and I have plans to go to dinner," Jake said with a smile. "Might as well go to bed exhausted but full." Jake put his arm around Clisty's shoulder. "Becca, we thought you and your husband might join us."

"Terrific! I'll give Jason a quick call." Becca reached in her pocket and pulled out her cell phone. She pushed a speed-dial key. "Hi, Honey. What ya doin'?" she asked as Clisty started to leave the room.

"I'm going to run in and change quickly," she explained as she slipped into the next room.

"You mean in your tiny-house bedroom?" Becca teased and then turned back to her phone call. "I'll dash home and pick you up. Be ready to go out to dinner."

"See you there," Clisty called after her. Clisty's so-called bedroom *suite* wasn't big, but not little either. It was more ... compact, just another room she wanted to keep free from clutter. She quickly took off the dress slacks she wore to the court house. Finger pressing the crease in her pants, she hung them on a clip hanger. When her stomach rumbled and grumbled again, she began to hurry. A fresh blouse was her pick for the top. New Levis, along with her Reeboks, were her other choices. Later on the news, she'd only be on camera from the waist up. She popped out of her room. "I'm ready! Let's begin."

Chapter 4
A Meal Together and a Plan

As Clisty and Jake rode down West Jefferson Boulevard toward Casa Restaurant, the street lights came on, brightening the redbud trees on both sides of the street that were in full bloom. They added splashes of purple to the darkening wooded areas along the road. Clisty smiled as the last of the setting sun danced in and out of the trees as they passed.

"Look, Jake," Clisty's voice was soft. "Spring has finally burst forth in all her glorious color. Shades of green are everywhere, on trees and shrubs, and look at the brilliant pastel of the flowers. It looks like a real crayon box full of magic." She folded down the visor to check her peach tinted lip gloss in the mirror. In the reflection, she saw Becca's car close behind.

At the corner of Jefferson and Engle Road, Jake pulled into the parking lot, turned off the ignition and came around the car to open the door for Clisty. Since they preferred to maintain the appearance of a purely professional relationship—a crime blogger with a direct line to the police department—they wanted to keep their budding romance to themselves. That night was a luxury for Clisty. Jake treated their dinner like a date.

The smell of garlic and freshly baked Italian bread drifted outside and greeted them as they entered the restaurant. Her last meal, if you call a few spoonsful of soup "a meal," was about 4 PM. Clisty's world stopped when the verdict came in.

Casa's dining room was full of hungry patrons twirling spaghetti artfully around their fork with the help of a skillfully placed spoon. Spices perfumed the air adding fragrance to the pictures of Italian villas with wide vineyards that hung on the walls. It seemed like everyone stopped what they were doing as the clatter of silverware gave way to low mumbles when Clisty walked across the room. Besides being a beautiful woman with dark blond hair, she had to admit she was becoming a local celebrity. She suddenly wondered how her personal life might change once she started broadcasting her segments on the American News Magazine. No more stealth shopping adventures around Fort Wayne.

Jake carefully selected a table in the back of the room. They both liked being out of the center of attention, in the background when they were out-and-about. Besides, a table in the middle of the room meant there was no solid wall to protect Clisty from someone who might approach her from behind. That was a hold-over-fear from when Treadway tried to kidnap her. Jake pulled out her favorite chair in any restaurant, the one against the wall.

Clisty was still experiencing relief following the early verdict on Treadway. The jury's deliberations had been short. She wished Jake would gather her in his arms and sweep her off her feet right there in the restaurant. But, all eyes were on them. Neither of them wanted their picture posted all over social media in the next few seconds.

Becca and her husband, Jason, walked in just as Clisty was fluffing her nest … adjusting her chair, straightening silverware, and repositioning her water glass several times.

"We're here," Becca sang out. "This is great." She smiled broadly as she and Jason sat down. "I have a feeling this is something more than a friendly dinner." Becca winked with sparkling eyes.

"Well … it is," Clisty drew out slowly as the server handed each a menu.

"Can I get you all something to drink?" The perky waitress asked with her pen poised for business. Everyone placed their order and the server withdrew from the table.

"*It is* … what?" Becca stretched the hanging sentence out with a wide expanse of her hands.

Clisty leaned forward, lowered her voice and tried to make up for the volume of nearby conversations with exaggerated pronunciation. "As you know, I'm supposed to leave for New York in the morning to talk to the network boss and sign my contract." She leaned her elbows on the table and placed her chin on her folded hands. "Becca, the network needs for you and Griff to come, too. Since I have chosen you as my local and network producer-director and Griff the cameraman, Mr. Funderbird thought it best for you two to make a network connection. Also, while we're in the east, we'll do a *Heartland* story in Connecticut before coming home."

"Really?" Becca let out a muffled squeal. Looking around to see who might be watching, she lowered her voice to a whisper. "Really?" She pretended indifference by mechanically cutting a piece of the restaurant's locally made bread and slathering it generously with butter.

"Yes … really," Clisty echoed with a giggled "And … Mr. Funderbird said you and I can bring our husbands, at the network's expense. I have none," she said as she took a breath, "but you do."

"So Jason can come with us?" Becca nearly choked on the bite of bread as she muffled a gasp. Looking at Jake, she asked, "What about Jake?"

Clisty lowered her head and whispered, "We're not married."

Jake reached for Clisty's hand. "It's all right, Babe."

"I have an idea," Jason suggested as he scooted to the edge of his chair.

"Here we go," the server placed full glasses and cups in front of them.

Jason watched the waitress leave, and then began again. "Becca and I both get a free ride to the Big Apple. I'm not even an employee. Becca has told me that you, Clisty, have certain standards of conduct that, well, harken back to days of old." He looked at his coffee cup as he tipped the drink toward him. "Our airfare and room will be paid for by the network. Jake, if you go, you will have to pay the full tab, room and airfare. Since Becca and I are lucky enough to have a free ride, we could pay for half of yours if you're willing to accept our offer."

"Gee, I don't know," Jake began as Clisty drew his hand closer to her and kissed his knuckles.

"Thank you Jason," Clisty said and then turned. "Please Jake. I would love for you to be there, too," she begged, clinging to his hand.

"No, Babe. I mean, I don't know about taking help with the hotel bill from Jason and Becca." He squeezed Clisty's hand. The right corner of his mouth raise in mischief. "I haven't had a vacation in three years. I had no place I wanted to go and no one I wanted to spend my free time with ... until you. I even kept on working through my paid vacations." He smiled again at Clisty. "I can pay for my own hotel room, even at New York prices." He turned back to Jason, bowing slightly," But, thanks. You're a real friend."

"Okay, man, but that means I'll have to carry my guilt all over New York City with me." Jason threw his red cloth napkin over his eyes and his shoulders sagged.

"Guilt?" Jake asked as his eyebrows rose.

"Yes, guilt." Jason cocked his head. "Clisty has to be there for the big appointment to sign her contract and ... she's your girl; it's her career; and, it's her big opportunity. Even Becca and Griff have a connection with the new show. I have nothing to do with any of it, except that I'm married to the producer." He stopped, "Okay, another idea. Becca and I will at least take you guys out for a great dinner after Clisty's meeting with the network's big boss."

"I'd enjoy that," Jake said and looked at Clisty. "That is, if you're okay with it. I don't know your schedule."

Just then, Albert and Carol Sinclair stopped at the table. Al kissed the top of his daughter's hair. "Hail, hail the gang's all here," he said with a smile.

"We didn't know you all would be here." Carol put her hands on Clisty's shoulders and hugged.

"Join us," Jake offered.

Carol waived her hand as she backed away from the invitation. "We just finished eating, but, thanks."

"What did you have?" Becca asked.

"Lasagna … as usual," Carol blushed.

"As usual," Clisty and Al repeated in unison.

"Okay, you two," Carol gave in. "I've tried nearly everything on their menu and I like lasagna best. I have that most of the time." Carol leaned closer to her daughter's ear. "Clisty, your dad has finished my studio. Maybe you can come over to see it tomorrow. He did a wonderful job."

"Studio?" Jake questioned.

"Al and I took some classes while we wintered in Florida for a few months. He took woodworking and I took art classes," Carol offered with a smile.

"What art classes, Mom? Painting?"

"You know me, Clisty. I do enjoy painting. But, pottery and jewelry making were fun, too. I'm a jack of all trades and master of none."

Clisty took her mother's hand. "How about, Carol of all trades and enjoyer of all?"

"I like that," Carol said as she nodded. "Dad is going to teach a little woodworking at our craft workshops."

"They'll make a treasure box with dovetail joints and a wooden lock." Al smiled as he measured out the size with his hands.

"Clisty, something I didn't know and maybe you didn't either," Carol raised her eyebrows. "Emily Treadway taught Faith to do crewel embroidery and Faith has agreed to teach beginning needle-art."

"You're kidding, Mom. That's amazing. The woman who helped her husband hold Faith captive, also taught her to embroider. Well, good for her."

Carol was nearly jumping around; her excitement about her plans was obvious. "We'll all have fun, the teachers and the participants. Why don't you come over tomorrow to see our studio and get a feel for where this all started?"

"I'm sorry, Mom. I can't. I'm leaving for New York tomorrow."

"New York?" Al gasped.

Carol threw her hand to her mouth. "I can't keep up with your new life, Honey."

"Me either," Clisty groaned. "Sometimes I wonder if I'll ever get used to being on the go all the time."

"Call me when you get back," her mother suggested. Carol slipped her hand in the crook of Al's arm. "Be safe. Have fun."

"Bye you two," Clisty called after them. Turning back to Jake she picked up the thread of the previous conversation. "Jake, what you said before, about dinner in New York ... does that mean you're coming?" Clisty inhaled deeply, holding her breath.

"It does," Jake agreed with a huge smile. "The police department can shuffle some schedules. I've filled in for all those other guys and gals many times."

"Then, I'll be able to breathe," Clisty admitted. She sipped some coffee in order to stall while she thought about the words she wanted to use. "I know I'll be traveling all over the country getting stories for the show. I'll be gone several days a week. But ... this one is a special trip, a launching of a completely new life for me, a new concept in reporting, stressing the positive, rather than mopping up after the negative. And, Jake, I'm glad you'll be there."

"Clisty, are you anxious about this promotion?" Becca's eyes narrowed.

"No, I think I'm neither nervous nor anxious with you guys around. But, I'm still excited. It's more … excited beyond any words to express!" she said as she laughed. "This is a great opportunity and all of you will be with me. I can do this." She inhaled the perfume of the black coffee still steaming in her cup. "What a beginning!"

"Well, then …" Becca summed up, "we'll need four rooms with Griff along, too. What did Jason say, 'Clisty has certain standards of conduct that harken back to days of old?' So—"

"I …" Clisty drew out as she caught a glimpse of Jake smiling his Cheshire cat smile. It warmed her inside. "I never thought I'd be able to be with anyone, not even married." Her voice caught in her throat as tears gathered in her eyes. "After that filthy, stinking animal grabbed Faith and me, dragging Faith away … I didn't want a man to touch me, not ever again … except a hug from my dad. I'll admit it took a long time before I was completely comfortable with Daddy." She sipped at her glass of water with shaking hands. "I vowed, I'd never let a man touch me … except my husband someday. It's not old fashioned. I call it … Clisty's fashion."

Chapter 5
The Contract – Written, Spoken and Unspoken

The next day and many miles later, Clisty swiped her key card in the hotel door lock and opened it into a wonderland of elegance and light. It was a large room with bed, small couch, two side chairs, TV and mini refrigerator below a console matching the dresser. The west wall of windows looked out on Avenue of the Americas, or Sixth Avenue as New Yorkers called it. She looked down from the seventh floor at all the traffic flowing northward and smiled. Excitement was everywhere and matched her feelings exactly. Would she still be as thrilled once she read the fine print in her new contract? Truthfully, her attorney in Indiana had found no problems.

"I'll put your bag up here," Jake offered as he lifted Clisty's suitcase onto the luggage station on top of the low dresser. "I'll get you settled and then take my things across the hall."

"Thanks, Jake," she said as she looked around the room. She threw herself onto the couch laughing. "I really cannot believe all of this," she said as she clenched her fists and pounded them on her thighs in glee.

"I am woman ... hear me roar?" Jake's eyebrows rose as he smiled.

"No! I am Clisty Sinclair. I have arrived!" she corrected him as she laughed.

The door was still open when a bell captain knocked on the jamb. "Miss Sinclair? Someone left this basket for you at the desk. Would you please sign for it?"

"Sure," she agreed with a huge smile. She pointed at the coffee table in front of the couch as a spot for the hotel worker to place the large wicker basket of assorted fruit. Clisty reached in her purse and handed the bell captain a tip before he excused himself.

A clear plastic holder with a small card attached was stuck in the foil that secured the fruit in the basket.

To our most talented teller of stories from the heartland.

Welcome to New York and BNN.

Bradley Funderbird.

"The fruit looks good," Jake said as he inspected the contents. "I'm hungry. It could be full of anything edible and it would look good to me. I'm starved."

"Please, take some," Clisty offered. "There is no way I'm going to be able to eat all of this. It smells fantastic now. I don't even want to think about how the uneaten pieces will perfume the room in a few days."

"Yuck," Jake moaned. "I have an idea," he spun around, his mind off the basket. "Your appointment at the station isn't until 2 PM and it is now ..." he flipped his wrist over, "11:30. We can go down, find some lunch and enjoy the beautiful spring day."

"That sounds wonderful," she clapped, jumping up. "I'll change for my meeting while you take your stuff to your room. See you in," she paused, "fifteen minutes."

"Do you think you should call Becca's and Griff's rooms?" he asked as he gathered up his luggage.

"Becca said she wanted to rest before going over to the network office. She's not part of my meeting, but she wants to look around the corporate office to get a first impression. Besides my contact with the network, the rest of the New York based team want to meet all of us. I won't bother Becca and Jason this time. As for Griff, he wants to sleep a lot. You and I can have a light lunch, go to my meeting, and then the others can meet us at the network before we all go for our late dinner."

"Sounds like a lot of food, but I'm hungry enough, it will work for me. I can come back here while you have your meeting."

"You will not! Jake, come with me to the meeting." Clisty walked him to the door, her arm entwined in his. "I'd better hurry. See you shortly."

Jake turned back at the door. "They want to see you, Babe, not me. You're their new star. But ... if you want me to come, I'll wait for you in the lobby of their building."

"Okay, great," she agreed with a wide smile. "That will be close enough. I'll know you're there." She sighed as she closed the door behind him.

Quickly, she grabbed her cell phone and connected to her mother back in Fort Wayne, putting the phone on speaker. As the phone rang, Clisty moved about, opened her luggage and started removing clothing. "Hi Mom, just letting you know we arrived safely."

"Good," Carol Sinclair said as she exhaled with a whistle. "What does your room look like, Honey?"

Clisty looked around the room again and basked in the spring sky that sent magnificent light into the room. "It's amazing. I'll take some pictures later and text them to you. Just letting you know the flight went well. Gotta run now. Bye."

"Bye, Honey. Have a wonderful time."

Clisty pulled some dresses and other clothing that needed hangers out of her suitcase. Hanging several pieces in the closet, she arranged them in order of type and length, and cringed. Becca reminded Clisty of her over-organization just yesterday. She quickly mixed the pieces up a little: long, short, pants, tops. A powder blue suit and lacy blouse, chosen for the day, made her feel both professional and feminine. Slipping on beige heels, she studied her reflection in the mirror.

"You're done," she said to her image and smiled. When she turned and looked out the window at the vastness of the city, she changed her mind. From the bottom of her suitcase, she pulled out a very dressy but much lower heeled pair of shoes. "This city is all about walking," she talked to her likeness in the full length mirror as she changed her shoes. "Okay— now you're done."

• • •

After sharing a light lunch of tuna sandwich on a pretzel bun with Jake, she polished it off with an Olde Brooklyn ginger ale in Hilton's Herb N' Kitchen Restaurant. Then they headed outside where the city swarmed with the buzzing sound of many languages. To the south, they could see the red and blue neon lights on the marquee of Radio City Music Hall. The earthy perfume of roasting nuts drifted across the street where a vendor sold his nutty goodness. "That smells amazing." Clisty smiled as the doorman opened the door of the stretch limousine the network had sent.

Once in the Lincoln, Clisty grabbed Jake's hand and held on. He gently folded his other hand over hers and smiled. The car smelled new, with a blended aroma of various hides all around her.

Clisty closed her eyes and inhaled. "I wonder if there's a perfume spray called Lincoln Leather."

Outside, people clogged the wide sidewalk beside the street full of yellow taxies and other dodging and weaving vehicles, large and small. Clisty and Jake said nothing. They relaxed and enjoyed the excitement of the moment as they rode up Sixth Avenue.

Uptown at the network's office, the impressive building with its row of American flags all along the front captivated Clisty. When she got out, her hair blew in the fresh spring air in sync with Old Glory. Jake squeezed her hand as they walked through the huge doors and entered a lobby with high ceilings and polished brass everything.

"I'll sit right here," he told her as he walked toward to a cluster of wing-backed chairs. "The network's gift shop is over there. I'll get something to read. When you're done with your meeting, I'll be waiting for you," he said as he pointed to the burgundy leather chairs.

"Great. And, Jake," she smiled nervously, "thanks for coming. I like knowing you're down here. I'll admit … I'm scared to death." Clisty waved her finger tips at him and grabbed the first elevator she came to. As the doors began to close, Clisty looked back and saw him watching her. Warmth filled her until she could feel her cheeks turn a rosy red.

As she stood facing forward, she vowed she wouldn't watch the numbers tick off on the floor counter bar centered above the doors. Determined to rise above her anxiety, she chose to pretend she didn't care how long it took to get to the top floor, or how much farther the elevator car had to rise. She chose to whisper a small prayer for calm and guidance. When the car stopped, her eyes darted up to make sure she had arrived at the proper floor before stepping off.

The wide hall that led to the network CEO's office, professionally decorated all along the space with portraits of the network's news personalities, stretched to large glass double door. As she pulled on one of the long brass door handles, she stopped in mid-stride, absolutely amazed. Hanging over the receptionist's desk was an additional picture, with the caption, *Our Newest Star – Clisty Sinclair*. Below her name: *Stories from the Heartland.*

"Miss Sinclair," the receptionist greeted her with a broad smile. "We are so happy you're with us." She was a friendly, blond woman that Clisty guessed would be about five feet ten if she were standing.

"Thank you," Clisty responded and looked quickly at the name plate on the woman's jacket. "I'm happy to be here, Megan."

"Have a seat right over there," Megan offered, pointing to a cluster of chairs. "I'll tell Mr. Funderbird you're here."

Clisty saw the chairs that lined the wall, but it was the floor-to-ceiling windows that drew her closer. The view was breathtaking. Far below, Central Park was alive with budding trees of multiple shades of green, peppered with large beds of colorful blossoms. The distance to the ground made the scene look like as an Impressionist's painting, with splashes of color rather than clear details. The silent movement of vehicles moving in and out of the park was hypnotizing.

"Clisty?" a voice called behind her. "It is marvelous, isn't it?"

"Mr. Funderbird," she startled and turned. "Sorry, I was lost in the beauty of it all."

"That's easy to do," he agreed. "Come on in," he said as he ushered her into his large office with a huge mahogany desk and credenza. A rough fieldstone fireplace with a dark polished beam mantle above it was on an adjacent wall. In front of it, there was a conversation area with caramel colored leather chairs on an antique carpet with red, blue and gold tones. "Please," he pointed to one of the comfortable looking chairs, "sit down."

"Thank you," she said. And, so it began. They reviewed the contract he had sent by email for her lawyer to go over. Line by line, the agreement was fine. Nothing needed to change. At the bottom was a paragraph detailing her total income, broken down by paycheck, with examples of which expenses to charge to the network, and how to file an expense report. They were all routine items it seemed to Clisty, until she read the salary line again. Her stomach fluttered and flipped. She had never dreamed she would ever earn that much money, certainly not before her thirtieth birthday, or after thirty for that matter.

"If everything is to your satisfaction, I'll have you sign it," he said as he offered her his gold pen.

"Yes, sir," she almost laughed from nervous excitement. She doubted, however, that laughter was appropriate.

"Well, I'm relieved that it's all done," Mr. Funderbird said as Clisty also sat back. "It's too bad you're not married," he revealed slowly. "There have already been some reports that you may be too pretty for news. Some people may not be as jealous if you had a husband."

Her mouth flew open as she gasped, "Will I be safe?"

"We may have a body guard travel with you when you're out in the heartland. But, I am glad you aren't married," he admitted.

"Really," she responded slowly, wondering why he would say such a thing. "That's not a legal interview question you know, Mr. Funderbird."

"Indeed I do know. I'm glad you aren't too intimidated to call me on it. But, that wasn't a question. It was a statement," he looked at her over his glasses and smiled. "It's of no matter anyway … really. Your private life is your own business. It's just that you are starting the Heartland series and it's kind of nice you won't need a pregnancy leave in the first several months." He laughed and added. "You know that has happened. We have a young group of newscasters here," he said as he laughed again. "If you're already married, the viewing audience will think you're pregnant every time you hold a flower pot in front of you."

"No, I'm not married," Clisty told him. She thought about Jake and the newness of their relationship. They had hardly actually dated. "I assure you; I am currently married and will not be getting married anytime soon."

Chapter 6
The Network Gift Shop Image

When the elevator doors re-opened on the first floor at BNN, Clisty saw the gentlest, strongest, wisest, warmest, and most gorgeous man she had ever known, waiting for her in the lobby. She wondered if she had made the assurance of no marriage too soon.

"Hi Babe," Jake called out. His glistening eyes wheedled their way into her heart.

Clisty felt her face, lit with joy, light the entire lobby. How could anything be more wonderful? The new job … and Jake. Just as quickly as the thought crossed her mind, she wondered again how she was going to juggle it all.

"How did the conference with Funderbird go?" Jake asked as he jumped up and pulled her to him.

Clisty didn't even think to look around. No one in New York knew her, at least not yet. Even a tour group passing through the main floor, laughing and snapping pictures, didn't point their cell phones in her direction.

"It went great." She didn't release her hold on him. "He was especially glad I wasn't married. Single, there would be no down time for babies and pregnancy leave."

"What?" Jake stood back and studied her expression. "He can't ask you if you're married or how many children you have, want, or don't want."

"He didn't ask me. He assumed I wasn't planning on marriage anytime soon, maybe based on our conversation … and he filled in the blanks. He said he was happy to hear I wasn't married."

"He asked someone back in Fort Wayne," Jake summed up and then studied her some more.

"Probably ... maybe," she agreed. "I promised him I wasn't married or getting married. It can't be a reason for hiring or not hiring someone anyway. But, he didn't ask me, so I guess it's okay," she sighed and shrugged.

"Are you disappointed?" he whispered as he held her close again.

"Disappointed in what?" she asked, all the while realizing she was disappointed in something, but didn't know what it could be. She had just signed the most impressive contract she had ever been offered. Even her attorney in Fort Wayne was impressed when Clisty gave her the advanced, review copy. Since she would be living in Indiana, where the cost of living would be much less than in New York, in a way she would get an additional raise before she started working.

"Are you disappointed in the fact you promised not to get married?" Jake hummed in her ear.

"Are you done already?" Becca asked as she and Jason breezed into the lobby. "Where's Griff?"

"Yes, my meeting just finished," Clisty answered as she pulled away a little but stayed tucked under Jake's arm. She blushed and fidgeted with the buttons on her blouse attempting to compose herself again. She wasn't jittery from the excitement of the contract ceremony with Funderbird, but from the thrill of Jake's warm breath in her ear.

Becca jabbed Jason lightly in the ribs and winked. "Were we interrupting something?"

"Here in the main lobby of the Bryson News Network?" Clisty denied, smoothing her clothes again. "Hardly."

Jake quickly jumped in for the rescue, gently patting Clisty's arm. "Griff? We haven't heard from him yet today. As for the contract, it is all signed and ready for the files. You two showed up just in time."

"Great," Becca agreed as she eyed them. "It's nearly three o'clock, so ... since people in New York don't eat supper until the next morning, we can see some sites and still get into any restaurant we want before the rush."

"That sounds wonderful," Clisty said, finally gathering enough composure to enter comfortably into the conversation. "I'd like to see the Empire State Building and the Metropolitan Museum of Art," she suggested.

"Good ... and I know Jason would like to hear some good jazz," Becca added.

"Becca, no," Jason denied. "This is Clisty's trip ... and yours ... not mine. Let Clisty decide where she wants to go."

"The network included you," Jake reminded him.

"Jazz sounds good to me too, Jason," Becca offered. "Then tomorrow, Clisty, Griff and I will meet our contact person."

"Okay…jazz it is, maybe after supper," Clisty thought aloud. When her cell phone rang, she checked the screen. "Griff," she announced. "I'm putting you on speaker." Clisty gave him the list of probable sights, the supper schedule, and the late music.

"Sounds okay," Griff agreed. "I'd like to skip the Empire State Building and supper. I have a friend here in town I'd like to join for a burger. We could meet you for jazz. Just call and let us know where."

Clisty looked at Becca with a grin, "A friend? Mr. Silent-one? Where did you two meet?" she asked.

Griff, the man of few words paused, and then offered, "Her family moved east when we were both juniors in high school. She's just a Facebook friend, but I told her we could connect in New York." His voice pumped with excitement. "She said she saw the segment you did on Faith Sterling Treadway and would like to meet the new celebrity in town. My high school girlfriend, now my wife Sara, and Tina's boyfriend would double-date in high school. Tina will bring her husband, Kevin, along for burgers, I think. Hopefully, she can find a babysitter."

"That sounds wonderful, Griff," Clisty marveled and high-fived Becca. "We'd all be happy to meet her." She pressed the "end call" button and put her hand to her mouth, embarrassed. "Doesn't that sound silly? Tina wants to meet me."

Becca winked as Clisty concluded her call. "Can you imagine?" she said, her eyes grew large in surprise. "Griff is actually going to talk to someone. *Talk*, I said. We are not in Kansas anymore, Toto."

Looking down the marble hallway, Clisty edged toward the network gift shop. "We will have our fun today and maybe not turn in 'til late. Hope we can all get up on time tomorrow to film the segment in Connecticut. We might not get back to the gift shop with time on our hands. I'd like to pick up some souvenirs to take home … and maybe something for Griff, too."

Inside the store, bright lights bounced off glass counters and display cases. Shelves were full of books written by some of the network journalists on topics ranging from the mid-east to children's books with pictures of smiling families. The delicious aroma of leather emanated from the side of the store where jackets, vests, and belts hung. A rich pale mauve, southwestern style leather jacket with short fringe along the bottom and a mountain range hand-tooled into the hide grain caught Clisty's eye. It was the words etched beneath the mountains that captivated her, *The Heartland*. A melodic background loop of various news program theme songs filled the room with soft advertising. *Wake up America's* theme was the catchiest, ending with a bugle call. Along the wall, faces of network newscasters and well known anchors smiled from coffee mugs and posters.

"It won't be long before your face will be on one of those mugs," Jason observed as he studied the cups that hung by their thumb loop.

A young woman behind the counter smiled when she saw Clisty. "Oh, Miss Sinclair, I'm glad you stopped in. Let our manager get your picture so your mug will adorn our display soon."

"My mug needs a little fresh lipstick first," Clisty said as she rooted in her purse for her tube.

"Larry," the salesclerk called out to a round man with glasses perched on the end of his nose. "You heard Clisty Sinclair was in the building. She's here. Get your camera. She's ready to pose for you."

"Let me buy one of those gorgeous jackets first," Clisty announced as she pulled a size small from a hanger. She tried it on, smiled and took her credit card from her purse.

"I'll take care of your purchase, Miss Sinclair, while Larry gets his shot."

"Okay," Clisty agreed. The newest American News Magazine's glittering personality fumbled at first with a pink blush and then quickly applied a fresh coat of gloss to her lips. "I'm as ready as I can be with absolutely no notice what-so-ever." She looked at Becca with pleading eyes. "Does my hair look all right? What am I saying? I don't want to know if it's in a wild flurry since I just came from the president's office. I want to delude myself with the pretense that it looks like I just stepped away from a professional make-up table."

"You always look good," Jason offered and then quickly added, "in a friend-to-friend kind of way."

"Your hair looks great, as always," Becca assured her. "Don't I always check your hair before you get behind the camera or make a super-blogger guest appearance at WFTW?"

"You do," Clisty agreed and looked at Jake. "Okay?"

"Absolutely marvelous," he said with a secret smile.

Becca studied the pair carefully. "Have we missed something?"

"Not a thing," Clisty denied as she reached for her package and credit card. "I'm just thrilled with the new jacket." She handed Jake the sack with the BNN logo on the side and reached for his hand. "I'll tell you what, Larry. You only need a close up anyway," Clisty suggested after the man returned with a camera in hand. "So, I'll just hold onto Jake here. He'll be off camera. It'll be okay. So much has happened, I feel wobbly."

Becca's eyes grew large. "Are you all right? Are you sick? We drive over to Connecticut tomorrow."

"Always the director," Clisty saluted with three fingers to her eyebrow. "I'm just thrilled with it all," she added as she squeezed Jake's hand.

"On three," Larry announced and counted. A sudden burst of light sent small black dots into Clisty's field of vision. In that instant, her new life as a national celebrity began.

Chapter 7
Engaged in Secret

Much later that evening, back in her hotel room, Clisty reveled in the joy she had experienced that evening. "I am stuffed," she moaned in glee as she fell backward onto her the bed. "Full of the excitement and thrill of New York; overflowing with the magnificent view from the top of the Empire State Building; completely overstimulated with the improvisation of the jazz musicians; and absolutely filled to overflowing with the most wonderful meal I have eaten in ages." She held onto her stomach as Jake closed the door. When she heard it latch, she leaned up on her elbow.

"I promise to be a perfect gentleman," Jake whispered, his voice hoarse with tension.

"Oh, darn," she teased.

"Does that signal a change in the game plan?" He knelt with one knee on the bed and leaned in as their lips moved closer.

Clisty sat up reluctantly. "I wish I were that kind of girl for you, Jake," she rubbed her hand on his thigh and sighed.

"I'm glad you're not," he admitted as he straighten up and put his arm around her. "And, I do understand. You have come a long way since you were nine years old. But, I do think ... since we both want more ... we have a problem."

Clisty's turquoise eyes grew large as the question she had to ask nearly choked off her breath. "What are you saying? Do you think we'd better not see each other as much? How will that work?"

"No ..." Jake drew out slowly but assuredly. "I think we should get married."

"Jake," she gasped as she flew into his arms, "do you mean it?"

"Of course, I do. That's what my parents did, Babe. They actually made a commitment. They didn't make a game of their lives."

Clisty jumped to her feet. "But, I just promised Mr. Funderbird this afternoon that I wasn't getting married anytime soon."

"It isn't the network's business," Jake insisted as he got up and took her in his arms. "In some states it's illegal to ask if a job applicant is married. A promise of not marrying would certainly be off limits."

"But, I did promise," she moaned and then paced over to the window. "Wait, Mr. Funderbird was more concerned that I would need family leave time just as my series was starting, than whether I'm married."

"Then," Jake began, "let's get married and not tell anyone."

"When? Where?" she asked. "How can we keep it a secret in Allen County Indiana? Everyone knows me there, and … we're not residents of New York."

Jake raked his hand through his hair. "When we get back home, we can drive down to Brown County, apply for a marriage license, and then go back down near the Memorial Day weekend and get married."

"The network may have an interview for me over the holiday weekend." The sparkle in Clisty's eyes flickered. "But, it won't matter," she thought aloud. "We can find the farthest, most obscure area of the state and get married. Then, when we're ready to tell everyone, we'll plan the big costume party where I wear the long white dress and you wear the tails." She jumped into his arms. "Wait?" She stopped. "White dress? Our formal wedding could be several years after we get married, depending on the demands of the job."

"It isn't the color of the dress, Babe. It's the veil and person who is wearing it. Just wear flowers in your hair and no one will be the wiser."

"Oh, what fun!" she squealed.

"Clisty?" Becca called softly from the hallway as she knocked on the door. "Everything okay?"

"Busted," Jake whispered and grinned.

Clisty threw her hand to her open mouth and clasped the other hand on top. She went to the door and, turning to Jake, she crossed her fingers. Before she let her in, she asked, "Becca, look around there in the hall and see if my pen is on the floor."

Jake's brow furrowed as he grinned and shrugged.

While she spoke, Clisty put her hand on the door lock. Her question covered the sound of the lock. "Is it around there anywhere?" she asked as she opened the door.

"No ..." Becca said as she looked around. "Oh, hi Jake," she added.

"Were you still awake, too?" Clisty asked. "Jake and I were going over any safety issues that might come up tomorrow."

"Good," Becca said and looked around. "I heard noise in your room and thought I'd better check on you. Glad you were here Jake."

"Right," he answered and said no more.

"So, do you have any tips you could pass on?"

"Tips?" Clisty asked.

Becca looked at her with a blank stare for a second, then added, "Safety tips?"

"Oh," Clisty began slowly. She started by rattling off a list of tips she had posted several months before on her blog. "Number one, if someone near you makes you feel uncomfortable, listen to your inner sense of danger. You're intuition is usually right."

"Okay," Becca said as Clisty began to innumerate them with a touch to her index finger.

"Don't make eye contact. Ignore them while paying close attention to where they are within your own personal space or bubble. Eye contact could be interpreted as a challenge of power." Clisty stated. "Alfa dog and all."

Jake stepped closer and added, "Clisty, let's demonstrate the move I was just teaching you." He picked up Clisty's hairbrush off the dresser and handed it to her. "Okay, again, hold it like you were going to stab me."

Clisty took the knife-brush and held it in an attack position. Her eyes grew large as her mind chased the possibilities around. Obviously, this move had not been rehearsing. She crouched a little, smiled and decided to play the game.

"Now, watch Becca," Jake instructed. "If someone threatens you with a knife like Clisty is acting out, hit their arm quickly, pushing it up," he went through the actions in slow motions. "Give a quick jab to the groin," he explained slowly without touching Clisty. "Then, turn and run like crazy."

"Wow!" Becca's expression lifted in wide-eyed amazement. "Can I try it?"

"No!" Clisty gasped as she backed way. "You might forget it's a demonstration."

"Okay," Becca said slowly with her head down. "Besides, I'd probably fall over, I'm so tired." She turned to leave, and then stepped back for Jake to walk out first. "We'll see you in the morning." Becca turned to leave while Jake touched Clisty's hand and slowly let go of her little finger.

"Night," Clisty said as she yawned. She caught Jake's eye as he left and smiled softly. After locking the door and throwing the dead bolt, she turned and flopped down onto the bed. When her cell phone rang she quickly picked it up from the bedside table and saw Jake's name on the caller ID.

"Hi," she whispered hoarsely.

"If you're serious about waiting to cuddle, I'm glad Becca came in when she did. I won't sleep all night, but I will have the most wonderful fantasies."

"Me too," she admitted as she rolled over. "If others knew about my stay-away game, they would think I was delusional."

"Delusions can be good when they lead to a beautiful reality," Jake said. "Are you aware that you agreed to marry me, Clisty? What about a ring?"

"I can't wear a wedding ring," she reminded him. "Unless it's on a non-wedding ring finger and any other stone than a diamond."

"We'll pick out gold bands in Fort Wayne and use them in the ceremony," Jake said, his voice dancing with excited creativity. "I'll have yours fitted with a bail and a small cross inside the ring so you can wear it as a necklace. It will look like a cross within a gold circle, a symbol of eternal love."

"I knew you were creative. And your ring?" she asked.

"I'll have it designed with a similar cross placed inside and mount it on top of a gold money clip," he said.

"This could be more fun than if everyone knew about it," Clisty said and laughed. "I'll wear the necklace all the time."

"There will still be attractive men in New York and across the country who will assume you're available," he cautioned.

"Then ..." she thought quickly, "Jake, I don't know how we'll manage it, but come with me as I travel around," she begged.

Jake paused for a minute while the silence grew louder. "Airfare could get expensive. If I can arrange my schedule with the department, we'll tell Becca and Griff I'm going along as a bodyguard."

"That will be perfect," Clisty exclaimed. "Mr. Funderbird said they might hire a bodyguard. I'll tell him about you. Maybe there's a way to keep your job with the police department and do this, too. Some sort of flex schedule."

"If the network wants to hire me … that would be even better."

Clisty responded immediately, hoping Jake wouldn't have time to fill in the spaces with worry or doubt. "I'll check with the network tomorrow."

After they said good night, she turned to her open laptop on the desk. For the first time, posting a blog didn't sound as exciting as it had. Exhausted, she knew she still had to make contact with her followers. She not only had to write the post before she went to sleep, it was the heart of the new plan. A smile crossed her face as she repeated softly, "The heart."

Crime Beat

✷

From the Heartland

1:45 *AM*

This blogger is writing you from New York City. Do not dismay. I continue to be your Fort Wayne, Indiana super blogger. In fact, this blogger signed a contract this afternoon to bring you stories about Heartland Heroes six times a year. On BNN's American News Magazine, I will lift up people who use their talents or creative inventions to help others.

ADDITIONAL OFFERINGS

In addition to this blog and the program segments on the American News Magazine, the Bryson Scruff Publishing Company will publish my True Crime novels you have so graciously supported.

My work will be the same, only different. The blog, www.crimebeat.blogsmith.com, will post as usual. Bookstores will shelve my novels twice a year as you have become accustomed.

The difference will be the wonderful opportunity to bring everyone a new kind of news. Rather than watching broadcasts about hate and anger, lies and deceit, the Heartland stories will lift up wonderful people who sacrifice their time and money to create and develop inventions and programs that will do nothing for them personally, but will benefit others. In some cases, the one lifted up has a talent that they teach or use to advance another's wellbeing. I know you will support this greater effort as you have supported my local newscasts and this blog, *Crime Beat.*

Share

SEE YOU AT THE BOOKSTORE

I will be back in Fort Wayne in time to sign copies of the *Crime Beat* series of blogs expanded into a novel. In August, I will be at Barnes and Noble Booksellers at Jefferson Pointe. I will sign the True Crime novel, *The Lottery Loser* from 7 to 9 PM. Come during those hours so we can chat. I'd love to meet you.

SAFETY FIRST

As I walk along the exciting streets and through the beautiful parks of New York City, a serious issue comes to mind, safety. Not for fear the city may be dangerous. There is danger in every situation if dangerous people are in your path. Self-defense classes will enhance your sense of empowerment. This blogger would find it difficult to demonstrate self-defense moves by drawing stick-figures. Those of you who have followed this blog over time know that I am brilliant at illustrations through scribbles. You cannot actually experience the defensive moves that way, however. The YMCA in your town may offer self-defense classes. If you cannot find a class, a local university may be able to recommend one. Shop around.

Share

Contact: clistysynclair@ebox.com

Chapter 8
Breakfast with a Side of Planning

The next morning, during breakfast at Penelope's on Lexington Avenue, Clisty made an announcement. "We have that Heartland story assignment in Connecticut so I did a little research early this morning. Stamford is only thirty miles from Manhattan. Considered part of the Greater New York metropolitan area, it's in the Bridgeport-Stamford-Norwalk Metro area. It should take about forty–five minutes to get there, depending on traffic."

"Wow," Becca exhaled. "Did you sleep with your head on a Triple A tour book?"

"Yes, I did," Clisty teased. "How did you guess?"

Becca shrugged, the corners of her mouth turned down. "Okay, so we stop at the network around twelve noon; meet Nicole, your research assistant, scheduler, and our life-line to New York; pick up the van; and get to Karl Kramer's home by our 2 PM appointment with him and his wife." She checked her watch. "It's 9:30 now."

"Right," Clisty agreed as she poured a second cup of coffee. "I want to talk to Mr. Funderbird about Jake being my bodyguard. Yesterday, the boss talked about needing someone to fill that job."

"You guys need a bodyguard?" Jason's jaw dropped.

Jake dug his fork into his three egg omelet with sausage. "We live in strange times." He popped a dangling string of cheese into his mouth.

"Maybe I should go, too," Jason suggested. "I was going to stay here in the city while you went over to Stamford."

"You can come along today, Jason, unless you want to sightsee in New York," Clisty offered. Her smile widened as the server put her Penny Egg Sandwich with scrambled eggs and American cheese on a croissant in front of her. Clisty spotted the woman's name tag. "Thank you, Trinda." She looked at the beautiful display laid out on her plate and refused to take a bite until she snapped a picture of it with her cell phone. The first bite had to taste the best so she held it in her mouth a few seconds just to savor its yumminess. With the flavor still hugging her mouth, she picked up the thread of conversation. "Jason, it may be the only Heartland interview you get to observe."

"That sounds good," Becca agreed. "You don't have to, Jason, if you don't want to. We'll all be safe. Why would anyone want to attack us? We're going to interview a man who only wants to help other people." She sipped from her cup of very hot coffee.

Jason's brow furrowed. "It'd like to see the interview. I'll have to trust Jake to keep you all safe on other assignments." Changing the subject, he seemed to study his plate the server had just put down. With the tip of his fork, he tasted a corner. "The goat cheese in my omelet is pretty good."

Clisty and Jake stared at Jason but it was Becca who asked, "Goat cheese? Jason, since when do you like goat cheese?"

"I've never tasted it before," he admitted. "But, I'm out of my comfort zone anyway here in the city, and I'm willing to try new things." He smiled as he held his chin high.

"You're out of your comfort zone?" Becca asked, her voice climbing.

"Yeah," he admitted. "I never thought I'd like New York City. Now, here I am, having a great time. There's so much to see. Last evening, we saw a guy with green hair. It stood straight up at least five inches above his head. I don't usually see that in Indiana."

They all laughed and settled back for a relaxing breakfast. When the coffee refill came, there was a scramble for the pot. Clisty won.

Trinda floated past their table with a large platter of cinnamon pecan rolls above her head. She placed them on the next table over.

"Trinda." Clisty grabbed the belt to Trinda's apron as she walked past on her way to the kitchen. "Are there any more ambrosia, cinnamon scented rolls in the back?"

"Me too," Jake echoed, followed by Becca and Jason.

"Sure, sweetie," Trinda agreed as she glided on.

Becca put on her producer hat and asked about the afternoon's appointment. "Nicole just emailed some details of this morning's assignment. What is this interview with Karl Kramer about?" She took another bite of her breakfast sandwich.

Trinda returned with four cinnamon pecan nutty, sticky buns. All four of them stared at the plate. Clisty reached first and selected the smallest. "I think my eyes are bigger than my stomach and maybe my olfactory sense as well."

She blotted her mouth on her napkin. "Karl Kramer is a man over fifty-five, maybe more. Nicole said he has invented something that will be a real blessing to elderly people. That's all she told me."

"That's all she said?" Becca asked, putting down her croissant.

"They haven't told me more on purpose. The idea is, they want me to experience the excitement of hearing the details of the person's contribution to the lives of those around them at the same time as the viewers at home." Clisty blew across the surface of her cup. "Um, good coffee." She closed her eyes and smiled. "Oh, Nicole did say, there is some danger in revealing the information. The Kramers received some threats. That's why Mr. Funderbird may want you to be our security, Jake."

"Threats?" Jake asked. "I didn't know about threats. Why? Specifically, what were the threats?" He put his fork down. "We all know more and more celebrities are being stalked, and some attacked."

"Nicole said it was star-crazy people that Mr. Funderbird feared," Clisty assured them. "In Kramer's case, it's some sort of jealousy regarding the inventors and their invention. Perhaps, it's someone in their background or their family. Anyway, I should learn more about the threats when everyone else does, during the interview. It will be a surprise to me when it's a surprise to you."

"I like that format, if it works," Jason joined in. "There may be some surprises you don't want to deal with on camera."

Becca put her roll down. "I can think of one reason it may not work. If you don't know what Kramer is going to talk about, Clisty, you can't develop provocative and interesting questions ahead of time."

"It's more like a conversation than an interview," Clisty answered. "That's what the Network wants. But, I agree. We'll see how this one goes. We may have to make changes for the next interview."

"So we can refine the show's format if necessary?" Becca asked.

"We know the format will have to change from time to time," Clisty explained.

"Depending on the interviewee," Becca nodded.

"Right," Clisty agreed. "If someone has received an award, there would be no real surprise. Everyone would know about it. In cases like that, we'll have to develop interview questions or run the risk of staring at each other in front of the camera. In today's case, it's an invention. A few questions about the inspiration for the idea, and development of the invention are logical conversation prompts. The public and I will learn about it during the interview. So, surprise and excitement on my part will set the emotional tone for those at home."

"The emotional tone?" Jake asked and smiled at Clisty over the rim of his cup.

"Well—" she smiled back coyly but looked into the bottom of her cup, not at Jake. Meeting his eyes would give everything away. "I'm game for secrets and surprises."

Chapter 9
Security and Transportation

A cacophony of chatter and activity erupted from the lobby at network headquarters when the four of them arrived. Employees were hurrying out for a quick lunch as visitors to the building hurried in. Perhaps the tourists hoped to see their favorite news anchor or visiting celebrity as the BNN journalist did the work of informing the nation.

Clisty pointed to the chairs and then the elevator. "I'll run up to the top floor and talk to Mr. Funderbird. You guys wait here for ten minutes then go up to the sixth floor. I'll join you in Nicole's office. She has the keys to the van and our itinerary."

"Okay," Becca agreed. "Jason, you haven't seen the gift shop yet. Let's go in there."

Jake smiled and gave Clisty a sideways hug. "I'll get a newspaper."

"Newspapers ..." Clisty teased. "I seem to remember those."

"Okay, okay," he surrendered. "I'm old fashioned."

"Me too," she whispered as she backed away, then turned and walked toward the elevator.

Inside the mahogany paneled lift-car, she pushed the button on the bronze panel for the top floor. When the doors closed, she smiled. All the way to the top her mind rolled back to the night before and the plans she and Jake made. They were actually going to get married and ... it would be their secret. Wow!

When she hopped off, her heals clicked down the hallway. Breezing through the double doors, she smiled at the receptionist who looked up and smiled.

"Miss Sinclair, it's good to see you. I heard you coming."

"Please, Megan, call me Clisty. Miss Sinclair sounds like you're addressing a kindergarten teacher." She paused only long enough to catch her breath. "Is Mr. Funderbird available? The team and I have a few minutes before we leave for the interview in Connecticut."

"Did I hear our newest news reporter?" Funderbird asked broadly as he walked into the outer waiting room. "Come in, Clisty. I know your schedule is tight."

He walked over, sat down behind his desk and pointed to the facing chairs on the other side of the desk. "Please."

"Just for a moment," she said hesitantly, slowly slipping onto the edge of one of the deep leather chairs. "Yesterday, you mentioned the possible need for a security person to travel with us."

"I'm glad you brought that up," he said as he quickly shuffled through a short stack of papers on the side of his desk. "Here it is." He waved a single sheet of paper in the air that looked to Clisty like a copy of an email. "Dr. Kramer said his computer received this email last night about 3 AM." Mr. Funderbird pulled gold rimmed readers from his lapel pocket and began to read. "Kramer, the find-my-way Walking Buddy was not your idea. I can prove it. Watch your back. Everybody in town knows where you'll be today. The newspaper thinks you're a hero and announces your every more. That news lady had better get out of the way, too."

"Wow, are we sure his invention and the subject of our interview was Dr. Kramer's idea?" Clisty asked. Her eyes squinted as she mulled over the possible consequences of stepping into a two-way feud.

"Our advanced team asked for testimonials from friends and neighbors. It's all good. We also had him send proof of patent ownership. Network lawyers looked over everything." Funderbird threw both hands out, palms up. "Again, no problem."

"That all sounds great," Clisty affirmed. "Careful vetting and safety are what I wanted to run by you. Looks like they vetted Karl Kramer thoroughly, he looks legitimate." She cleared her throat and boldly brought up the other topic. "As to the security issue, I may have a solution." She thought for a minute then asked the question that had troubled her. "How did the note-writer know about my involvement? I haven't done the interview yet?" Clisty began to feel a darkness surround her. She shook it off as she remembered Jake.

Mr. Funderbird's expression fell. "The network ran a brief promo about your new Heartland segment with the Kramers." He said no more, leaned forward, folded his hands and listened intently.

"Sergeant Jake Davis paid his own way to come to New York with us. He was the Fort Wayne police sergeant and SWAT team leader who helped us track down Faith Sterling's captor into Illinois and brought him to justice. He knows our producer, Rebecca; the cameraman, Griff; and me. We would all feel very safe with him around if you are planning to hire a security person."

"I remember Sergeant Davis from your clear and complete reports. Is he still on the Fort Wayne Police force? That would give him credibility when we run the credits." Mr. Funderbird's face brightened. New ideas seemed to take place in the moment. "Will he resign from the force?"

"No, not at this time. For now, he would arrange his schedule so he can work with us on a part-time basis, taking his 'weekend' on the date or days we travel."

Funderbird stroked his chin. "You will be living in Indiana with Fort Wayne as your base. So, the connection is very logical. I'll call Davis' Captain and see if he has any problem with an affiliation there in the department, while working for me, too. You said he came to New York with you. Take him along today. I hope he's not needed."

"Thank you," Clisty said as she exhaled slowly. "I feel so much better."

"Great," he affirmed as he stood up. "Now, Nicole Bernard is waiting for you. She has the keys to the van for today's interview and a voucher for you to pick up a new mid-sized van at a dealership there in Fort Wayne. That way you can have the van assigned to you maintained and serviced locally." He paused a moment and added. "I think I'll have Davis take care of scheduling all the vehicle maintenance for you. Not that you couldn't do it yourself. But, you will be your own satellite office there in Indiana and will have many more details to handle than the average news reporter."

"That would be a big help, Sir." Clisty thanked him as she stood up, extending her hand.

"Please, Clisty, 'sir' sounds so stuffy."

"That's how my parents raised me," she assured him.

"Then, when I hear you address me as sir, I'll consider it a nickname." He shook Clisty's hand and led her to the door. "Have Jake come and see me before you fly back to Indiana. I'll have the legal department draw up a contract for him." Mr. Funderbird stopped at his office door. "Tell Davis not to worry. I'll find out what his current salary is and match it, plus a sizeable raise. If he thinks it will work for him, he can transfer into full time with the network whenever he wants to. The network will pay his travel expenses, along with the expenses for the rest of you. Legal will look into a carry permit for Jake so he's all set the next time he's in New York."

"That would be wonderful," Clisty said, careful not to use the word, sir.

•••

On the sixth floor, Clisty walked quickly down the hall to Nicole's door. The Indiana trio was waiting in the hall. She grabbed Jake by the shoulder of his jacket and pulled him aside.

"Do you still want the job?" she asked hoarsely, so excited she nearly jumped into his arms.

"Job?" he asked, his eyes darting from Clisty to the Landers couple. "What job?"

"Hi everyone," Griff called out as he walked toward them. "Thanks for dropping a bread crumb trail for me to follow. The desk clerk at the hotel told me how to find you."

"I'm glad you're here," Becca sighed in relief as she put her hand to her forehead. "We'll be leaving for Connecticut soon." She narrowed her eyes. "By the way, you could have called one of us to find our location."

"I always show up," he said with a bow. "Eventually ... and on time ... within reason."

"Welcome aboard," Clisty greeted him with a salute. "Nicole is waiting for us."

"What job?" Jake whispered again as they all followed Clisty into Nicole's office.

"Security," she answered quietly leaning toward him. Her hand shielded her mouth. "We'll talk about it later. Mr. Funderbird is expecting you to act as security today in Connecticut. Okay?"

"Okay? It's great."

Clisty added, "He wants to see you before we leave for Indiana."

Nicole, a round blond woman in an oversized cardigan sweater, stood up as the entourage entered. "Miss Sinclair, I am so happy to meet you in person. This whole assignment is going to be so much fun, and I get to be a part of it. Thank you."

Clisty reached out and gave her a hug, then leaning back she added, "Nicole, please call me Clisty. Or, I'll have to call you Ms. Bernard."

"Oh, please don't," Nicole said with a laugh. "And, anyway, that is Mrs. Bernard. I've been Mrs. Bernard for twenty-six years. Please call me Nicole. I'll feel so much more a part of the team."

Clisty took her hand. "I'm glad to be a part of the team, too." Turning to Jake, she added, "I'd like you to meet Sergeant Jake Davis. He's our new security person and will handle the maintenance on the new minivan."

"I am?" Jake asked, looking from Clisty to Nicole.

"He is?" Becca questioned and patted him on the shoulder. "Congratulations!"

"New van?" Griff asked. "Wow! I haven't driven a new anything for — not ever."

Jason shook his head in amazement. "It's feeling more and more like the Twilight Zone."

"Fantastic, Sergeant," Nicole affirmed him. "Before you go back to Indiana, make sure I have your email address, cell phone number, Social Security number for Personnel and your full name. I'm going to have to sit down. This whole thing is an Olympic event." She flopped in her chair and laughed.

"Will do," he agreed. "And ... it's Jake Davis."

Nicole pulled out her desk lap drawer and brought out a keyring. "Here are the keys. It is completely outfitted with cameras, lights and all you'll need today," she said as she handed them over to Clisty. "I don't know which one of you will drive. You'd all better let me copy your driver's licenses. Then, I don't care who drives. I'll let you guys fight over that. In a few minutes, I'll call our insurance carrier and pass on all of your information."

"No fight," Becca said with a flip of her hand. "Griff drives when we're on the road."

"I like the sameness of that," Clisty agreed. "I have a feeling things are going to change faster than I will be able to control them."

Becca put her arm around Clisty's waist, giving her a hug. "Isn't it nice that you won't have to control any of us? We all know our jobs."

"And, all of you do them with precision and polish," Clisty agreed as she relaxed her body and took a deep breath. "You are all a blessing to me," she added and looked at Jake.

Jake tapped Clisty on the shoulder. "I'll run up and meet Mr. Funderbird quickly. Why don't you all go down to the gift shop for a few minutes? Mr. Funderbird should know we have to leave soon. I won't be long."

"We'd better get going," Becca reminded him. "Don't make it more than … say … seven minutes."

"Seven?" Jake asked with a chuckle. "Not seven and a half?"

"No," Becca began with a grin. "Let's go down and wait for Jake."

Griff raised his hands like the trail boss of a wagon train. "Head 'um up. Move 'um out." He laughed and added, "Road trip!"

Chapter 10
An Invention – A Blessing

The ride out of New York City into New Rochelle, where they picked up I-95, then into Connecticut at Greenwich, was slow going. Even though they started a little after twelve-noon, the traffic was rough. One man in a black two-door sedan with dings in both right and left front fenders darted back and forth in front of them. Griff couldn't get around him because the man would swerve from one lane to another in an instant. Clisty held on to the grab bar to the right of the windshield until her hand hurt, waiting for the crash everyone was preparing for. They all breathed a sigh of relief when the man in the crumpled sedan finally pulled off on an exit ramp and disappeared. Clisty was glad she didn't have to drive. Once the guy left the highway, the front passenger seat gave her the opportunity to enjoy the scenery. Dangling her hands below the seat, the numbness, a result of her tight grip on the safety bar, finally went away.

The city of Stamford glittered off to the right of I-95, the Connecticut turnpike. Mammoth office buildings stood up straight on high pedestals; travelers could see them as they drew near the city. Griff pulled off the highway at Southfield Avenue and headed toward Twilight Cove. The scent of salt water from the mighty Atlantic that lay at the mouth of the inlet, lightly flavored the air.

Karl Kramer's house was a waterfront home with a fantastic view of sunlight bouncing off bubbles that babbled at the water's edge. Seagulls strutted along the beautiful terrace that stretched from the house to the dock, past Adirondack chairs painted sunny yellow. A boat bobbed gently in the deep water access of the private dock while

Sandpipers soared above on the winds of the sea. Dr. Kramer greeted them at the door, eyeing all the equipment.

"Good afternoon," Clisty began with a relaxed smile. She was surprised at how comfortable she felt with the upcoming interview. Yes, it was a national broadcast, seen on televisions coast to coast and some other countries, but the interview would be no different than the hundreds she had done in and around Allen County Indiana as she gathered information for her newscast or blog. "I'm Clisty Sinclair; this is Rebecca Landers our producer; and our cameraman, Griff."

"Glad to meet you, Miss Sinclair," the doctor answered with a firm grip. He opened the door wide.

As soon as the door cleared the frame, a streak of black wet fur dashed into the house, stopped and shook sea water all over the floor. A big Labrador, weighing at least seventy-five pounds, wiggled and flopped, depositing the evidence of his recent swim off the dock. Obviously, Dr. Kramer was not going to push the big animal around, but the entry smelled like wet-dog.

Kramer put both hands on his hips. "Oliver," Kramer ordered, "out!" The dog turned, tucked his tail between his legs and slumped his way back outside as Jake held the door. "I am so sorry," Kramer apologized.

"Don't you worry about it," Clisty said. Laughing, she added, "These two gentlemen are Sergeant Jake Davis, our traveling security person, and ..."

"I'm nobody," Jason interjected as he stuck out a strong hand in friendship. "I'm a tag-along, Becca's husband, enjoying my first trip to New England. I can wait in the van if you would be more comfortable."

"Don't you think of it," Kramer said as he put his hand on Jason's shoulder and drew him in across the threshold. "The early folks settled Stamford in 1641 with friendship and open doors. I've lived in this house since the mid-eighties and I see no reason to be any less hospitable than our community ancestors. Oliver already welcomed you."

They entered onto medium toned hardwood floors of varying board widths and polished to a matte luster. "This will make a perfect room to set up in," Griff observed as they walked into the living room. "You have great west facing windows. The sun is high and the light shouldn't be a problem. If we use the fireplace as our backdrop, I'll aim the equipment away from the windows anyway," Griff said as he surveyed the large room. The room had warm sunset yellow colored walls, sea blue fabric on overstuffed furniture, and off-white coffee and side tables with wooden tops the same honey color as the floors.

"That sounds great," Becca agreed. She pulled her iPad from under her arm and used the screen to preview the space the camera would see.

Dr. Kramer stroked his arm and made a suggestion. "I don't want to tell you how to run your interview, folks, but, do we have to sit on dining room chairs with our knees three inches away from each other?" he asked. "That looks so confound uncomfortable when they do that in news interviews, and frankly, it looks silly."

Clisty didn't want to laugh because truthfully, she felt the same way. "The idea is that all distractions are stripped away. Only the subject of the interview and the interviewer are in the shot."

"I understand that," he agreed. "But, it still looks silly. It's like two people perched on the head of pins, pretending they're comfortable." He paused and looked out the window toward the water beyond. The green terrace of the northeastern spring was soothing. "If you want to just focus on me, you can pull the camera in close enough to see nothing but the wart on my nose and the hair in my ears, if you'll just let me sit on a comfortable chair... considering my arthritis and all." He pointed to the couch and chairs.

"I want you to be comfortable, Dr. Kramer," Clisty stated firmly as she looked around the room. "May we rearrange your furniture?"

"Sure," he agreed.

Becca studied the room for a second. "We could move the couch perpendicular to the fireplace on one side, with the two chairs facing it on the other. That beautiful coffee table could be in the middle between you two, and the end tables would be beside the wing back chairs. Turing on the lights will add the warmth we want. It would look like you had that arrangement all along."

Kramer smile. "If the lights aren't on, it looks like no one's at home." He stepped back and studied the setup. "I may like it enough to keep it that way after you leave. I could enjoy the view of the water from the new angle."

Clisty ran her fingers over the top of the coffee table. "These tables are wonderful. They blend perfectly with the floor."

"They should," Kramer said as he puffed out his chest. "When I had the carpet replaced with this hardwood flooring, I popped the table tops off and replaced them with extra flooring boards. After they were sanded, I polished them with polyurethane to protect the wood from spills and the salt air."

"You did this work yourself?" Jake asked as he squatted down and inspected the workmanship more closely.

"I did," Kramer answered with modest pride. "I'm always reinventing something."

"Jake and Jason," Becca pointed, directing the furniture arrangement. "Please move the furniture. Dr. Kramer is already giving us good material and we're not even set up yet."

"I'm not ancient, unless you call sixty-one over the hill," Kramer said. "I can help move the furniture I put there in the first place." He turned and excused himself. "Oliver baptized the floor. I'll get something to wipe up the water."

The men pushed and pulled the furniture, flipping the pieces from one side of the room to the other, careful not to scratch the floor. Griff put the flood lights in front of the windows, facing them away from the glass and toward the fireplace.

As Kramer finished mopping the floor, Becca asked, "Do you have any pillows?" Looking around she pointed, "Oh, out here." She darted over to a small four season sun porch next to the living room. "There are tons of them out here." Gathering up a half dozen decorative pillows, she came back with full arms and plopped them on the sofa. One of them was a coarse weave cream linin with an embroidered sea shell on the face side; two were Bahaman sea blue accented with nautical ropes, and the other three were the same fabric as the furniture with cream piping on all sides.

"Good idea, Becca," Clisty agreed and sat down on the edge of the side chair next to the fireplace with several pillows at her back. "Dr. Kramer, if you will prop the remaining pillows behind you, you'll be comfortable and still look alert and focused."

"We don't want to appear to be falling asleep," Kramer quipped and smiled. Sitting on the end of the sofa nearest Clisty, he scooted out to the edge, and wedged the pillows behind him. "Just so I don't look like an old coot that needs pillows to prop him up."

"Believe me, Dr. Kramer, no one will mistake you for an old coot," Jake assured him with a laugh. "I hope I have half the energy and a third of the creative ideas you have when I'm a few years older."

"Thanks."

"Besides, sixty is the new forty-five," Jason agreed.

"Really?" Becca asked as her eyebrows rose. "Where did you read that?"

"I made it up," Jason admitted without a twinge of embarrassment. "I know I've heard something like that and, I fully agree."

"You're hoping you're right," Becca teased.

"Dr. Kramer has proven me right," Jason boasted, pointing at the homeowner and inventor.

Becca just rolled her eyes. Again, she pointed the iPad at the new staging in the room to get an idea of the focal point for tapping. "Looks good, people."

Clisty breathed deeply. *No different* than all other interviews, she reminded herself again. And, so it began.

Chapter 11
The Interview

Clisty pulled her e-tablet from her bag as Griff adjusted the lights, flooding the two in brilliance. "I may not use these discussion prompts," she explained to Dr. Kramer as she looked down at the interview questions she pre-loaded on the tablet. "We're just going to have a conversation. But, there are some points I want to include in our talk and not forget to ask. I may also use some terms, like *evening*, since the show will air in the evening. I'm well aware of the time of day."

"Got ya," Dr. Kramer acknowledged.

Looking directly into the camera lens, Clisty began. "Good evening," she addressed the future TV audience. "And, welcome to Stories from the Heartland. I'm Clisty Sinclair. We've come to Stamford, Connecticut, just north of New York City, to meet Dr. Karl Kramer, a physician affiliated with Stamford Hospital."

"Thank you for coming, Miss Sinclair," Kramer greeted. "This is an exciting opportunity for me to inform your audience of a device for helping loved ones with Alzheimer's disease. That's important since one in ten people aged sixty-five and older, or ten percent of people in the US in that age population, has Alzheimer's dementia."

"How many people are we talking about doctor?" Clisty continued, pleased with Dr. Kramer's knowledge and his ability to communicate.

Kramer continued. "With the additional two-hundred thousand people under age sixty-five with younger-onset Alzheimer's, according to the Alzheimer's Association's 2017 report, more than five-million Americans are living with Alzheimer's disease."

"That seems impossible," Clisty whispered as she thought of her parents living almost twelve-hundred miles away in Florida six months out of the year. How would she recognize subtle changes in their ability to remember or process ideas when she doesn't see them every day?

"Of course, they aren't all wondering around, lost and alone," Dr. Kramer assured her. "They begin by forgetting things. Luckily, there are medications to slow the process. Eventually, they get lost in their own neighborhood and that's where my invention comes in."

"You've invented something that helps Alzheimer's patients who have advanced to the point they aren't able to find their way home?" Clisty asked.

"More than that," Kramer said as he leaned into the conversation with enthusiasm. "When these folks are out for a walk, they may not recognize any of the buildings or signposts around them."

"You have invented something to help them?" Clisty asked with wide eyes. "That's wonderful. In your medical practice, do you treat patients with Alzheimer's?"

"We all do," he explained. "People with Alzheimer's disease come into every hospital and practice, usually for unrelated conditions. Their children or other family members bring them to the dentist, optometrist, family practice physician and medical specialist. These patients are part of every practice in some way these days," he paused and smiled. "I wanted to help them."

"Tell us about your invention, Dr. Kramer."

Kramer turned his hand over, exposing his wrist and the watch around it. "This is it. It's many things. First of all, as you can see, it's a timepiece for those who want to wear a watch, and it's also a camouflage for the Buddy."

"The Buddy?"

"Yes, that's what I call it, the Walking Buddy. You have your spouse, family member or friend's voice with you at all times, telling you where you are and what scenes you're passing ... your Walking Buddy." Dr. Kramer inched farther out to the edge of his chair in excitement. "It has a GPS locater in it that can detect the walker's location. In addition, a voice programed to sound like your spouse, son, daughter, etc. ... your Buddy ... will name each of the buildings, parks and sites as you pass them. Their family or friend's picture will appear on the screen in place of the clock face if the GPS detects the owner is lost. The voice can be programed to say, 'If you're ready to go home, turn right here, Daddy,' to help the walker who has wondered away. The Buddy will be able to tell if the walker has forgotten which way is right or left, and redirect them if they turn wrong."

"Dr. Kramer, that is amazing!" Clisty sat back as her hands flopped on the armrests of the chair. "With the number of Alzheimer's patients we have, your invention has come just in time."

"I'd like for you to have this one," Kramer said as he reached for a small box on the coffee table in front of him.

"Thank you!" she said, smiling broadly. "I love presents. I certainly did not expect to get one today."

"I'm not saying you need the GPS feature," Kramer laughed. "I do know everyone can use a new watch."

Clisty opened the box, threw back her head and laughed. "Karl," she gasped as she took the watch out of its packaging, "this has the logo of the Bryson News Network on the front. How did you do that?"

"We can customize a watch for anyone's tastes or needs," he said, beaming with pride. As Clisty released the watch from the packing and put it on her right wrist, Kramer's attention was distracted to the front entry when a woman with maple syrup colored hair entered. "Honey, I am so glad you're home," he said as he stood up and motioned for her to come in during filming.

"I'm sorry, Karl," she apologized with her hand over her mouth.

"Honey, come in and meet Miss Sinclair." Kramer greeted his wife with a hug and a kiss on her cheek. Turning to Clisty, he added, "Karen left work early to get here. I hope the interruption won't hurt the interview."

"Not at all," Clisty said as she offered her hand to Karen Kramer. "We'll edit out your entry and go directly to your introduction."

"Great," Karl exclaimed as he pumped his fist in victory. Patting the cushion beside him, he added, "We're going to need more pillows."

Karen saw the throw pillows and started to get up. "There are some more in the corner of the sunroom in that sea captain's chest."

"I'll get them," Jake offered. When he returned, he fluffed them behind Karen and stepped out of the camera shot.

Karen leaned toward Karl, "I'm sorry I'm late. When my graduate assistant came in to take over my class, he gave me a letter that had arrived in the departmental office." With her voice even lower, she added, "It was another threat. I had to wait for the police."

"Threat?" Clisty quickly asked, her face drawn as she remembered the note Mr. Funderbird read.

Karl reached for his wife's hand. "Karen is a professor of computer programming at a nearby university. She took my ideas and wrote the program to make the Walking Buddy functional. Karen is my wife and partner in life, as well as my partner in the Buddy Program."

"So you two co-own the business?" Clisty asked.

"Yes," Karen answered, "with complete survivor rights. The University has no rights to the company, neither its patent nor its profits."

"Neither does the hospital," Kramer explained. "And, I have no partners in my practice. So we are safe on all fronts."

"Except for whoever wrote the threatening letter?" Clisty asked.

"Well ... there's that," Karen admitted slowly.

Clisty leaned in closer as if they were going to share a secret. "What did the letter say?"

"Letters," Karen corrected.

"More than one?" Clisty sat back in surprise.

"Actually three," Karen sighed and pursed her lips. "Today's letter was the third. They have all been addressed to me." She gripped Karl's hand more tightly as Griff zoomed in for a close-up of them on the couch. She rooted around in her large bag and pulled out the note. "This is a copy. The police have the original."

Clisty took the paper in her fingers, studying it for a moment. "There would be no fingerprints on this letter since it's a copy. I'm sure the police will run a complete analysis on the original."

"Yes," Karen agreed. "They said they'll check for finger prints, type of paper, and so on."

Clisty handed the letter back to Karen. "Do you mind reading it?"

"Will that be all right with the police?" Dr. Kramer asked and looked at Jake.

"Reading the copy should be okay," Jake nodded.

"Okay," Professor Kramer agreed. As she looked at the paper and cleared her throat, her hands started shaking. "I warned you," she began reading from the note. "If you keep selling my invention, I will not be responsible for my actions. You will have brought destruction on yourself."

"I hear two things," Clisty said slowly, enumerating them on her fingers. "One, the writer claims the Walking Buddy is his or her invention." She touched the next finger. "Second, either the company or you personally could be injured."

"The first element is the strangest." Karl put his arm around Karen and patted her shoulder reassuringly. "No one else worked with me in planning the concept of the Walking Buddy. I discussed it with no one until I had it completely formed in my mind: the watch face, the GPS locating element, the prompts from familiar voices with their pictures on the screen, even offering the various company pictures and logos on the face of the watch. When I had it completely thought through, I told Karen and asked her to write the programs necessary to make all phases operate."

"So, except for your wife, your business partner, no one else knew you were even working on it," Clisty concluded.

"Right," he agreed. "I hold several, unrelated patents," Kramer said with a modest smile. "I don't talk about any of my ideas until they're in production." He lowered his eyes. "Not that I'm smarter than everyone else; but, I did tell people about my plans with my first idea. Some got really excited and jumped right in, wanting to help. They offered suggestions, too many, until I was so confused it took months to unravel the helpful ideas, from the ... not so helpful." He stroked Karen's shoulder, smiling into the camera. "Brainstorming is good ... but not with people who have no idea about the product, its purpose, or how it works."

Clisty smiled knowingly. "I understand. So, when the concept for the Walking Buddy was fully developed—?"

"That was when I talked to Karen." he concluded.

Karen lightly massaged her husband's knee and smiled. "We sat at the dining room table and planned the entire project."

Clisty paused, forming her next question carefully. "Did you have some of your better students participate in programing the Walking Buddy as a class project?" She eyed Karen for any indication of hesitancy.

"No, absolutely not," she stated flatly. "I didn't so much as doddle a line of code while at school. I told no one."

Dr. Kramer enumerated each step in the preparation. "When we were ready, we filed out the patent papers together and each of us signed them. With the patent in hand, we went together to the company we had chosen to manufacture it, Boston Technologies. Finally, we began the distribution process. We didn't involve anyone else until then."

"Have any Alzheimer's patients used the device?" Clisty looked at the Walking Buddy on her own arm. It was stylish and functional.

"Yes, we asked for volunteers from a neurologist's practice, Dr. Jeffery Jorguson," Karl replied as he looked at Karen. "But, we didn't tell him anything about it until we held the patent."

"Let's talk about distribution," Clisty suggested as she looked up from her brief list of pre-written questions. "Were there any criteria for inclusion in the test group?"

"The first criterion was approval by Dr. Jorguson. Since he had already diagnosed the patients, knew their medical history and the progression of their disease, he was the one qualified to accept or reject them." Karl stopped, put his hand to his chin and looked at the camera. "Can I say something off the record?"

"Of course," Clisty answered and motioned to Griff to stop filming momentarily.

"Miss Sinclair, there is no way Jorguson could claim the Buddy was his idea. He knew nothing about it until after it was already in production," Kramer whispered.

"Sometimes, more than one person happens to come up with the same idea at approximately the same time," Clisty suggested. "Did you tell Dr. Jorguson about the letters you received?"

"No," Kramer recoiled. "Absolutely not. Jeff is a friend. I don't believe he has anything to do with the threats."

"Okay," Clisty agreed. "Let's go back to the distribution." She looked back at Becca and nodded. "We'll pick it up again."

Becca kept her eyes on Clisty. "Action," Becca directed.

Karl leaned forward, resting his forearms on his knees. "Under the neurologist's direction, we separated those who received a Buddy into two groups. The first group was those who had early onset Alzheimer's. A few of their symptoms included problems performing tasks at work or in social settings. They also have increased trouble planning or organizing. The second group includes those with moderate Alzheimer's ... like forgetting some of their own personal history or having an inability to recall their own address or phone number. They also may not be able to choose clothing appropriate to the season or weather. Those folks are the ones who can become confused about where they are or the day of the week, and have a growing risk of wandering off or becoming lost. The patients in severe or late-stage Alzheimer's require around-the-clock help with activities of daily living and personal care. They may even have increased difficulty with communication. They did not receive a Buddy, since they would not be walking alone. The first two groups would continue to benefit from being out and about, enjoying a walk and running errands."

"If they get confused or lost, a familiar voice directs them home?" Clisty concluded.

"Right," Karen agreed. "The GPS tells them where they are, and uses that to prompt a familiar voice to tell them how to get home."

"That is amazing and indeed a real blessing," Clisty said, affirming the Kramers' creativity and caring. "Is there anything you want the viewing audience to know about the Walking Buddy?"

"Not at this time," Karl Kramer answered with a strained smile on his face.

Clisty looked over the Kramers' heads and saw Jake, Becca and Griff smiling back at her. She knew her first interview was a success. "That wraps up our visit with Dr. and Professor Kramer from here in the Heartland. We are thankful the network has recognized the need to bring positive stories of encouragement and hope from real people."

Karen put her index finger to her lips, like she was about to pass on a secret. "Clisty, there is another issue I didn't want to get out to the public until the police had made a thorough investigation."

Clisty looked around at the team. The cameras were off and Griff turned off the lights as well. Clisty's eyes quickly adjusted to the warm glow of the table lamps. "Jake, is there any problem with Karen sharing her information at this time?"

"It isn't going to be taped," he thought aloud. "Karen, this team is guided by certain professional standards. No one is to talk about any of the interview outside of this immediate circle. As a college Student Affairs chairperson once said, "We need to keep the circle small.""

"Thanks to all of you, I do feel very comfortable in this circle." Karen stood up and walked over to the long expanse of windows. "The other day, we were just getting home from work. I had picked up Karl at his office since his car was in the shop. When we got out of my SUV in front of our garage, a man threw a baseball at me ... at us maybe ... and shattered the windshield. If the ball had gone all the way through the glass, he could have killed me. We saw no one else around. The ball was like a huge bullet." She paused and looked at Karl for confirmation.

"I know she's right," Karl nodded. "He had some arm. He must have thrown at ninety miles per hour, like a professional."

"You said, *he*," Jake observed. "Are you sure the pitcher was a man?"

"I'm not sure of anything right now?" Karen blustered. "But, I would think there would be very few women who could throw a ball as hard as the one that blasted at me."

"Clisty," Karl added, "I agree. The field of possible throwers would be narrowed to a very few men and even much fewer women."

83

Chapter 12
The City

Back in the city on the Hudson, Clisty and the team dropped off the company van at BNN. "Thanks Nicole." Clisty handed her the key and placed her other hand on top. "I'm finding you are indispensable."

"Thank you, Clisty. I feel like I've found a new friend." Nicole waved as Clisty left.

Riding down on the elevator, Clisty overflowed with excitement. The smile on her face grew beyond her ability to contain it.

When the elevator doors opened on the first floor, she nearly jumped out. "I want to run in here," Clisty motioned to the gift shop.

"The gift shop?" Becca asked. "If we're going to sightsee, I'll pick up a few things while you're in there."

"You could," Jake suggested. "I'm pretty sure they would deliver your packages to the hotel's front desk."

Clisty gave Becca a quick hug. "As long as you don't take more than a minute or two." She walked in the store and looked around. "It's right over there." A stack of pamphlets and maps nested on a rack near the gift shop door. She noticed them when she was in the shop earlier.

"The Metropolitan Museum of Art sits on the edge of Central Park on Fifth Avenue," Clisty read from a guide. She waved the pamphlet in the air. "This will help."

"Wouldn't your Walking Buddy be able to show you the way around New York?" Becca asked as she pointed to the Buddy on Clisty's arm.

"Probably," Clisty admitted. "But, I haven't read the directions yet." She looked at it again and smiled.

"Okay," Jake began, "we didn't get to see the Museum yesterday. I know you wanted to go there, Clisty. That would be a good place to spend a few hours. We'll hit the highlights. We can go back to the hotel from there and change for the Broadway musical this evening when we're finished."

"Thanks, Jake," Clisty grabbed his arm and hung on. "We don't have much time but we can see what we can see." She looked at the pamphlet again. "With 1,500,000 square feet of art in the Met, those highlights will flash by like lightening."

Outside, the flags along the front of the BNN building flapped in the wind against each pole. All four of the team inhaled deeply at the same time. It was a beautiful day. Clisty almost thought she could smell the blueness of the sky. The brilliant color was a blessing to the day.

"Since we are saving every minute," Jason suggested, "let's all cram into a taxi. We're on Sixth Avenue and the museum is on Fifth, but I don' know how far uptown we would have to walk to get to Central Park."

"Absolutely," Jake agreed. He walked to the edge of the sidewalk and flagged down a cab. "Jason, you hop in the back with the ladies and I'll get in the front with the driver."

"No, Jake," Jason said.

"Get in the cab, Jason," Becca ordered, pushing Jake into the back, then Clisty, and then Becca jumped in. Jason climbed into the front before the cab left the curb.

The cabbie dropped them off at the wide expanse of stairs that led to the entrance of the largest art museum in the country. "We're on a run," Clisty announced with a giggle as she darted up the steps, laughing all the way.

They hurried over to the security line and stopped. "There's no fast lane here," Clisty observed. "They have to check every bag."

"It's a good thing I had the two coffee mugs of Geraldine Vega I bought at the gift shop for Mom and Dad delivered to the hotel. That's one package that doesn't have to be inspected."

"I don't know if we'll have time to run into the Met's gift shop, however." Clisty fumbled with her Walking Buddy and wished she had taken the time to program it. It could have been useful.

They quickly purchased skip-the-line smartphone tickets and Clisty grabbed a few diagrams of the displays in the huge space. While they stood in line, Jake made a decision. "We will all follow Clisty while here in the museum. This is her few hours."

Clisty smiled. "If we have the time, I'd like to see the major exhibits: Monet, Degas, Renoir, and Van Gogh for sure." She pulled out her guide and handed it to Jake. "You were military. Can you find the shortest route to the French Impressionist Art? It's the largest collection outside the Louvre in Paris."

Jake looked over the map. "The paintings you want to see are inside the 19th century galleries. Come on," he said, handing the map back to Clisty. He took her hand and added, "Follow us or, follow the signs," he added as he pointed to placards prominently placed around the museum. "If you get lost, call one of us on your cell phone and we'll find a meeting place."

"This building is amazing," Becca drooled as they walked through the Grand Hall with its inverted arches high above. "Wonder what it would be like to film in here?"

"Watch, *When Harry Met Sally* again. A scene from that film took place here." Clisty hurried on to the first display. The four of them paused at each painting. Then, they whipped past the masterpieces, with one art treasure whirling into the stately stance of another. At the Renoir exhibit, Clisty moved in closer to get a better view of the artist's rendering of *The Bay of Naples*. Suddenly, she heard the sharp blast of a whistle. "Step back, Ma'am," a museum guard ordered with insistence. "You must stay a few steps back from the paintings."

"Oh, I'm sorry," Clisty stepped back, blushing. "Mother likes to paint. I told her I'd study the brush strokes if I get a chance to see it up close."

"Well, you did," the guard snapped.

Clisty and Jake stepped back with Jake's hand resting on Clisty's shoulder. "We can see it from here just fine."

"Who knew?" Becca whispered.

Clisty put her hand to her mouth. "I guess I should have," she whispered in agreement with the guard. "It does look much better from back here."

"Shall we move on?" Jake asked.

"Right," Clisty agreed. "There are more Renoir paintings or we can move on."

Clisty lifted the map from her pocket again and pointed, "There, that exhibit. Walk past the center steps and turn right."

"Lead on Sergeant," Becca announced with a swish of her hand.

Jason looked at his watch. "We're making really good time."

As they neared the landing at the top of the wide staircase, Clisty let go of Jake's arm, brushed her hair off her forehead, and swept it out of her eyes. At that very moment, a man in jeans, a long sleeve flannel shirt and a baseball cap, rushed up behind her, and pushed her with full force. Clisty crashed into Jake causing him to lose his balance. Rather than falling down the steps, Jake shifted his weight to his right leg and grabbed Clisty. Then he went into tackle formation and together, he and Clisty rolled in the opposite direction from the steps.

"Clisty!" Becca screamed running to her side. The Monet scarf Becca hurriedly purchased in the gift shop when they first arrived and wrapped around her waist was rapidly jerked off. She wadded the scarf and tucked it under Clisty's head.

Jason chased after the assailant in fast pursuit.

Jake inspected Clisty's head, turning it gently. There was no blood, no scratches or bruises. "You okay, Babe?"

"Yes, yes," Clisty waved her hand in the attacker's direction. "Get him, Jake!"

Jake took the steps down, two at a time. Leaning over the banister to the right, he saw no one moving in an erratic manner. On the other side of the steps, the same was true. As Jake searched the Grand Hall, Jason returned. He hopped up a few steps and searched right and left from that elevated position.

"Sorry, Jake," Jason apologized. "He got away."

"Clisty …" Jake caught his breath, turned, and ran back upstairs. By the time he got to the landing at the top of steps, Clisty was on her feet. Jake grabbed her, sweeping her off her feet. "I'm going to take you to the E.R."

"We have Broadway tickets, Jake. I am not going to the hospital. I just fell down." She threw her arms around him. "Besides," she laughed, throwing her head back, "you make a comfy giant pillow." Brushing off her clothes, she added, "I am ready to go back to the hotel. But, I'll sneak out the window if there's any more talk of doctors."

"From the seventh floor?"

"Of course." Her eyes twinkled. "I am Clisty Sinclair, remember. I have arrived."

Chapter 13
A Night Out

In the hotel that evening, Clisty checked her image to see if her little black dress was appropriate for the Broadway Musical, *My Honeysuckle Rose*. The network was generous and gave tickets to all five of them. "Okay," she said aloud as she twirled slowly in front of the mirror. She stopped when she heard a quiet tap from the hallway.

"Ready?" Jake asked when she opened the door.

"You tell me," she said with a laugh, lightly dancing around the room.

"Well," Jake sized her up from toe to head, "you look great, except ... some may wonder why you're not wearing shoes."

"No one knows me here," she announced with a little smile of satisfaction.

"Yet," Jake finished her thought.

Clisty's body shook a little as her shoulders drooped. "That is the part I'm not looking forward to, having everyone watch my every move because they think they know me."

"That's one of the many things I love about you." He pulled her close and shut the door with a backward shove of his foot. "Most people would want the celebrity status above all else."

"Hopefully, we'll have at least a little private life," she whispered. "Do you think we'll be able to live together after we're married without others finding out?"

Jake shook his head. "I don't know. What's really strange ... now days, people wouldn't care if we lived together ... but the network wouldn't like it if we got married."

"You have to remember, I'm from Indiana, not Paris, France." Clisty tapped Jake on his suit jacket with the tip of her finger.

"Yes ... I know. But it's 2020, not 1820." Jake teased.

"I know, give me time," she coaxed, although the corners of her mouth told him she agreed. Clisty wanted to send Mr. Funderbird a wedding invitation, but she just wasn't ready. "Mr. Funderbird wouldn't say anything negative. I'm sure he wouldn't care. It's just that he and I were talking and, I already promised him I wouldn't marry anytime soon," she sighed deeply as she buried her head in Jake's chest. "I want to honor my word."

"See, I can add another thing I love about you, Babe." He gathered her in his arms. As he leaned to kiss her nose there was another knock on the door. "The busy-life begins," he said with a smile.

"Becca," Clisty remarked as she opened the door and looked around the hall. "Where's Jason?"

"He's going to meet us in the lobby. Griff called and said he was going on down. I came up to see what you're wearing."

"Black dress, black shoes ...." Clisty blushed as she looked down at her feet. "My shoes are in the closet." She pulled the pair of black patent leather wedge heals out and slipped them on. "Now, I'm ready."

"Good," Becca announced. "We match ... well, sorta. We have the same theme going on, short-skirt evening wear." She checked Clisty again and then looked at her own reflection in the mirror. "You're in black with white accents and I'm in white with black trim. I'd say we look more like New Yorkers than Hoosiers."

Clisty turned to Jake, "See. What did I just say? Now, I'm really confused." Turning back to Becca, she admitted. "I think you're right."

"I like Indiana," Jake protested in jest.

"So do I," Clisty agreed and gave him a side-by-side-hug. As she did, she wondered how many hugs would come casually from the hip in the future. "Remember, I negotiated a new contract placing my home base in Fort Wayne." She stopped and studied her reflection again. "Still, I would hate to think that my wardrobe will consist of only black dresses for the rest of my life."

"That's your choice," Jake reminded her. "You care less about what people think of you than anyone I know. You do your own thing, and proudly." Another sideways hug as he whispered, "See … another thing."

"Right, Clisty," Becca echoed. "I like you in light blue."

"Me too," she agreed. "I love color." She picked up her door card, slipped it into a small black clutch bag and threw her white shawl with beaded trim around her shoulders.

Chapter 14
A Casually Dangerous Walk

Later, in an historic theater on Broadway, while Clisty, Jake and the others stood for the final curtain call of *Honeysuckle Rose*, in Stamford, Connecticut, the Kramers enjoyed a late night stroll with Oliver. The chirping of crickets danced on the clear night air and floated on the perfume of white, spring-blooming honeysuckle. Karen knew of Clisty's show tickets and smiled. Both of the Kramers drank in the sweetness of the evening as deeply as possible.

"Do you think it's safe to walk out here at night?" Karen asked. "Remember what happened a couple of days ago?"

"Karen," Karl dropped his jaw in surprise. "Of course I remember. And, I remember the other threatening notes you received. I do worry. But, Karen, we can't hide in fear." Karl looked up at the star-scattered sky and sighed. "I can't think about that now." He was quiet for a minute. "Can you imagine how many people will see our little Walking Buddy when the show airs on the American News Magazine? Thousands."

"I looked it up online," Karen agreed as she gripped Karl's hand more tightly. "Ten or eleven million viewers will be tuned in. I'm so excited, I could explode."

"Don't do that," Karl dropped Karen's hand and hugged her. "I want you around to help me enjoy all the rewards of this great invention of ours."

"Karl," she began to ask slowly as they started walking again, "have you ever thought about what you'd like to do with all the extra money we could make off the Buddy?"

"Oh, wow," he gasped and started to dance around like a child enjoying all that life had to offer, with Oliver tangled in his leash around Karl's legs. "Money? Real extra money? No insurance forms to fill out, no liability insurance payments to make, no complaints from the patients who came in fifteen minutes late, then griped about sitting an extra five in the waiting room." He untwisted himself from the dog.

"Yes," she twirled and spun around with her hands out wide. "Money," she sang out for emphasis.

"Actually, I have thought about it ... some ... a lot." He kicked a few pebbles with the tip of his shoe. Oliver chased one of the pebbles to the end of his leash, checking it for a source of possible food. "Karen, I'd like to start a foundation. I've actually thought recently about an old idea," he said as he looked up and saw an approaching car. Grabbing Karen by the wrist, he pulled her off the pavement. "Watch out mister," he choked as the words caught in his throat. Watching the car speed away, he dismissed the near-accident and continued. "Our foundation may have to change to *college professors who are hit by approaching cars.*" Oliver barked after the vehicle and stood in the street watching it disappear.

"Okay," she said as she stumbled a little while backing away from him. "What else ... besides assistance for clumsy Profs?"

"Well, as you know, Dad was a minister." Karl took a deep breath and looked up, expanding his universe. "I'd like to help children and families of pastors. They don't make much money. I'd like to pay for piano lessons for the kids, buy their special team uniforms, and pay for sports camp. We could send teens to college who want to prepare to serve in the inner city and in under-developed areas. They wouldn't be able to make those sacrificial choices once they graduate because they wouldn't make enough money to pay off their huge student loan debt."

A car buzzed by sending a small spatter of loose gravel to the side of the road. A man leaned out the window and called, "Sorry."

"No problem," Karl shouted back, waving.

"The small foundation would be a wonderful idea, Karl. Maybe, we can do all of that," Karen agreed as she stuck her hand into her pocket for warmth. "I'm a little more selfish than you are," she whispered. "I'd like for us to have money to travel a little, go places we never had the time to go before, see small towns before they're gone, and taste the rest of life while we can still enjoy it."

"You know, Karen," Karl added, "that's not selfish at all. A lot of our income has gone to help our children come out of college debt free. A small practice doctor doesn't make as much money as some people fantasize. Not when they run their practice in the only way I want to practice medicine, slow and personal."

"You don't have a lot of family income left over when you treat so many patients who have medical needs but no insurance or ability to pay." Karen kissed him and continued her dance of joy. She threw her head back and shouted, "You are my hero, Karl Kramer."

Karl suddenly stopped and stared across and down the road in disgusted amazement. Oliver growled, held his ears high, his tail higher, and paced back and forth.

Karl pulled on the dog's leash and stared at the car. "What is that guy doing?" he asked as he watched the approaching car. "That doesn't look like the same car from before. He's acting the same though. Get way over, Karen," he warned as the oncoming headlights grew larger and began to cross the center of the road.

Karen didn't move but stood frozen on the berm of the road. With her arms spread out in disbelief, she argued with the driver, "How much road do you need?"

"Karen, Honey," Karl pleaded, reaching toward her. "Get in the ditch if you have to." He watched as the car slowed down and sat there, breathing, in the middle of the road.

Karen started backing up further off the road. She couldn't seem to move far enough for that driver. "You couldn't possibly want all of it. Think about it!" she sassed.

Then, the sound of crunching, flying gravel filled the night. A thud and then silence except for the idling of the car's motor ... then the squeal of tires.

"Oh, Karen ... no!"

Chapter 15
The Early Call

Clisty woke up the next morning around 9 AM. Bright beams of light streamed through the narrow empty spaces between the tall buildings visible from her window. After a brilliant performance of an exciting new stage musical and a late night supper the evening before, they had all gone back to the hotel. Clisty and Jake were exhausted. They said their goodnights and retired to their separate rooms. Now the morning brought another schedule: extra time to sleep in, then pack and get to the airport by 5 PM for a 6 PM departure, arriving in Indiana in time to get a good night's sleep.

Clisty nearly drug herself out of bed and stood for a minute at the window. When she finally finished waking up, she realized she'd better stop being a window display and flipped the curtain closed. With the clothes in her hand in which she intended to travel, she hopped into the bathroom. In the shower, she sang strains from the previous night's Broadway musical:

I'm glad I found you
My honeysuckle rose.
Why you chose me
Only heaven knows.
You're Sweet as honey —
All I need of love.
Angels brought you,
From heav'n above.

When her cell phone rang, she didn't want to leave the warm water and fragrant sweet bubbles inside the glass oasis. She sighed deeply, reluctantly grabbed a large white towel from the rack and wrapped it around her. Fumbling with her phone, she hoped she wouldn't get it too wet. "Clisty Sinclair," was her brief greeting.

It was Nicole Bernard. Clisty was surprised. Was there another assignment already?

"Clisty, we know you spent yesterday afternoon with Karl and Karen Kramer," Nicole stated very professionally, not the friendly, jovial new friend from yesterday.

"Yes," Clisty drew out.

"Karen was struck by a car last evening." Nicole delivered the news with a strained voice.

"What? How is she?" Clisty asked as she held her breath.

"She's in very serious condition," Nicole informed her and added quickly. "Dr. Kramer is by her side."

Clisty bunched the towel behind herself and slowly slumped down on the desk chair. "What are her injuries?"

"We know that both of her legs were broken, her right shoulder, and she has a head injury ... a concussion."

"A concussion?" Clisty fired back as she began to rock back and forth. "Their invention is to help people with memory and brain problems. I don't know if that's good or even more tragic."

"I know," Nicole agreed and waited while the impact of the accident soaked in. "We heard on the scanner they airlifted her to New York Presbyterian – the Allen Hospital, part of the Columbia University Medical Center on Broadway here in New York City. They have fine doctors there who can help her. Her other injuries will also be analyzed to see what needs to be done." Nicole was silent for a few seconds. "The hospital is about eleven miles north of your hotel, Clisty. The network wants you and your team to go to the hospital, check on her and comfort Dr. Kramer. If Dr. Kramer will permit a short interview, we'd like you to talk to him on camera ... and his wife too, if possible."

"Okay ... right." Clisty's stomach churned, adding to her discomfort. She and Jake had planned to have a leisurely breakfast of eggs and smoke-cured bacon with buttered toast.

That would be out now. "We returned the van yesterday. We'll take a cab to headquarters—"

"I've arranged for Allen and Eric, two BNN drivers, to bring the van to you at the hotel at ten o'clock. They'll be at the Sixth Avenue entrance. Eric will drive a second car and bring Allen back to the network."

"Nicole, I can see how helpful you will be to all of us," Clisty said. "I want to say thank you for all you do, in case it gets too hectic later to tell you." She hung up and called Jake, Becca and Griff.

"Oh, my goodness," Becca gasped when she heard the news. "It's a good thing they had right-of-survivorship. What if something happened to one of them?"

"It's good they thought of it. Nicole didn't say if it was life-threatening. She did say that Karen is in serious condition. I'm sure Dr. Kramer could use our support. You tell Jason. I'll call Jake and Griff." She quickly changed her clothes and readied herself for a long, hard day.

Chapter 16
Karen Kramer

As they drove up to the bright red awning over the entrance to New York Presbyterian Hospital, they were all silent. The jarring wail of incoming emergency vehicles filled the morning air and brought them back to the reality of Karen's grave condition.

Before they got out of the van, Jake commented quietly, "Things change really fast." He looked at Clisty. "I don't intend to put off anything important."

Clisty blushed and lowered her eyes so the sparkle wouldn't give them away. "You guys get the equipment, then, wait for a minute while I go in and see if I can find where Karen is. The equipment might scare the staff inside."

"HIPPA regulations won't let them tell you where she is," Jake reminded her.

"I'll figure out something." Clisty didn't look back as she walked confidently into the lobby.

The hospital didn't smell of germicidal disinfectant cleaner like Clisty expected. Whatever they used, it was odorless, but something began to nag and sting at her throat almost immediately.

Griff followed her into the hospital as planned, catching up before she went through the second set of doors. "I have an idea. It could expedite the search and perhaps get us out of here more quickly. Professor Kramer was brought to this hospital," Griff suggested, "not because of two broken legs, but because of her head injury." He hoisted the camera higher on his shoulder. "Try asking where the neurology department is. That's where they took my cousin after he got a concussion from his motorcycle accident."

103

"Perfect, Griff," Clisty agreed. Leaving the others to wait near the entrance, she hurried into the lobby and headed to the receptionist's desk.

A woman with a toddler balanced on her left hip, darted back and forth in front of her as she tried to navigate the bustling hallway. The woman was pushing a double stroller that rocked a sleeping baby. The crackle of crepe soled shoes hurried up behind her and passed Clisty on the left like faster moving traffic. A man with greying clumps of wavy hair shuffled past Clisty and patiently hung onto the greeter's desk. His panting wasn't hard for Clisty to hear.

"May I help you?" a volunteer in a light blue smock asked when it was Clisty's turn. Her quiet expression was encouraging.

"Thanks," Clisty said as she smiled sweetly and watched the man beside her. To get out of his way, she quickly asked, "Hey, I forgot where the neurology department is. She was brought in sometime during the night."

"Oh, well then," the lady in blue thought out loud, "she may still be in the E.R., depending on how many tests they need to run."

"I didn't think about that," Clisty said and turned to start down the hall toward the E.R. just as the film crew came through the doors.

"Is that a camera?" the gate-keeper in blue cautioned. "There are privacy laws you know."

Clisty stopped and pretended to look for something in her purse in order to hear the conversation between Griff and those at the front desk.

"Yes, Ma'am, I do know," Griff answered as the man with the camera. "But, we were asked to come into the hospital. I brought this small one." He changed the subject, declining to say who requested the interview. He turned matter-of-factly and followed in the direction Clisty was heading.

Various signs led the way to the Emergency Room. Down a long hall, and then left through double doors. When Clisty arrived, she encountered a well-organized frenzy of people with buzzers, beepers and cell phones all bleeping at the same time. Karl Kramer was pacing outside one of the examining rooms.

"Miss Sinclair?" Kramer gulped as he opened his arms and welcomed her with a relieved hug. Standing back he asked, "How did you find out?"

"My assistant at the network called. They monitor the incoming news in real time." Clisty looked over Karl's shoulder and saw the crew coming. "The network asked us to get an interview, if that's okay with you. I know you must be very upset. I don't know if an interview is even possible for you."

"An interview?" he questioned in surprise.

"We don't have to, Karl," Clisty explained quickly. "This whole thing must be hard for you. I don't even know how badly Karen is hurt. But, with the threatening letters and all—"

"Being a doctor," he began, as a shadow of worry crossed his face, "doesn't really prepare you ... at least it didn't prepare me ... for an unexpected accident," he cleared his throat, "involving your own wife."

"Do you have children who need to be called?" Clisty asked, wondering if she could be of any help.

Karl began to pace again. "Heather and her family live in Florida. I called her the minute we got to the hospital." He paused and looked around as Becca, Griff and Jake walked up. "Hi guys."

Jake handed Karl a cup of coffee in a vending machine cup. "You can have this one, if you want it." He gave the cup in his other hand to Clisty.

Karl took the cup and smiled a weary smile. "Thank you." He drank a swallow and watched the steam rise from the surface. "Steve and his wife and kids live in New

Rochelle but the kids are on spring break. They're all in Florida right now. I called them and will let Steve up-date them on his mother's condition as soon as I know what all of her injuries are."

Clisty sipped a little from the hot liquid. She couldn't believe that a drop-down, vending machine cup of coffee could taste so good. "This is great, thanks."

Becca came up beside Clisty with her cell phone screen glowing. "Look at this," she whispered.

The words in the crawl across the bottom of the screen caused her to stop and catch her breath. "Police are looking for Dr. Karl Kramer," she whispered. "He is not accused of anything at this time and is only a person of interest." She turned the screen to Jake and nudged for him to read it.

Jake said nothing but stepped toward the doctor. "Sir, are you aware the police are looking for you?"

"For me?" Karl asked, blinking in apparent confusion. "Why wouldn't they know I'm here with my wife?"

"That is the usual procedure, Doctor," Jake explained quietly. "When there has been an incident, the police rule-out people in the victim's family and circle of friends first."

"Victim?" Kramer slowly lowered himself onto a chair in the E.R. waiting room. "It was an accident. There was no victim, not this time." He stopped and waved his hand, clearing the air.

Jake smiled and reassured him softly. "The police must have a reason to talk to people. Do you want me to call them and let them know you're here?" he asked.

"Yes, yes of course," Karl agreed and looked up as a man approached. "Jeff, what are you doing here?"

The man reached out and reassured Kramer with a friendly embrace. "It's on the news, Karl. How is Karen?"

"I don't know yet." He nodded in agreement when Griff raised the camera and focused the lens. "Jeff, I'd like you to meet some people." He gestured toward Clisty and the crew. "This is Clisty Sinclair with BNN … and her crew, Rebecca Landers and Griff on the camera. The other gentleman is Sergeant Jake Davis, their security."

"Security?" Jeff asked. "Has there been a problem?"

"Some threats," Clisty offered.

"Now, with Karen's accident—" Karl didn't finish but turned to the TV crew. "Oh … sorry, this is Dr. Jeffery Jorguson, the neurologist I told you about."

"Yes," Clisty acknowledged, transferring the microphone to her left hand while extending her right. "The physician who supplied the patients."

"Miss Sinclair, I see you have one of our watches," Jorguson observed, then quickly added, "Karl and Karen's watch I should say." He rubbed his chin and admitted, "Since my patients are benefiting, I do feel like I'm part of the whole project."

"It is a great idea," Clisty agreed.

"Have you seen all the features yet?" Jeffery asked.

"No ... just the time. So far, I haven't programed it." Clisty stepped back as an E.R. doctor approached them.

"A TV camera?" the woman in green scrubs asked with raised eyebrows.

"It's all right, doctor. I'm Karl Kramer, Karen's husband. I've given them permission to film her progress. How is she doing?" He spoke softly with a tremor in his voice.

"I'm Dr. Blout." The E.R. physician nodded at all of them and shook Kramer's hand. "She does have a concussion, Dr. Kramer. It is serious, but so far there is not much swelling. Her right shoulder has been set, but her legs are going to require surgery to insert a rod in at least her right leg, to stabilize it. The orthopedic surgeon will check the x-rays again and he may just set the bones in the left one."

Dr. Kramer slapped his hand to his chest and exhaled. "That sounds better than I feared. Is she conscious? Can I talk to her?"

"Yes, she has a terrible headache so try not to ask her too many questions." He looked at the camera crew. "Just family."

"Can they come in for a minute?" Karl asked. His face was taut and drawn. "Karen may say something important about the person who hit her and they would have it on film. Besides, they are all family now."

"For just a few minutes," the doctor cautioned. "I don't know what she can tell you. Her thinking may be fuzzy."

"Karen?" Kramer asked with a tilt to his head. "She's the most detailed person I know."

"Follow me then." Dr. Blout led the way into the small examining space.

Clisty watched for changes in Kramer's expression or body language. She was glad Griff was discrete as he filmed the scene from the back, unnoticed, while his lens saw everything.

Kramer went to his wife's side. With a trembling lower lip, he appeared to fight hard to hold back his own tears. "Honey," he gasped, kissing her scratched face and swollen blackened eye. "Someone has come to see you."

"Clisty?" she asked through a foggy voice. "I thought I heard you."

"I am so sorry to bother you, Karen," Clisty apologized as she took a step toward the examining table and her new friend. "I had to come. I know, I know, the network asked me to. But, Karen, I came because you're a friend." She extended her hand to Karen. When she saw the cast on her arm, she patted it gently. "Is it all right if I ask you a few questions?"

"Yes," she said as she reached for her husband's hand. "If Karl stays right here."

"I'm not going anywhere, Honey," he said, his smile assuring but appearing tired.

Clisty moved a little closer, touching the crisp white sheet that covered her. "Your accident happened very late at night, or early in the morning. Can you tell me why you were out at that hour?"

Karl kissed Karen's hand and answered with background information. "Clisty, first, you don't know what happened earlier." He looked at his wife and took a deep breath. "Hours before Karen's accident, we were out for a late walk with Oliver. Someone in a car toyed with us, aiming his sedan in our direction, even crossing the midline. Finally, he got so close Karen fell in the gravel as he sped away."

"That was no accident," Clisty whispered as fear gripped inside. "That was deliberate."

Karen reached for her head and frowned when she felt bandages. "Then, later, during the night, someone called from Karl's office. We had set up our Buddy business there in a spare examining room. The caller said the Buddy program was hacked and I needed to go in and check the program."

"What?" Kramer gasped as he clutched Karen's hand to his chest. "I had no idea why you were out late. Why didn't you tell me? I would have gone with you."

"You were sleeping," Karen whispered, her face drawn tight in pain. "I didn't want to awaken you. So ... I dressed quickly and went out to assess the damage."

Clisty leaned the mic closer. "What happened? Did you see who hit you?"

"No, only a streak of dark blue." She closed her eyes and shuddered. "A small truck or a sedan ... I don't know." She shook her head as Karl bent down and kissed her forehead through her blood-matted hair.

"Did you recognize the vehicle?" Karl asked. "Did the car look like the one that had taunted you earlier?"

"I don't know," she mumbled … her eyes heavy. "Maybe … I … don't know."

"Thank you, Karen." Clisty leaned down and carefully kissed Karen on the forehead, wondering how the Kramer's act of kindness had gotten to that point. She looked at Becca and nodded. In the entrance to Karen's examining area, Clisty saw two men in suits talking to Jake. They looked in her direction. She guessed the police had come for Karl Kramer.

Chapter 17
Buddy is the Cause

Clisty watched from the hall as an orderly wheeled Karen's E.R. gurney out of the cubical. Karl walked beside her, holding her hand. Night visitors, burdened with their own loved one's injuries, hurried out of the way as the gurney pressed on through a group of hospital workers in various colored scrubs. When they reached the elevator, Clisty turned to the team. "Let's go." They jumped on just as the doors closed. Jake turned back to talk to the men in suits. Kramer reached over to Clisty's wrist and pressed a button on the side of her Buddy watch. She thanked him, but wasn't sure why he did it.

Karl smiled at the Buddy and wrung his anxious hands together. "I'm a fixer. At least I can do something."

When they got off, Karl hurried to keep up with Karen's transport nurse. Clisty looked for a sign to direct her and saw one labeled, "Surgery Waiting." She pointed to that area as the others came up. Becca and Griff said nothing but slipped into the lounge and sat in silence, staring blankly at the television mounted high on the wall.

At the end of the hall, Clisty saw them pull Karen's examination bed through another set of double doors. Watching Karl, Clisty saw him go limp. When tears began to stream down his face, he pulled a white handkerchief from his hip pocked, blew his nose and wiped his eyes.

"Come over here, Karl. Griff will have his camera off," Clisty said as all four of them sat down in the waiting area near the ubiquitous fish tank.

"I flipped the button on your watch to the 'on' position," Kramer began, "to activate your GPS. Maybe, if

111

Sergeant Davis has a GPS in his phone, he can find you here on this floor."

"Right, but visitors aren't supposed to have their cell phone on in the hospital," Clisty added.

"The GPS signal in the Buddy won't interfere with medical equipment," Karl explained distantly. His tired eyes revealed his distraction.

"That's fine, Dr. Kramer—"

"Please, Clisty, people who know me, call me Karl," he said as he looked toward the television, although his blank expression revealed he didn't seem to see the program.

"Karl," she repeated. Becca and Griff watched and listened.

The fish swimming around in the tank, darting from one end to the other, mesmerized the team. Colorful choral and water grasses added interest and another layer to the hypnotic trance.

"Clisty," Jake called from the hall.

She looked up, smiled and went out to talk to him. At first she said nothing but reached around and gave him a sideways hug. Karen and Karl's marriage popped into her mind. What would it be like to love someone for thirty-five years and then nearly lose them? She could not imagine.

"Clisty, these men want to talk to Dr. Kramer," Jake said as he looked over at Karl and motioned for him to come into the hall. When Kramer walked up, he assured him, "It's just routine."

"Dr. Kramer," the man on the left began, "I'm Detective Frank Shanahan; this is Sergeant Hafner. We're sorry to interrupt you now. We know you're worried about your wife."

"She's just gone in for surgery," Karl explained. "Talking to you may take my mind off of it. What can I do for you?"

"Can you tell us what your wife was doing out at that hour?" Hafner asked.

"We just had a chance to talk to her before she went into surgery to have her legs set and rods inserted," Kramer rubbed his eyes. "She was able to tell us a little."

"We?" Shanahan asked.

"Yes," he answered. Turning to Clisty, he said, "This is Clisty Sinclair. She and her producer, Rebecca, and cameraman Griff had interviewed me and my wife at our home yesterday afternoon for BNN's new segment, *Stories from the Heartland* on the American News Magazine. They were at our house when Karen came home from the University. She just now told us that she went to the office late last night after receiving a telephone call. The caller said someone had hacked our Buddy program."

"Who would have been at the office to call her at that hour of the night or early morning?" Shanahan questioned.

Kramer blinked his eyes and turned to Clisty. "I didn't think to ask her. Her accident came as such a shock. She is going through a lot right now."

"I'm sorry, Detective," Clisty joined in. "I didn't ask her either. I was just glad she was conscious. I did find it odd that someone would hack a program that only helps people."

"Yes, Ma'am," Shanahan agreed. "We live in odd times. Even hospitals are hacked."

Clisty shook her head in disbelief. "Karen was very weak. She couldn't say much."

"We understand," the sergeant assured her. Turning to Karl he asked, "Dr. Kramer, why didn't you go with her to the office?"

"I didn't know she left. She said she didn't want to awaken me." Karl's voice, strained with grief and worry, cracked under the stress.

"Yes, Sir," Sergeant Hafner agreed. "Did she say anything else?"

"Um, I ... yes," Kramer answered slowly. "She said she remembered something blue."

"A streak of blue," Clisty added.

"Yes," Kramer answered, re-energized. "She wondered if it could have been a dark blue truck or maybe a sedan." He rubbed his hands together and sighed. "Do the police have any information? Hit and run is such a cowardly act."

"We've just begun our investigation." The sergeant looked at Clisty and the film crew. "These next questions cannot be filmed."

"Oh, of course," Becca chimed in. "We'll wait over here." She pointed to the waiting room chairs.

Clisty didn't say anything nor did she go away. She stood quietly and listened, hoping to disappear from the sergeant's conscious view.

"It may not have been a hit and run, Dr. Kramer." Hafner narrowed his eyes. "There were no tire marks ... no skidding. Can you think of anyone who might have wanted to do your wife harm? Or, you for that matter."

"Karen had no enemies in the past. But, just recently, she received several threatening notes," Kramer explained and nodded in Clisty's direction. "She had gotten one yesterday before she came home, while the TV crew was at our house."

The sergeant looked at Clisty. "Did you see the note?"

"Yes," she thought back. "Well ... a copy. When we went to their home to interview them about their invention, Karen came in late. She had called the Stamford police about a note she received and had to wait for them to get to her office at the university. The Stamford police have the original note."

"Did you read the note yourself?" Hafner asked.

"Yes, I saw the note and handed it back to her for her to read. It said ... something about warning her."

"Warned was the word he used, as in the past," Jake, who was silently listening, corrected. "He had sent threatening notes before."

114

"That's right," Clisty remembered and agreed. "He referred to the Walking Buddy as 'his creation.' He said, 'If you keep selling MY invention, I will not be responsible for my actions.' Then he said something like, 'If you don't stop selling it, you will be responsible for your own destruction.'"

"Good memory," Kramer said. "That is what the note said and it's similar to the other notes she received."

"Do you have any idea who may be behind the threats?" Shanahan questioned.

"We told no one about our project," Kramer stated emphatically, "at any stage of the development ... not a single person. When it was completed, we patented it. Only then, did we take it to a manufacturer and approach marketing people."

"Is that all?" Hafner questioned.

Karl paused and closed his eyes. "Oh yes. Remember Clisty, we talked about the guy who ran us off the road while we were taking a walk earlier in the evening."

Clisty looked at Karl. "Yes, but Karen didn't get a good look at him either." She looked over at Jake and added, "I don't remember any other details."

Kramer rubbed his hand across his forehead. "I can't think of anything."

"Here's my card," Hafner offered. "If you think of anything else, give me a call, text, email, whatever is your preferred form of communication." He reached in his pocket and pulled out another business card and handed it to Clisty.

"Yes, I will," she said. She had no more information but many more questions.

"One more question, Dr. Kramer," Shanahan asked. "Why did you have your wife airlifted to New York City?"

"She had a concussion," Karl replied. "We are currently working with people with Alzheimer's Disease. We know the tragedy that a head injury or progressive memory loss can cause a patient and their family. I wanted to make sure everything possible was done to help Karen."

Shanahan smiled briefly. "Has she had recent memory loss?"

"Absolutely not," Karl threw up both hands. "She wrote the program for our Walking Buddy."

"Great," the detective said as he folded his note pad and put it in his jacket pocket. "I'm sure any brain injury would damage her ability to share in the success of your invention."

"What?" Kramer asked with a bewildered expression on his face. "I don't even know how to answer that." His shoulders fell and his face went white. "She is going to get better. It will take time, but she'll be fine. We're going to travel and … set up a foundation. We have plans."

Clisty said no more. That last interaction between Detective Shanahan and Dr. Kramer answered a lot that flooding her mind. Perhaps, the police had finally gotten to the reason for their need to talk to Karl. They seemed to have him on their suspect list. She wondered what other unexpected information would twist the Kramers' story, from good to tragic. She hoped it would all land right-side-up in the end.

Chapter 18
Alone in a Crowd

They arrived at the airport that afternoon in time to find their flight had already lifted off. "Let's check the departure board and see if there's another flight this evening." Clisty darted between the legions of travelers, dragging her wheeled carry-on over to the panel of arrival and departure screens. A boy in a ball cap ran into her as his thumbs flew over his cell phone key board.

"Hey, watch it lady," the boy griped with one hand on his hip. "I almost dropped my phone."

Clisty ignored his comment. Suspecting the boy's absorption with the tiny screen was his usual interaction with the world, she doubted he'd hear her anyway. She stopped in front of multiple screens, with her purse and laptop balanced on top of her luggage, and searched through the list of airline departures.

"There's a plane that leaves at 6:45 PM," Jason observed as he perused the board.

"I'll check if they have any seats," Clisty offered. "With all the over-booking these days, I doubt it."

Over at the check-in counter, the reservations agent looked at her computer screen and reported dryly, "You missed your plane? Now you need to reschedule five people for Fort Wayne, Indiana."

"Yes, that's right," Clisty responded. She looked at the agent's nametag, *Jamie.*

"How are you doing?" Jake asked as he came up to the desk.

Clisty smiled. "Don't know yet." She reached over on the counter and took Jake's hand.

He squeezed hers gently and looked around to see if the other three were watching.

Jamie removed the small reading glasses perched on her nose and pointed at the screen with the stem. "I can get three of you on Delta at 4:30 ... and two more at 5:00 PM on American Airlines. That will get each flight in at 9 and 9:36 PM."

"I can live with that," Clisty said as she took out the network's credit card to pay for the tickets.

"I hope that card has been activated," Jake said with a wry smile.

"Nicole said she had everything ready to go." Clisty held her breath and hoped that included the plastic.

"You'll be boarding soon," Jamie said and handed over the boarding passes. "Place any checked luggage on the belt."

Clisty and Jake turned and walked back to the others. "You three can take the 4:30 flight. Jake and I will be on the 5:00 PM. Take your luggage up to the counter and check it in."

"Jason and I will be okay taking the later one," Becca offered as she picked up the larger of her two bags. "Come on," she directed Jason who had sat down and folded his arms across his chest.

"No, that's all right," Clisty corrected her as she checked her watch. "Your plane leaves in fifteen minutes. Jake and I will have a small wait and then be right behind you." She glanced over at Jake, then back at Becca and smiled. "You need to hurry."

"Griff," Becca nudged his shin with the tap of her foot. "Get up. We have to check our bags and then get down to our gate in the next few minutes."

"Great. Home in enough time to get to bed early." He yawned and gathered his few belongings.

Becca rolled her eyes, patted Jason on the back and hurried over to the ticket counter.

"So ..." Jake drew out as he watched the other three out of the corner of his eye, "what did you have in mind?"

"Well," Clisty grabbed the front of his shirt and pulled him to her. "I was dreaming of a quiet dinner by an open fire, sweet conversation, and then a long cuddle on the sofa as we watch an old movie." She slipped her arm through his as he took his luggage over to Jamie at check-in. "But, we'll have to do that another time." Looking at her watch, she added, "We have nearly an hour, so that's more time alone together than we've had in weeks."

Jake had a puzzled expression. "Your watch is off. We have a half hour."

Clisty checked her wrist watch and then the Buddy on her right arm. "I was looking at my own watch. I'll have to tell Kramer, his Buddy is working great. But, with only a half hour, I'll settle for a Starbucks in Gate D's waiting area."

"Even a few minutes alone with you would be wonderful ... anywhere." Jake looked at the signs above each concourse. "This way," he pointed. "There's Griff and the others running into that gate area."

"Jake," Clisty pointed at a coffee kiosk on the left side of the hall. Without checking the menu board, she knew what she wanted. She ordered café mocha ... Jake a cream steamer. "I want to post on my blog when I get home. The caffeine and chocolate will help me stay awake." With the steam still rising through the drinking spout, they walked over to chairs by the window where they could watch the arriving and departing planes.

Clisty brushed off the seat with the Starbucks napkin before sitting down. "You know we're not really alone. There are people all around us. Remember, with your work as our security, we will be together in a crowd many, many more times, two guppies in a fish bowl," Clisty sighed.

"We don't have to look out. Our world is in the private confines of our glass bowl. When we get married, we can close our door to the rest of the world for a while each day." Jake drank several swallows from his cup. "I'm just not sure how we'll be able to keep Mr. and Mrs. Davis away from the public's awareness."

"Mr. and Mrs. Jake Davis ..." Clisty whispered.

Jake leaned in toward Clisty. "Unless you're thinking you want to keep your own name."

"I'll have to keep my name professionally, Jake," she said, her brows furrowed.

"I understand," he said as his fingers tapped on his cup.

When she looked up at him, her face softened. "But, in the ceremony, I want the pastor to say, 'I now pronounce you, Mr. and Mrs. Jake Davis,' even if no one else is there to hear it but us."

Jake looked around the concourse waiting area, reached over and put his hand behind Clisty's head. He pulled her closer and let her rest her head on his shoulder. For that moment, they were alone in the crowd.

Crime Beat
✬
From the Heartland

10:45 PM
Arrived home from New York this evening after this blogger signed a contract to expand the outreach of *Crime Beat*. Hop aboard as this might get bumpy.

THE TREADWAY VERDICT
As you know, the verdict on the Ezra Treadway case came in. Guilty on all counts. Many of you helped with the research that went into bringing that man to justice. Remember, www.crimebeat.blogsmith.com is more than an entertaining read. The bits and pieces you sent in on the "Contact" email connection were pieced together to form a whole. Thank you for that.
The entire story, from the beginning when Treadway kidnapped Faith Sterling and attempted to seize this blogger, through the verdict and a glimpse at Faith's new life, will appear on BNN's American News Magazine. An exciting component will be the first Heartland Hero we will lift up. In the Treadway case, it will actually be Emily Treadway. While that may seem strange, since she is the wife of the violent kidnapper, Ezra Treadway, Emily's bravery helped Faith survive the many years locked in the second floor of the Treadway home. That courage is in need of recognition. Ezra refused to allow books or educational materials on the second floor. Emily was able to sneak a cell phone into Faith's room so she could read books that carried her out of her small drab existence and to places far and beyond anywhere she would ever go. Emily's brother secretly

hooked up a small projector to cast images on the wall for science and other subjects. Go on BNN's website for more information.

| Share |

A NEW MYSTERY TO SOLVE

Already, this blogger has encountered a new mystery. Along with that crime to solve, will be our next Heartland Hero. The amazing invention will thrill you. The mystery will enrage you.

To protect the identity of the one injured, at this time the co-inventors will remain nameless. I can ask you, however, an important question. If any of you great readers have knowledge about the traffic injury that happened last night in Stamford Connecticut, please contact this blog and/or the Stamford police. Contact information is below. That would be a great beginning.

| Share |

JOIN THE BLOGGER ON TV

We will add a new twist to our segment, *Stories from the Heartland,* on the American News Magazine on BNN. If an occasion arises, like the above request for information regarding the traffic injury in Connecticut, and you WANT to appear on television, we have a way for you to do that. We can arrange for you to Skype in your information. If appropriate, we might use it on our segment on BNN's program. Please, continue to contact this blog with any information you may want to share. An email rather than a Skype message will insure you won't be on TV. Your comments will add an element of teamwork.

| Share |

SEE YOU AT THE BOOKSTORE

Reminder: Join me as I sign copies of *The Lottery Looser* at Barnes and Noble Booksellers at Jefferson Pointe in August. Come and join the conversation.

Share

Contact: clistysynclair@ebox.com

Chapter 19
A Stalker

Two weeks later, Clisty was running unusually late. She and Becca had gone to the Chrysler dealership in Fort Wayne earlier in the day. That set her schedule back ... something that rarely happened. Time was important. The order for the company van included outfitting it properly for the team's use. Cameras, computers, and lights all had to have their own built-in niche in order to keep them steady while traveling. Their driving distance to interview-locations would vary, from nearby to hundreds of miles in some cases. The team would fly for heartland stories farther away. Everything would require careful packing to insure safe arrival. Even with the timely order of the great new van, delivery would take several weeks. Black Beauty, as Clisty laughingly named it, would be ready soon.

The network had scheduled an early showing of her segment in order to hype the interest of the viewing audience. It would be on that evening. Her compulsive nature didn't leave room for darting in her house at the last moment in a huff. Friends and family would be there soon.

Clisty was just hurrying in the door of her apartment with shopping bags in both hands when a man followed her over the threshold. As she put the bags on the kitchen island, she turned. "Who are you?" she gasped as she grabbed her chest.

"I'm a fan, Clisty," he oozed with sticky warmth.

She felt her hands begin to shake but tried to remain in control. "I'm sorry, you'll have to leave," she ordered with a firm voice. "How did you find me?"

The man was probably middle-aged but it was hard for Clisty to tell. He was obviously mentally unhealthy, with his eyes darting wildly around the room and his appearance unkempt. He had yellowing teeth and a greying complexion, which combined, made his age hard to guess. He offered a disturbing smile through missing teeth.

"I've watched you on the news every day. Then, I saw you again when WFTW interviewed you about your blog. They said your number of followers had grown a ton. So, I called the station and they gave me your address."

Clisty knew that wasn't true. It was Tuesday. Since her first segment on the American New Magazine, *Stories from the Heartland,* would air in a little while, it would expose her to instant national recognition. Neither the local station nor the network would give her address ... to anyone. Her heart pounded until it felt like she couldn't breathe. "They have a privacy policy. They wouldn't do that."

"Then," he smiled broadly, "you must have sent out solar rays or left bread crumbs along your way."

"My name isn't Gretel," she tried to sound light but her body suddenly felt heavy and weak.

"Clisty?" Becca questioned as she came up behind the disheveled man in the stained jacket and dirty knit cap. "I have the cola," but she couldn't get past the man who blocked the door. With his back to her, she put her fingers to her nose and raised her eyebrows.

The man didn't turn but stayed planted in the doorway. "I got here first," he said as he laughed.

"Becca," Clisty tried to sound calm but couldn't get a grip on the tremor in her voice. "Will you hurry down and see if Jake is here yet."

"Sure," she agreed lightly. "I'll put the drinks on the floor here by the door." When she turned, Clisty could hear her run down the hallway.

"I'm sorry I can't invite you in," Clisty said with exaggerated turned down lips. She pretended to busy herself, getting ready for friends and family, but didn't take her eyes off the creepy man. "I'm expecting company in a minute."

"That's what they all say," the shabby looking man hissed. "I haven't seen you in a long time. Where have you been?"

"I've been right here," she answered without giving him any information. Once she was past the initial shock, she could see the man was ill. If she were giving him a mental health exam, she would have noted: dirty-scraggly hair, smelly torn clothes, and filthy broken fingernails—too many checks on the list of instability. She tried to slow her breathing, knowing it would slow her heart and calm her nerves. "I'm sorry, you'll have to leave," she said as sweetly as she could and still have a tone of authority.

"I came for you, Clisty Sinclair," the rancid man said with a menacing grin and took one more step into the room. "You know we belong together."

"If you're trying to scare me, it won't work," Clisty said as she stiffened her back.

At that moment, Jake burst into the room, grabbed the man around the shoulders and forced his hands behind his back. "You okay Clisty?" he asked as he gripped the man tighter.

"Yes." She grew weak and slipped onto a bar stool. "Or, I will be."

The grizzly man tossed and twisted, resisting arrest. When they all heard the wail of a siren, Jake said, "Becca called 911 on her way to the front door to look for me. They'll take this guy away and book him at the station."

"Sergeant Davis?" one of the officers stopped abruptly as he entered Clisty's apartment.

"Thanks for coming, guys," Jake said as he handed the intruder over to the two uniformed officers. "Book him under possible home invasion, intimidation, and trespassing. He's your arrest."

Jake's eyes followed the man as the other two took him into custody. "Hey," Jake called after him, "what's your name?"

"Hiram Hubley," the little ratty man called back over his shoulder. "Make sure the princess knows my name."

Jake leaned toward the last officer. "I want to know if someone sent him, if he knows Miss Sinclair in any way, his motive, and what his plan was."

"Got ya," the officer said as he closed the door behind him.

Jake turned and reached out for Clisty. "I am so thankful I was just arriving when Becca called 911. Who was that guy?"

Clisty fell into his arms, burying her head in his shoulder. "I have no idea. I've never seen him before."

Becca burst back into the room, out of breath. "I saw them take the guy out. Who was he?"

"Neither of us knows," Clisty said as she went over to the sink and filled the coffee pot, busying herself. "We do know his name, or at least what he said it was ... Hiram Hubley."

"Hiram Hubley?" Becca's nose wrinkled up. "Who in the world is Hiram Hubley?"

Jason came in as the confusion continued. "Hiram Hubley?" he asked. "That doesn't even sound like a real name."

Clisty picked up the mug into which she had poured the last bit of the breakfast coffee, and absent-mindedly put some crackers on her plate. "I don't think he had the emotional creativity to make up a name."

Jake brushed his shirt sleeves back into position around his wrists. "Hiram Hubley was the man who was just ushered out of here."

"Everyone will be here in a short time," Clisty gasped as she looked at her watch. "The American News Magazine will be on in a few minutes. We'll all watch *Stories from the Heartland* together. Mom and Dad will join us; as well as

Faith and her daughter, Pooky; and you, Becca and Jason. Griff is coming but I don't think his wife can come."

"Too bad for Griff—but it sounds like fun," Becca agreed as she prepared a plate for herself. "I hope that Hiram guy didn't spoil the evening for you."

"No, I'm fine," Clisty sighed. "This is all a little too exciting for me, though" she admitted as she wiped the counter with a tea towel. "What will it be like when people across the country recognize us wherever we go?"

"This week has been exciting for Karen and Karl Kramer, in spite of what happened to Karen," Becca said. "After tonight, everyone will know who they are, too."

"Oh, my goodness, yes," Clisty agreed as she answered the door. "Mom, Dad," she greeted with open arms. "Come in."

Faith and her daughter arrived behind the Sinclairs. Pooky had on a princess shirt Clisty assumed her new grandparents bought for her. Faith and Pooky had nothing besides the clothes on their backs when she and her mom came back into Indiana from Illinois.

"Faith, I am so glad you're here. You too, Pooky," Clisty added as she bent down and tussled the little girl's hair. Turning, she walked over to the kitchen and took some more mugs out of the cabinet. "Coffee, Pepsi, cheese and crackers, fruit bites and cupcakes. They are all here on the island. Everyone, help yourself." She looked down at Pooky and took a square box from the cabinet and a spoon from the drawer. "How about hot chocolate for you, Pooky. As I remember, you are a cocoa lover."

Becca reached for a dark chocolate cupcake. "I'm glad you didn't forget the sugar."

Clisty's mother sat on one of the bar stools with a package wrapped in brown paper in her hand. "I've been using my studio a lot. I brought this for you." Carol handed Clisty the package secured with string.

"Mom!" Clisty's surprise was evident. She took the package and pulled a paring knife from the drawer. Popping the string, she spread the package on the counter. "Oh, Mom," she wilted. "This is beautiful."

Clisty held the 12 by 16 inch oil painting, framed with a scooped ribbed design in an antique gold finish. There was a green tone on the scoop that went perfectly with the seascape inside the frame. The sea foam blue and white bubbles of the tide were the focal point, complimented by a large palm tree that arched the left side of the painting and across the top. Seagulls soared above the waves. Clisty could almost hear their choking call and the beating of their wings. "Mother, it is wonderful," she sighed.

"Thank you my dear. Most of your walls are bare. I thought you would have room for this."

"Oh Mom, I sure do. And, very soon I will come over to see your new studio," she promised.

"Aunt Carol?" Pooky started to ask. Carol wasn't really her aunt but Faith and Pooky's grandmother, Roma believed children shouldn't call elders by their first name. "Did you paint this?" the child asked.

"I sure did," Carol responded with a huge smile.

"It is beautiful!" the little one squealed, careful not to touch it. "I love to paint. Momma and I painted as part of my classwork this year."

"Good, Pooky. Uncle Al and I have been developing an idea. We're not ready to talk about it, but we might need your help when the time gets closer," Carol said as she tickled Pooky's neck.

"I'll have to ask Mama first," Pooky reminded Carol with a tone of authority.

"Wouldn't want it any other way," Carol high-fived the child.

"How about a cupcake, Pooky?" Becca asked as she put a small desert with more icing than cake on the little girl's plate.

Pooky reached for the chocolate delicacy as Becca added, "Stay up here at the bar."

"I promise," Pooky said with a grin as she crossed her heart with her finger.

"Dad," Clisty called to Al across the room. "Would you bring over a picture hanging strip tomorrow and hang Mom's painting? You can let yourself in." She pointed to the wall next to the fireplace. "Right there, I think."

"Sure will," her dad smiled the smile of a father put to good use.

Carol folded up the brown paper and put it in the trash. She wound the string around her finger and placed it in a drawer. "That would be nice," Carol agreed. "I was wondering, Clisty, have you heard anything from the Kramers today? It's been over a week since someone hit Karen. That poor woman, she's been through a lot."

"I can't imagine," Faith joined in. "Broken legs and right shoulder plus a concussion."

"Only you would see Karen's situation as worse than your own, Faith," Clisty said as she shook her head. "Eighteen years as a captive, never allowed outside, and you can still empathize with someone else."

"But," Faith corrected with a smile, "I had no broken bones."

"Everybody …. it's coming on," Albert Sinclair announced from the armchair nearest the TV.

Carol smiled and rolled her eyes. She bowed deeply. "You would know, oh master of the remote."

"Okay, okay," Clisty teased. "Behave, you two."

Jason filled a paper plate with crackers and cheese and poured a cup of coffee. "Did Clisty tell you someone broke in a little while ago?" he asked the Sinclairs.

"Technically," Clisty put up her hand, "he didn't break in. That would require breakage of some sort. The door was still open and he only stepped *in* a few steps. But, yes, he did invade my home."

"Who? What did he want, Honey?" her dad asked as he sat up straight, leaned on the arm rest and balanced himself on his elbow. "Was he dangerous?"

Clisty looked down, running her finger over the rim of her cup. She didn't want to think about Hubley anymore. She wanted to revel in the success of her new program. "He said he came for me."

"For you?" Albert nearly leaped out of his chair. "Who was that guy? Do you need for me to put another deadbolt on your door when I come over?"

"Hiram Hubley," Clisty stated with conviction. "That's what he said his name was." She threw her head back and howled. "I will not be afraid of you, Hiram Hubley." Then she stopped and added, "But, I'll have to admit, another deadbolt does sound good."

"Wait a minute," Jake stepped in, his brow knitted. "He actually came looking specifically for you? I didn't know that. And, you didn't know him from anywhere, not even a hanger-on in the background of places where you interviewed followers and others? How did he find you?"

Becca put her hand to her mouth. "I don't like this."

"Don't like what?" Jason asked as he came back to the island to re-fill his plate.

"I'll tell you later," Becca said as she kissed his cheek and helped him add more food to his plate.

"No," Clisty whispered, feeling more vulnerable all the time. "I would have noticed him if he'd been around. He gave off that vibe that raises the fear center in your brain that's impossible to ignore. He said, 'You dropped bread crumbs.' I have no idea what he meant. I told him I'm not Gretel." She glanced down at the Walking Buddy she had transferred to her left wrist. "I am wearing a GPS," she started to laugh until realty set in and the humor faded.

"He meant," Jake rubbed his chin, "he had actually followed you, somehow. He was either following directions someone gave him or he followed you home. I doubt he was tech savvy enough to know anything about GPS locations, so a hacked Walking Buddy is likely out of the question."

"I wasn't at any one place today," Clisty whispered as the hair on the back of her neck stood up. "I ran errands and wrote my blog." She crossed her arms and folded them against her body. Maybe if she wrapped herself up in a small package it would compact her size, making her a smaller target.

"He didn't have to follow you today." Jake's eyebrows raised and his voice elevated. "He may have followed you another day or … many times."

"So, you're saying …" she stopped and nearly gagged, "I have a stalker?" Clisty was overwhelmed as the theme music to the American News Magazine filled the room. "Why? How did he find me? Or, doesn't he care who he stalks?" Clisty chuckled as she tried to make a joke out of what could have been a very dangerous situation, a frequently used defense mechanism of hers.

Jake wasn't laughing.

Carol rubbed her hands over her arms and visibly shuddered. "This conversation is making me feel creepy."

"Let's not talk about it anymore," Albert announced with a smack of his hand on the arm of the chair. "I'll go to the hardware store tomorrow morning and get another lock for your door. I'll have it on by 10 AM." He sat back with the plate of snacks Carol had handed him. "Maybe we can install a surveillance camera in the hallway, focused on your door," he concluded. "Don't see why the landlord would complain, given the fact he will have a famous TV star in his building." He popped a cracker in his mouth and added, "Maybe you should move home with your mom and me until this blows over."

"Daddy!" Clisty whispered with a quiet hiss. "I'm not coming home for spring break."

"Maybe a small home in a gated community would help," Carol suggested.

Clisty rolled her eyes but didn't tell anyone that her stomach was rolling at the same time. "I appreciate all of your suggestions, but I'm staying right here for now."

Becca balanced her plate on her knees and tapped her fingertips together. "The house isn't a bad idea, Clisty.

You'll be working out of your home here in Fort Wayne. Maybe we could put in a large office and a small soundproof room for a studio."

Clisty mulled over all the brainstorming and tried to smile. She looked over at Jake who had given no suggestions. "We wouldn't have to buy another expensive TV camera. Griff would have the professional video model in the van. All we'd need is the camera's wheeled pedestal. What do you think, Mr. Security Man?"

"Living alone may get harder for you …" he said as he smiled. "But, I think you'll sort it all out and find a solution."

The American News Magazine began and the talk of housing stopped. Clisty and Jake sat on the bar stools, creating a balcony for viewing. With their hands linked, the silent messages that passed between the two spoke of alternative security measures, not shared with the others.

Chapter 20
Another Buddy Attack

It felt late. Everyone had left her apartment after the viewing party but Clisty was still restless. Actually, it was only 11 PM. She was used to being up late writing her blog after the eleven o'clock news. Some nights, she didn't post until 2 AM, depending on the evening's activities and how quickly she could get away from the news room. Eleven was still early for her.

Jake had just left to go to the police station to check on the stalker. He said he wanted to ask the guy some questions himself. When her cell phone jangled, she jumped. *Why do I have a standard bell ring?* She mumbled to herself as she reached for the phone on the coffee table. *I should download a lullaby for any incoming calls after 8 PM.*

"Hello?" she answered.

"Clisty, this is Karen Kramer."

"Professor Kramer? It is so good to hear from you. How are you feeling?" Clisty sat up quickly and shook her head to clear her tired thinking. "What did you think of our segment on the American News Magazine?"

"I loved it, Clisty. Karl and I were both thrilled. We watched it on the TV here in the hospital. Karl insisted they keep me a little longer due to the concussion." She paused for only a second and immediately added, "Something has happened. I thought you might still be up." Her voice sounded shaky.

Clisty wondered why Karen hadn't responded to her question about her health. "Karen? What's going on? Are you sure you and Karl are okay?" Clisty sat back on the couch, waiting for another announcement of bad news. "What happened?"

"Jerry Wintergardner," Karen sighed heavily into the phone, "one of our trial subjects—"

"Right ..." Clisty acknowledged, waiting for the rest of the story.

Karen exhaled slowly. "Jerry has had an accident ... similar to mine."

"Another hit and run?" Clisty's jaw dropped as she sat back.

"That's what the police are saying. Jerry has had a Walking Buddy for several months." Karen sounded tired. "Here, I'll let Karl talk to you. I'm still a little weak ... and so upset."

"Sure," Clisty soothed, holding her breath. "You get some rest. The police will get to the bottom of this."

"Clisty?" Karl chimed in. "We've had Karen's cell on speaker. I heard your last comment and ... I don't know how they'll begin to investigate any of this. They still have no idea who hit Karen and now there's this new tragedy."

"Maybe our show earlier tonight will bring forth a witness, Dr. Kramer. Sometimes, people don't know what they've seen until their memory is jarred."

"That would be great," he agreed. "And, Clisty, remember, it's Karl ... just Karl. The odd thing is, Jerry took a walk every day and had no problem finding his way home with the help of the Buddy. He loved the independence and the spring weather. This morning, while walking, the family voice on his Walking Buddy directed him many blocks out of his way, onto a road with no sidewalks. A blue car swerved and hit him. Clisty ... he's dead."

Clisty sat up straight, her eyes wide. "Dead?"

"Yes," Karl whispered. "He's dead, and Karen is so shaken. I'm even more concerned about her now than I was when she entered the hospital. She's supposed to be released in a few days."

"Karl, I am so sorry." Clisty's head was swimming as nausea gripped her stomach.

Karen's voice came back on the line. "I'm concerned that the hacker the whistle blower told me about that night, the one who called me back to the office, had something to do with this."

"You're saying that this was no accident? The police are confirming it? The Walking Buddy didn't malfunction?" The thought flipped around in Clisty's head. "What is going on?"

"I don't know, Clisty. The police have Jerry's Walking Buddy," Karen said weakly. "We're hoping they'll let us inspect it."

"If the hacker is responsible … why? What are they getting out of it? Running people down in the street?" The possibilities refused to materialize in Clisty's mind.

"What do you mean?" Karen asked. "How would a hacker benefit from redirecting an eighty-nine year old man into dangerous traffic?" She sounded like she was crying.

Clisty's head began to clear. "The old directive is … follow the money."

"Money?" Karl asked. "How would a hacker benefit monetarily from messing up someone's Walking Buddy?"

Karen jumped back in. "Karl and I are the only ones who financially benefit at all from the Buddy. We have no real partners. We don't owe anyone for product development or any other phase of construction."

"Karen," Clisty snapped to attention, "the notes you have gotten. They warned you to quit selling 'their' invention. At least, the person believes they have some right to the Walking Buddy."

"But, who?" Karen sounded helpless.

Karen didn't seem like the woman Clisty met at her home in Stamford. Clisty recognized that Karen was recovering and was in fact, still in the hospital. She was concerned. If Karen were to dwell on the negatives associated with the invention she helped create, it could slow or defeat her recovery.

"Maybe they're delusional," Karl suggested. "I can't see how anyone in their right mind would try to claim something when they don't even know how it works."

Clisty wasn't sure about that. But then, she didn't really know anything about psychosis or those who sit on the border of mental health, except for the warning signs she had blogged about. With Hubley, she had met a candidate for a delusional diagnosis. "You medical people will have to figure that out. But, let's get back to my hope that the program we just watched earlier in the evening may bring someone out from the shadows who has information about Jerry's death, once their memory makes some connections."

Karen sighed, sounding heavy in heart. "The police want Karl and me to come into the station and give our statements."

"What does your attorney say?" Clisty asked and then followed that question with another. "Karen, the more important question is, what does your doctor say about your bopping all over town? You're still in the hospital."

"Exactly," Karl agreed. "Just riding down to police headquarters and trying to get inside, would take a lot out of her. Also, she could easily get confused due to exhaustion. I don't want the police to misinterpret any possible confusion, and think she's lying."

"What about this?" Clisty asked as a new plan unfolded quickly. "I could bring the TV crew back east after my assistant in New York sets up a town hall meeting. Rather than putting you and Karen out there for ridicule from those given the Walking Buddy to test, I would lead the discussion … on film. That may draw out the note-writer who wants people to pay attention to them. And, if they aren't the hit and run driver, just the hacker, that person may not resist the need to smugly listen to others marvel at their brilliance. We may find the answers. At the least, we'll make the public aware. That will give us more eyes and ears that could possibly dredge up some answers to this mystery. I'll post an abbreviated entry to my blog to let those folks know. We might get information from followers."

"That sounds great," Karl responded with enthusiasm. "Should Karen and I be at the Town Hall meeting?"

"Of course you're welcome. If you don't think Karen is up to it … or her physician won't release her from the hospital, we'll understand," Clisty said as plans and expectations buzzed through her head. "Neither of you will be targets of a police interrogation. You can relax. Mostly, you can just listen. It may relieve your anxiety. We could arrange for a comfortable chair for Karen, maybe even a recliner, or a wheel chair." She changed her tone from enthusiasm to supportive. "You two are pillars of the community. Your friends will want to help. Someone is trying to sabotage the Walking Buddy which is a wonderful invention for those who need it."

"When can you come?" Karen asked with renewed energy in her voice. "I'm afraid someone else will be hurt because of the Buddy." Her voice cracked as she admitted, "I don't think I could stand that."

"I was racking my brain with dire possibilities." Karl's voice was low and serious. "If they are hacking into a tiny tracking computer on your arm," he warned, "someone could track down people they have a beef against … an x-husband, x-wife or boyfriend. I know they might be able to zone in on someone's location using their cell phone. It's all so frightening. I just don't see how they could do it with the Buddy."

Clisty paused and didn't say anything for a second. Her stomach flipped over and tied in a knot. "Like a stalker?" she asked, shuddering.

"Just like a stalker," Karl agreed. "Have we invented the perfect Stalking Buddy, rather than the helpful Walking Buddy?"

Clisty didn't tell the Kramers about Hiram Hubley. She didn't see how any good could come from worrying the Kramers more. Hubley lived in Indiana, not New England. If she focused on the forum, she might find answers to her own personal stalker, too. "I'll call the network first thing in the morning."

"Will you call us as soon as you find out when this taping will be scheduled?" Karen asked with angst in her voice.

"I sure will," Clisty agreed. "I haven't heard about our next story, so I can't promise it will be next week. Scheduling won't smooth out until stories begin to come in. This is all new. But, I'll let you know as soon as I know."

"Oh Clisty," Karen cried. She sounded short of breath. "If someone else dies or is injured I don't think I'll be able to live with myself." Her breathing seemed labored. "Let's get this fixed."

"Your note writer said something about bringing destruction on yourself. Don't do that, Karen. Don't give him the satisfaction of making you doubt your invention or your intention, not even for a moment. You and Karl only wanted to help others. For some reason, it sounds like the note writer directed his threats toward you, Karen. But, it's not about you. His twisted need is his own."

"Thanks, Clisty," Karen sighed again. "Deep down, I knew that … but I needed to be reminded."

"I want to thank you too, Clisty," Karl chimed in. "We both appreciate that. Okay, then call us when it's set up." He added, "And, the show was wonderful. I had no idea how badly I look with 1960s sideburns."

Clisty put her cell phone on the coffee table. In her usual compulsion to have everything in order, she began to pick up small finger-food plates, glasses and cups, and took them to the kitchen. Looking at her watch, she determined it was too late at that hour to call Mr. Funderbird about the follow-up segment. As the water ran in the sink, she pushed up her sleeves. That's when she saw it. She was still wearing

140

the Walking Buddy Karl and Karen had given her. Then, she remembered what the stalker said. "You dropped bread crumbs."

"Bread crumbs," she exclaimed aloud. "I stand corrected. I am evidently the real twenty-first century Gretel." She finally recognized she was more than a reporter. She was also a victim.

Crime Beat

✴

From the Heartland

11:30 PM

Good evening my friends. This blogger is sending a short post to ask for your help. I know you are out there and ready to lend a hand in our research and investigation.

THE MYSTERY WITHIN THE JOY

Many of you watched the American News Magazine on BNN and caught our segment, *Stories from the Heartland* this evening. Thank you for your support.

As you saw, a very creative couple, Dr. Karl and Professor Karen Kramer, have created an invention to help people with Alzheimer's disease. For those who missed the program, go to BNN's website at www.ByrsonNewsNetwork.com and click on the program that was aired this date.

Sadly, this blogger must request your help in solving several crimes related to the Kramers' invention.

1. Karen Kramer had received threatening notes weeks before the program aired. The note writer claimed the invention belonged to him or her. Have you heard anyone who bragged about being the "real" creator of the Walking Buddy?

2. A driver in what may have been a blue vehicle, taunted Karen while she and her husband were out walking in the evening.

3. A hit-and-run driver struck Karen's car late the same night, forcing her car down a steep ravine. She sustained two broken bones and other injuries. Again, a blue car may be involved.

4. Also, a driver hit a man who was testing the Walking Buddy. The driver killed the man and left the scene.
5. A stalker followed and invaded the home of some individuals involved in this wonderful invention.

As you discuss our new American New Magazine segment with friends and acquaintances, listen carefully for any clues that may help solve the above crimes. If you have a lead and would like to report it on camera, please Skype the clues to this blogger. If you don't want to be on camera, email your comments to the contact below. The police in New York, Connecticut, and/or Indiana may want to talk to you. We thank you so much.

This blogger greatly appreciates your help in solving these crimes. Your intuitive ability to search out criminals is amazing. You're a valuable asset.

Share

Contact: clistysynclair@ebox.com

Chapter 21
A New Plan

"Good Morning, Mr. Funderbird," Clisty greeted into her cell at 9 AM the next morning. "This is Clisty Sinclair." She tried to stay in an upbeat tone, hoping the morning, despite the over-head clouds, would warm her voice and calm her fears.

"Clisty," he roared through the phone. "I would have called you in a few minutes."

"Sorry, I can get back to you later if I called too early," she held her breath and winced.

"Young woman," he said with a laugh, "I'm in my office by 7:30 every morning ... sometimes on the weekends, too. This gives me the opportunity to tell you how great the segment was last evening. You were superb."

"Thank you, Sir," Clisty said as she saved a few of his words, tucking them into the corner of her mind to savor again another time. She closed her eyes, gathering her wits so she could smoothly change subjects. "As you know, Professor Kramer was struck by a hit and run driver."

"Yes," he began slowly. "We sent you and your crew to the hospital for real time news coverage."

"Two other things have happen ... well, one for sure. I don't know about the other." She looked out the window onto a gentle spring rain that had just started. Although it was beautiful in that golden-clean sense, she knew it was only a distraction from what she had to concentrate on. The gathering clouds began to cast a cool darkness into the room. "Last evening, I had a viewing party for a few close friends and family." She poured herself a cup of coffee from the pot she had made the night before. Popping the cup into the

145

microwave, she continued talking as the aroma of Folgers filled the kitchen. "A man I've never met before followed me into my apartment when I got home after running errands. He tried to enter, claiming he had tracked me down. I wondered if I sent off pings, signals from the Walking Buddy the Kramers had given me. Someone said they doubted the man was capable of tracking anyone electronically."

"Clisty," Funderbird gasped, "are you all right? Did he hurt you in any way? Where was your security?"

"No, I wasn't hurt. The man didn't even touch me," she said, relieved that he showed concern. Perhaps he would welcome a follow-up segment about the strange turn of events. "Rebecca Landers got here just minutes after the man stumbled in. She called 911. Jake, our security, arrived immediately after Becca and restrained the stalker until two uniformed police officers arrived and took him away."

Funderbird gulped, "Sergeant Davis thinks the stalker used the features of the Walking Buddy to find you?"

"No, Jake didn't think the man was capable of advanced planning," Clisty corrected. "But, the system may have been hacked."

"Good grief, they're hacking everything these days."

"So it would seem," Clisty sighed as the microwave timer sounded. Removing her cup, she sipped a tiny swallow, emptied the last of the coffee from the pot and made fresh. "But, the larger issue is regarding Jerry Wintergardner, one of the patients given the Walking Buddy to test. Someone killed him while he was out walking last evening … a hit-and-run driver, the same as Karen Kramer. They believe his Buddy was hacked, too."

Funderbird was silent a second. "Did we make a mistake lifting up a defective invention? A dangerous product?" Funderbird asked … his tone serious. "Do I need to call in our attorneys?"

"I don't know about the legal end of the business, Sir. But, I've met Karl and Karen Kramer and I believe they're genuine." Clisty paused a moment to let her testimony on behalf of the Kramers sink in. "I am proposing another angle."

"Okay …" he drew out. "I'm interested. What do you propose?"

"I'd like to take the crew back to New York or Stamford for a town hall meeting of patients and their families who were given a Walking Buddy to test. We would announce the meeting on TV, the network website, our Facebook page, Twitter, talk radio, the newspapers and, of course, my blog. We'll invite everyone who is interested. An inner circle will consist of those who already have a Buddy. If we're lucky, we'll coax out the one who is hacking the system. He wouldn't want to miss seeing the chaos he's caused. He'd probably relish hearing comments about how brilliant he is to hack a system that is not hackable. Police could be present in plainclothes to maintain order and make arrests if we are lucky enough for it to be necessary."

"Great! When can we do this?" Funderbird bellowed. "I can have our attorney monitor the event … a whole team of them … to check for any liability on our part. Just let me know when you want to do it."

"The Kramers want it filmed and aired as quickly as possible, before anyone else gets hurt." Clisty flipped on a light switch over the kitchen island as rain clouds dimmed her space and filled the room with a damp chill. "I'm worried about Karen, Sir. I know she is still weak from the attack on her, and she's taking all of this very personal."

"Okay, Clisty. Call Nicole to set everything up—the announcements and advertisements. Ask her to schedule a large studio here at the network and arrange your air and hotel reservations." Funderbird paused, then added with authority, "Get it done, Clisty. You will be great. Your segment may set new standards for investigative journalism."

"Thanks. I'll call Nicole immediately." Clisty placed her cell phone on the granite countertop and gave her full attention to her coffee. She tapped in Nicole's number and waited for an answer while she quickly became lost in her next exciting trip to New York. This one would be different. With all the details and intricate parts to the puzzle, there may be little time for enjoying the approaching summer in the city. Nicole's ring went to voice mail. Clisty left a detailed message, including travel, hotel reservations and the forum concept. She told Nicole she'd call her back.

Dressed in soft blue capris and an oversized blue T-shirt with a logo of the American News Magazine on the front, Clisty padded barefoot around her apartment between her coffee pot and her large new desk in front of the windows. When the doorbell rang, she caught a glimpse of herself in the mirror above a low entry table and shuddered. Her hair looked like Medusa without the snakes.

With the door ajar a few inches, she peeked around the edge and smiled sheepishly, then flung it open. "I guess you'll see me eventually before my hair is combed. I was hoping to make a better impression on you before that shock."

Jake grabbed her by the waist and lifted her off her feet and into his arms. "You are absolutely gorgeous. And, you would be beautiful with no hair at all." He was breathless with a voice full of love.

Dressed in a grey suit, it was easy for Clisty to see that Jake was working. "You're dressed like you're on duty, Gunny. Are you here to arrest me?" she asked as she snuggled her head into his chest.

"Don't I wish," he answered without letting her go.

"Sounds scandalous," she murmured in his ear.

Finally, he released his grip enough to step into the apartment and close the door. "I was going to take a coffee break and decided to check on the supply of java here at BNN's Indiana satellite office."

Clisty kept her arm around his back as they walked together to the kitchen island and secured that precious, fresh cup of dark, aromatic gold. "I am so glad you came, Jake," she said as they walked through her living room, over to the couch.

He studied the couch and chairs. "Do I have to keep everything this clean once we're married?" he asked with a laugh.

"I've thought about that," she said softly while placing her cup on the spotless tufted coffee table/footstool in front of them. "Maybe I'll finally feel safe when we're married and won't need to wonder what's hiding under every dust bunny." Her eyes rimmed with tears. Embarrassed, she quickly wiped them away. "Why is my safety linked to Faith's disappearance so long ago? I still cry about Faith's kidnapping, eighteen years after it happened?"

Jake took his handkerchief from his pocket and dried the tears that began to roll down Clisty's cheeks. "Because, it happened to your best friend … in your home … and he tried to kidnap you too. Honey, you were both just children …nine-years-old at the time. You were still forming deep and lasting memories."

"I guess so," she whispered, sniffing.

"I know so," he assured her, drawing her into his arms.

She remained silent, snuggled within the safety of his strong embrace. "There's something else …."

"That's what I wanted to talk to you about—our wedding," Jake said as he kissed her forehead. "I was thinking, we could drive down to Brown County and get a marriage license. I can take tomorrow off. What about you, are you free tomorrow?"

"Jake," she said as her heart sank, "I would love to but … I can't … not tomorrow."

"Okay," Jake whispered. "The next day?"

"Gunny, we … I don't know when we can get to Brown County. We have to go back to New York soon. Nicole will set it all up," she blurted out quickly and buried her head in his shoulder again.

"Back to New York? When? Why?" he stammered as he unwound his arm from her and leaned back on the couch cushion, flopping his arms heavily over the back.

Clisty interpreted his body language as withdrawal, not from the conversation but from her personally. "Can you go with us ... as security?"

"As security?" he repeated, his eyes avoiding hers.

"Well ... sure," she fumbled through feelings and words and confusion. Funny how loud a silent room can become when no one is talking. What else could she say?

"Another few days in a glorious city ... alone," Jake shook his head and started to stand up.

"Wait, Jake ... alone?" she asked, not believing what she just heard. "What do you mean ... alone?"

"Oh, I don't know," he said as his shoulders sagged again. He sipped his coffee quickly and checked his watch. "I'd better go. My break is up soon. I'll see you tonight." Starting toward the door, he turned and kissed her on the forehead.

"Jake ... I am so sorry. Trust me, I'll make it up to you somehow," Clisty apologized as she followed him to the door. "Don't be mad at me, please."

"Mad? I could never be angry with you, Clisty," he said as he stroked her cheek with the back of his fingers. "I'm just disappointed, Babe," he said as he wrapped his arms around her. "I want you so much it hurts."

Clisty said nothing at first. When she finally looked up at him, she knew he could see desire written in every sparkle of her eyes. "I know, Jake. Be patient. This job is going to demand a lot of my time ... our time. Your job is very important to the whole team." She sighed and began again. "Karen and Karl Kramer called already this morning, about nine. A car hit one of the patients who received a Walking Buddy, Jerry Wintergardner. He died, Jake. Karl suspects the Walking Buddy was hacked."

"What?" Jake gasped as his jaw dropped.

"The man was apparently using the Buddy to help him find his way home, but he ended up way off his route and was struck by another hit-and-run driver." Clisty went over to the fireplace and rested her hand on the mantel. She needed some distance from Jake so she could think clearly.

"When do we leave?" he asked as he joined her at the hearth and put his arm around her waist again.

"Nicole will set it all up. She should have everything ready in a matter of hours, a day or so at the most." She smiled again at Jake and the love he offered.

"Okay, I'll tell my lieutenant."

"Will he be upset if you have to give him a short notice?"

"Actually, he's okay with all of this. This morning he said he liked seeing the credits roll at the end of the program last night." Jake waved his hand across in front of his face as if displaying the writing on a marquee. "In particular, the acknowledgement, 'Security is provided with the cooperation of the Fort Wayne, Indiana Police Department and Lieutenant Frank Combs.' I guess if Frank is promoted sometime, the network will have to change the wording," he added as he laughed.

Clisty was relieved when she heard the deep smooth warmth of his laugh. "Becca will be here soon. Nicole will let us know when it's all set up and ready. I left Nicole a voice message right before you came in. I'll call her again soon and let you know the details."

Jake put his hand on the doorknob then stopped. Whipping around, he grabbed Clisty in a strong embrace. "I love you, Babe," he whispered hoarsely, jerked the door open and hurried back out into the hallway. He pulled the door closed behind him with a thud.

Clisty touched her mouth; her lips still trembled from their kiss. Rubbing her arms where her skin tingled, she swooped around the room, twirling and dancing. When she heard someone at the door again, she hoped it was Becca. She was too lightheaded to welcome anyone else.

"Rebecca," she controlled a squeal as best she could when she opened the door. "Get in here." She reached out for Becca's arm and pulled her into the apartment.

"Whoa," the young producer said as she put up her hand. Regaining her balance, she looked intently at Clisty. "What's going on with you?"

"Oh nothing?" she denied as she brushed her hair from her face.

"Nothing? Really?" Becca stood with both hands on her hips. "I saw Jake pulling away from the curb when I pulled up outside."

"Did you now?" Clisty sighed. "He stopped in for a quick coffee break."

"Coffee? Okay ... if that's what you want to believe. In my opinion, he can't go more than eight hours without seeing you."

"All right ... all right," she surrendered.

"Coffee? You said something about coffee?" Becca moved toward the island and the black coffee maker that sat on the coffee bar.

"Help yourself," Clisty said with a wave of her hand as if dismissing the thought. Turning back, she said quickly, "Becca, we're going back east, to New York in the next day or so."

"Really, why?" Becca filled her cup and walked back over to the living area defined by a white area rug.

Clisty rubbed her thighs in an effort to ground herself again in her body and not in her day dreams. "Someone is apparently hacking the Walking Buddy's system, causing injuries and even death. Nicole will be sending out ads and making arrangements for us to have a huge meeting of all those concerned, for a follow-up segment. It will be in the structure of a forum, or town hall meeting."

"Hacked?" Becca pulled her cup away from her mouth, nearly choking. "Hacking a device intended only for good ... to help Alzheimer's patients? Why?"

"I talked to the Kramers this morning, then Mr. Funderbird. None of us can make sense out of it." Clisty looked at her prayer angel that sat on the mantel and closed her eyes a second. "I called Nicole and left a message," she said as she checked her watch. "She'll be in the office by now. Becca, if you'll sit down and start a list of interview questions I can use during the forum, I'd appreciate it. I'll be talking to the Kramers, the volunteers who are current users, their families and care givers, and those who are in the community and are interested in bringing us some information or asking questions."

Clisty walked over to her desk, retrieved a yellow legal pad and pen, and handed them to Becca. Clisty sat down with her own list in hand and then dialed Nicole.

"No more talk about Jake and why you were so worked up when I came in?" Becca asked as she poised her pen over the paper.

"Nope," Clisty answered while a little smile turned up the corners of her mouth. Quickly, she dialed Nicole in New York.

Chapter 22
Sergeant Down

Nicole called back several times earlier in the day, offering new threads of questioning for the forum. The discussion ideas came in on posts people offered on the suggestion board of the network's website. Clisty and Becca sorted and categorized the additional messages that appeared on the network's social media page. Readers already started posting questions and comments on Clisty's blog. Information they added was both interesting and cleaver. So far, blog responders were far more interested in offering help than they were in appearing on television.

     Clisty wondered if Nicole ever left the office once she got in. She was always there to answer Clisty's call, with suggestions and further questions people suggested. Clisty hoped her new "re-visit" segment wasn't the cause of Nicole's over-time.

     Jake hadn't stopped by the apartment like he said he would. By 8 PM Clisty jumped every time her cell phone rang. Most of the evening, she fixed her eyes on the network's website and other contact paths. More information had flowed through the various channels than she had imagined. She completed some additional non-work related searches a little after 11:00 PM and rubbed her eyes. Finally, she leaned back in her desk chair and looked over at the TV screen.

     As she paused, she tried to remember if she had eaten anything for supper. For lunch, Becca had buzzed out for chicken salad at Kroger's deli. Clisty sliced a few grapes and threw them into the mix with a handful of walnut pieces. It was good. But, that was around noon. What had she eaten for supper? She thought for a moment and determined it must have been nothing. When she suddenly remembered a carton of raspberry yogurt in the refrigerator, she let her computer cool off for a few minutes, went into the kitchen, opened the "icebox," as her grandfather would have called it, and retrieved the Yoplait.

With a spoon in hand she slowly walked back to a wingback chair. It was only then that the rest of her world came into focus. What was the late night news reporter talking about?

"The shooting took place right before shift change," the middle-aged woman at the news desk announced.

Clisty thought the newscaster looked good. She liked the way she pushed her hair into a twist at the back of her neck. Her dark suit looked professional. Clisty didn't approve of middle-aged female newscasters in sleeveless, low cut dresses who looked like they were chaperoning a senior prom later in the evening. The news anchor's name was Stephanie Fisher. Clisty didn't see her at the station often as Stephanie's usual responsibilities included the noon news updates. That evening, Stephanie and Dan Drummond were at the news desk for the 6 PM news and again for the late edition.

"The sergeant was participating in the arrest of Paul Kiplinger, the suspect in the murder of Kiplinger's wife, Amy. Kiplinger snatched an officer's gun and fired. Those who were injured were taken to the hospital."

"What?" Clisty shrieked into the air around her. "Who? What did you say? Which sergeant?"

She grabbed her cell phone and called the television station, number six on her speed dial. It rang once, twice, and then someone knocked on her door. Jumping up she nearly spilled her yogurt as she practically threw it onto the coffee table, her cell phone still pressed to her ear.

"WFTW-TV," someone announced in the studio. The outer lobby personnel left for the evening. At the same moment, Clisty opened the door.

"This is Clisty Sinclair," she began speaking into her phone and then stopped.

"Hey, Babe, you should use the security door chain before you open up like that," Jake said with a smile. "I know it's really late but I saw your light on from the street and thought I'd say goodnight."

"Talk later ... bye," Clisty shouted abruptly into the phone, ending the call. Trembling, she jumped into Jake's arms and sobbed. The room spun around her as migraine-provoked tunnel vision blurred her sight. She could do nothing but cling to Jake. When her heart stopped banging around in her chest she could finally breathe. "I was busy all evening. I saw only the last few minutes of the news. They said a sergeant had been shot, but they had already given the name when I stopped long enough to listen." Her throat tightened to the point she almost couldn't talk. "Jake," she burst out sobbing, "I didn't know if it was you."

"Babe, I am so sorry," he apologized. He wiggled out of his suit coat even as he continued to hold her tightly in his arms. Loosening his tie, he added, "It was Streeter, my partner. He wasn't hurt badly. He'll be fine." With Jake's hands on each side of her face, he kissed her eyelids and the top of her hair. "I went to the hospital with him. I tried to call you, but your line was busy all evening." He didn't let go of her but picked her up and carried her to the couch. Putting her down on the sofa, he took off her shoes and curled up beside her, popping his own black lace-ups onto the floor beside hers.

"I thought maybe you were still mad at me for messing up our wedding plans this weekend." Her voice was soft and shaken.

"Oh, Babe, no," he soothed her. As he scooted them both down farther on the couch, Clisty piled on top of him. "I told you I wasn't mad ... just disappointed."

"Me too," she whispered, clinging to the front of his shirt with both hands. As she nuzzled down into a comfortable nest cuddled against his chest, she yawned and realized how sleepy she was.

Jake kissed her ear and murmured, "Are we okay now?"

"Now? We were okay from the first time I saw you," she sighed deeply.

He pulled his jacket off the floor with one hand and put it over her shoulders. "Good. Lay still."

"I'll smash you," she gulped, half crying and half teasing.

"A little lass like you isn't heavy?" he denied. "Besides, you feel too good for me to complain about your closeness." He reached for the afghan on the back of the couch and added it to the pile on top of them both.

Clisty lay there coiled up on Jake's chest, finally at peace with the rhythmic rise and fall of his breathing. "Jake," she mouthed sleepily, "don't go." Her eyes grew heavy but she didn't want to sleep. She might miss a whiff of his aftershave or his breath on the top of her head.

He unfastened the tie from around his neck, threw it on the floor, scooted down even farther and pulled her close. "I'll stay until you want me to go."

"Never. I don't ever want separation from you. Even when this job snatches us into an updraft, I want to be holding on to you."

"Don't worry, Babe," he assured her as he stroked her hair and caressed her back. "I'll hold on tight."

Funny how life changes so quickly you don't even see the turning. You look away for a single moment and when you turn back the world has changed from the previous view. Clisty had been so happy ... then her entire weekend changed. Will her new job's fast pace overtake her? Will she be able to keep up with the blur of emotions and activity?

Lying there in Jake's arms, thoughts of going back to New York drifted away. She dreamed only of cuddling with Jake forever.

Chapter 23
Interview Prep

Rumpled but content, Clisty awakened the next morning still tangled in Jake's arms. She didn't want to move a muscle. His warm body moved up and down in tempo with each of his precious breaths. Someone was chattering on the television she had neglected to turn off the night before, something about pancake syrup and butter. The Thursday morning sun cast streams of light that stretched across the hardwood floor. Like a sundial, the length of the beams told her it was early enough for Jake to get to work on time.

"Gunny?" she nudged him gently, actually hoping he wouldn't awaken. "Jake?"

"I hear you, Babe," he said as he yawned, moving only to pull her more closely to him.

"What do you think your suit pants will look like when you stand up?" she asked and chuckled when the image appeared in her mind. "What will you say if someone asks if you slept in your clothes ... considering the possible impression you'll make?"

"Actually, I wasn't thinking about my wrinkled pants. But, since you brought it up ... I'll simply say, 'Yes, I did sleep in my pants.' The rest of the story is none of their business." Jake kissed her forehead.

Clisty pealed herself off him and steadied herself as she stood on the floor. She wiggled and stretched, pulling her clothes into place. Looking down at Jake as he rested his arm under his head, she smiled. "You look wonderful...a bearded, mussed, totally wonderful specimen of a real man."

Jake jumped up from the couch and grabbed her with an intensity that amazed her, just as the doorbell rang.

"You've gotta be kidding me," he moaned and started for the door.

"No," Clisty whispered, her voice sounded forced. "Hurry into my bedroom and close the door," she giggled.

Jake forced a disappointed expression as the corners of his mouth turned down. Then he smiled mischievously. "Should I take my shoes, jacket and tie?"

His clothes lay scattered on the floor in front of the couch. Clisty gathered them for him. She quickly shoved them in his direction with a playful jab. His cell phone was on the coffee table so she collected that as well, moaning when the bell rang again. "Coming," she called out.

With her hand placed on the doorknob, she turned around to inspect the room for evidence of Jake's presence. Nothing was visible. In a matter of a few seconds, she formed an explanation for the room.

"Becca," she sang out as she opened the door but stood in the opening. "I just got up."

"So I see," Becca exclaimed, wide eyed. Studying what she could see of the living room behind Clisty, she added. "Did you sleep on the couch?"

"I sure did," Clisty admitted, still without budging. "I have no coffee, Bec. Would you run down to the coffee shop and get us some? I'll take a quick shower, but after the other night, I can't leave the door unlocked. Just knock."

"Maybe I should have a key," Becca suggested as she started back out of the apartment.

"No, I don't think so. I'd be spooked with keys floating around town." In her mind, she saw an image of Becca walking in while she and Jake cozied up on the couch. She tried to hide a cringe.

"Sure," Becca agreed as she studied Clisty's face. "Be right back with the coffee," she mumbled when Jake's cell phone rang from the bedroom. She started to say something, but smiled, slowly backed away, and headed toward the elevator.

Clisty tried not to slam the door but made sure she latched it and then jumped into action. She bent down and grabbed the cream colored afghan her grandmother had made, folded it lovingly and replaced it on the back of the sofa. With a few dishes in her hands she picked up from around the room, she called out, "Jake? Hurry!"

"Is she gone?" he asked as he peeked out the bedroom door.

"Well, if she weren't," Clisty said laughingly, placing the dishes in the dishwasher, "she would have caught you coming out of my bedroom." She hurried over and began pushing him toward the front door. "Jake … move. She'll be back in a few minutes." She kept her hand on him as he backed all the way to the door. "I'll lock it as soon as you're out." Reaching for the door, she stopped. "Maybe you'd better use the stairs. You won't meet Becca stepping off the elevator as you're stepping on."

"Got ya. I'll go home and change, check in at the precinct and drop by with a fresh can of coffee for your kitchen later this morning."

"I have coffee here, Jake," she said, her eyebrows pinched.

Jake smiled and touched his finger to his mouth and then to her lips. "I imagine you do," he said as he laughed. "But, you just told Becca you didn't. If we're going to be able to pull off this marriage game, you may have to learn to lie, or at least cover your misstatements with inventive stories."

"Oh," she squealed, pushing him out the door. "See you in a while." Leaning against the door for a second, she whispered, "Whew!" She slammed the door closed, locked it, and threw the deadbolt. Over in the kitchen, she pulled the Folgers from the cabinet and opened the freezer portion of her side-by-side refrigerator. Reaching for the Edy's vanilla bean ice cream, she pulled it out, put the coffee container behind it and replaced the tub. "This is going to be quite a marathon," she chuckled to herself as she thought about her blog, her next book, the TV show, plus the marriage chase across several states.

In her bathroom, she threw her clothes in the hamper and jumped into the shower. Face, shoulders, splash, splash … doorbell. Wrapping a large bath towel around her, she dashed back to the door. Her bare feet made wet prints on the floor. Clisty stretched up and looked through the security peephole at a smiling Becca holding a venti size cup of Starbucks in each hand. Clisty unlocked the door, peered out and checked the hall in both directions. "Come in … fast." She closed the door behind her, re-locking it.

"You're still wet," Becca observed stating the obvious.

Clisty looked down at her towel and the water marks on the floor. "I had to fold up the afghan first, and took dirty dishes to the kitchen."

"Of course you did." Becca shook her head and placed the paper cups on the island. She snapped several sheets of paper towel from the dispenser and began mopping up the drips. "You might want to dress before you sit down to drink your coffee." She nodded toward Clisty's towel and the bar stools. "The seat might be cold. It's a chilly morning."

"Right," Clisty said, blushing as she dashed into the bedroom.

Clisty slipped into matching pink undergarments, jerked on jeans, a lightweight heather-colored cropped sweatshirt, white socks and Skechers. She tied her hair behind her head with a twisty as she walked into the kitchen. "Okay, I'm ready for coffee," she sighed deeply as she slipped onto a stool, took the container Becca brought in, and poured the coffee into one of her own ceramic cups.

"What did Nicole say about the forum?" Becca asked as she threw the Bounty paper towel in the trash.

"She was organizing everything the last we talked late yesterday, at the end of her very long work day." Clisty handed the cup lid to Becca mechanically to add to the trash. "We should hear from her sometime this morning."

Becca pulled her cell phone from her pocket and brought up her memo app. "I have a few more questions for the forum participants."

"Good," Clisty agreed, nodding. "The general audience will have questions, too. As we talk, Karl and Karen might have comments or questions to ask or answer, prompted by what others add to the conversation. I would rather have too many questions than stand there with nothing to talk about."

Becca startled when Clisty's cell phone rang. "I'll think of a few more."

With adrenalin still pumping from the hide-Jake game she had played, Clisty grabbed the phone and took a deep breath. "Clisty Sinclair here."

"Hi Clisty, this is Nicole. I have the forum placed on the master schedule for Sunday evening ... in three days. You will all fly out Saturday. The non-stop flight is at 6 AM. I thought you'd all appreciate the one at 1:36, even though there's a three hour layover in Detroit. The four of you can have a nice supper in an airport restaurant. A LongHorn Steakhouse is at Gate A66 in the terminal. Then, catch up on the news in the VIP lounge and arrive at JFK in New York at 7:22 PM."

"Sounds doable," Clisty agreed as she added it up in her hand. "We can look over the setup at the studio on Sunday after lunch."

"That would work," Nicole agreed. "Then rest before taping at six. You would fly back to Fort Wayne on Monday afternoon. By the way, this new assistant job I have, coordinating New York with Fort Wayne, is fun."

"I'm glad, Nicole. And, the travel arrangements sound perfect," Clisty agreed. But, underneath it all, thoughts of a white sundress with special sandals and Jake in a crisp white shirt ... personal plans ... had to be changed. She and Jake had planned to secretly marry on the weekend, a wonderful late spring drive down to Indiana's beautiful Brown Country on Friday late afternoon, before their schedules became impossible. But, impossible had arrived early. When Becca left later that afternoon to pack, Clisty started again to check out some research of her own.

Chapter 24
Attack from the Water's Edge

The doctor released Karen Kramer from the hospital in the morning on the same day that Clisty, Jake and the team were getting ready to fly back to New York. Although still off her feet, Karen was able to put enough weight on her legs to transfer from a wheelchair to her bed or lift chair. Being home to absorb the beauty of the pink and yellow rain lilies waving near the water's edge behind the Kramer home was peaceful and healing. Karl had hired a home-health care worker to assist Karen when he had to be away.

When Karl opened the front door and wheeled Karen in, the house smelled like south-western chili, one of Karen's favorites. "Oh Karl, it is so good to be home." She clasped her hands together in joy as she looked out the massive windows toward the dock. "Look, there are sail boats on the water already," she gasped. "I can't seem to see it all or take it in fast enough. My eyes are bombarded with beauty."

Oliver slid in from the kitchen, prancing and dancing around, his whole body twisting in delight. He licked Karen's hand and nuzzled his nose in her lap. "Come on boy," Karl warned as he took the dog by the collar. "You're going into the laundry room for now."

"Karl, no. He'll be good," Karen begged as she scratched the dog behind both ears.

"Not now, Honey. I want to get you settled before Oliver tries to knock you out of your wheelchair." Karl leaned down to Karen's level and patted her arm. "After I take care of Oliver, do you want me to push you out to the terrace?"

165

"No," she sighed. "It's a little windy. Just look at the way those sailing ships are skipping over the water."

"Tamera?" Karl called to the health worker.

"Yes?" A woman called back as she slipped into the living room wiping her hands on a tea towel.

"Karen, you remember Tamera," Karl said as the nurse came in. "She has assisted other patients you know. Vicki Bradford, from church, is one that comes to mind. Tamera helped Vicki after she broke her hip falling off the stage when she and her Sunday school class built sets for last Christmas's pageant."

"Of course," Karen said with a smile as she extended her hand. "It's good to see you again, Tamera."

Karl patted Karen on the shoulder. "Well, it looks like you two girls are hitting it off already." He checked his Walking Buddy for the time. "Okay … I can get to the pharmacy and back in fifteen minutes, twenty if the line is long." He turned to Tamera, handing her Oliver's leash while maintaining control of the dog. "I'd like you to put Ollie in the laundry, please." He transferred his grip on the dog to Tamera's hand. "When will lunch be ready? It smells wonderful." He took the car keys from his pocket and jingled them in his hand. He had an errand to run.

"It can be ready in about fifteen minutes, Dr. Kramer. It will hold nicely if that's too early," she said as she smiled and threw the towel over her shoulder. "Chili will keep all day if you need it to."

As Tamera removed the dog from the room, Karl kissed Karen slowly on the forehead. "Are you sure you're okay, Honey?" he asked.

"Karl," she coaxed, "you hired Tamera to be here when you have to be gone. You're just going to the drug store. The doctor's office already called in my prescription. You just have to pick it up."

He closed his eyes and sighed. "I know. But, I hate to leave you." He lingered for a minute. "I've had you around a long time, my girl. I've become very familiar with those beautiful hazel eyes. I take care of many patients every day, but you aren't my patient. You're my wife."

"I'll still be here when you get back," she said and smiled. "Unless you find someone to talk to and linger. Then, I may have to eat without you. It smells so good; the aroma is far different from hospital food."

"Tamera," Karl started to say as she came back into the room. "I'm going to run to the drug store to get Professor Kramer's prescription." He watched as Karen settled in.

"All right," Tamera answered and looked at Karen. "Is that comfortable for you?"

"I'll be fine, Tamera. And, I'll feel even better if you take me into the kitchen so I can watch you prepare lunch."

"Absolutely," Tamera agreed as her face lit up.

"And, please call me Karen. I'm Professor Kramer at the University, not in my home."

Tamera smiled and nodded as she pushed Karen's wheelchair toward the kitchen, next to the living room. "I'll bet you'd like to see your kitchen again."

"Great," Karl sighed with relief and beamed. "Honey, you'll have a wonderful view of the water from the kitchen as well." He pointed toward the lake as he started out the door. "I'll be back soon."

"I'm enjoying working in your kitchen, Karen," Tamera admitted as she ran her fingertips over the white swirl marble counter. "It is designed perfectly for taking the fewest steps and still having plenty of counter space on which to work. I promise not to rearrange anything." Looking out the window, she added, "Everything white in here makes the blue water and sky seem like part of the room."

"Thanks Tamera. I designed the kitchen, and Karl plotted out the flower beds and dock outside. We planned the house to have a great view from any of the major rooms. The master bedroom is on the other side of the living room, also facing the water." She drank in the beauty beyond the large windows. "Now, what can I do to help?"

"I just washed the lettuce. It's been draining. If you want to tear it into bite size pieces, I can put a bowl on the table and you can make salad." Tamera went to the cabinets looking for a shallow dish, opening and closing several doors.

"Bowls are in the upper cabinet next to the cook top," Karen offered as she wheeled herself over to the 1950s, turquoise Formica and chrome kitchen table. "I'm ready to assist the chef," she said smiling broadly.

Tamera smiled as she put the bowl on the table. "My family had a dinette set just like that one, in black and white."

"Did you?" Karen picked up the lettuce and began tearing it into pieces. "We had one in this color."

"Ah," Tamera exclaimed with a laugh. "And, I have a sous-chef. Wow! I never dreamed that watching the Food Channel would elevate my position in the kitchen." She got a cucumber and some fresh onions from the refrigerator, a proper vegetable chopping knife from the drawer, and a cutting board, and placed them on the table in front of Karen. "Here's another tea towel if you need to wipe your hands. Lunch will be ready when you finish the salad. Do you want to eat here in the kitchen, in the dining room, or on a tray in the living room?"

"Oh, right here in the kitchen," Karen said as she began to chop vegetables, and watched the sunlight bounce off the waves that lapped at the terrace grass. As her eyes leisurely gazed on the water, her focus fixed on the area near the dock. "I wonder who that is?" she asked as a speed boat she didn't recognize silently drifted up beside the Kramers' assigned dock space. Like a huge snorting animal, it sat there with the motor idling.

"Nice looking boat," Tamera agreed as she walked closer to the window.

Absolutely mesmerized by the boat's movement on the waves, bobbing up and down, rocking back and forth, Karen dropped the knife on the floor. "Oh no, Tamera. I am so sorry. Fine helper I am. Now you have to help me," she apologized as she bent over, just as Tamera stooped to pick the knife off the floor.

POW, pa, pa, POW, POW—the rapid blasts from an automatic rifle shattered the kitchen window and exploded off pots and pans and Karen's favorite dishes that she displayed around the room. Glass shards flew everywhere sending tiny pieces into Karen's hair and into the salad she was making.

"Stay down!" Karen yelled as she slouched in the chair. Grabbing her injured right shoulder with her other hand she screamed in pain.

Neither of the women tried to look out between the window fragments to the once peaceful water. It wasn't until they heard the speed boat rev its engine and escape the scene that they came up from the floor and the shelter of the low-placed wheelchair.

"Are you all right, Karen?" Tamera asked quickly as she struggled to get up on weakened, wobbly legs. "Sorry, I'm pretty shaken."

"I think so," Karen responded, her voice shaking. "See if the land-line works. The phone is hanging over there on the wall. Call 911. If it's out, my cell phone is in my purse in the living room."

Tamera lunged for the wall-hanging, old-fashioned blue princess phone. "There's a dial tone," she gasped with relief and punched in the three digits. "This is Dr. Kramer's residence over on Twilight Cove. Someone just shot at us from a boat on the water, breaking some of the windows. We haven't checked for any damage. Send someone quickly. Please hurry. Professor Kramer just got home from the hospital a little over a half hour before the attack."

Karen watched as the peaceful water once again lazily lapped small foam bubbles against the weathered, grey wood planks of the dock. The explosion, just a few moments before, quickly dissolved into a picture of tranquil serenity. Tears welled up in Karen's eyes and spilled down her cheeks as her lips quivered in fear. "I don't know how much more I can take? I just got home, and home isn't as safe as I thought it would be. I wish Karl was home."

The sound of a police siren pierced the sudden calmness of the near noon hour and sent chills down Karen's spine. The same shrillness had beckoned to her while pinned in her car at the bottom of the hill just a week before.

When the doorbell rang she nearly leaped out of her wheelchair. Panicked by the involuntary trembling of her hands, she began to frantically wring them in an effort to regain control.

Tamera dashed to the door and flung it open to find two uniformed police officers. "Thank goodness you're here," she sighed deeply as she let them in. "Come into the kitchen."

"Officers Littleton and Garcia, Ma'am. Are you Mrs. Kramer?" the taller of the two policemen asked.

"No," she snapped. "She's in here." Tamera hurried into the kitchen and put her arm around Karen's shoulder. "Are you all right, Ma'am?"

"No," Karen whispered as she clung to Tamera's hand.

"As you can see," Tamera addressed the officers, "Professor Kramer just got out of the hospital. In fact, she came home about forty minutes ago. We were only in the kitchen a few minutes when there was gun fire from the dock."

"Does anyone else live here?" Garcia asked.

"My husband, Dr. Kramer. Right now, he's picking up my prescription." Karen's mouth was so dry her teeth stuck to her lips.

"Karl Kramer?" Littleton asked.

"Yes," she said as she blinked. Karen, still shaking from the gunfire, blotted her eyes with the tea towel. "He should be here shortly." She smiled faintly and added. "He's quite a talker. He may have been detained."

170

"Dr. Kramer has been my physician since I was a kid," Littleton said as he walked over to the shattered window and inspected the shards.

"Karen?" Karl shouted as he slammed the door and darted into the kitchen. His eyes spanned the floor splattered with broken glass and the jagged pieces that still clung to the window frame. "What on earth happened?" he gasped. Bending his knees, he got down on Karen's level, gathered her in his arms and sobbed.

Littleton assured them, "I'll call for a full crime scene investigation team to come out and go over the dock microscopically." He touched the radio attached to his shoulder. "We need a complete forensic workup of the area here at Dr. Kramer's residence. Thanks." He turned to Karen with a soft voice. "I'm sorry this happened, Mrs. Kramer...Professor. But ... if the shooter didn't get out of the boat, I have to tell you, we may not find much. He would have taken the crime scene with him."

"I'd like to take my wife into the living room and get her out of this glass, Tom." Karl reached for the handles on the back of Karen's wheelchair. Then, he stopped and turned back to the police officer. "Can I call someone to replace the window?"

"Not yet, Doc. The C.S.I. team will take pictures and process the room. They will let you know when they can release the house."

"The whole house?" Karen cried and buried her head in Karl's arm where it rested on her wheelchair.

"I'm sorry, Ma'am," Garcia apologized.

"Officer, my wife has a broken shoulder, two broken legs, and a concussion. A hit-and-run driver smashed into her car. Right now, I don't know how many days ago. She needs her home. Please, let us know the minute we can move back home."

"Dr. Kramer, I am so sorry for everything your family has been through," Littleton offered kindly.

"Thanks Tom," he said without taking his eyes off his wife. "Karen…" Karl suddenly stood up and looked out toward the lake. "Steve and his family just left on spring break. They'll be in Florida for the rest of the week. We have the keys to their home in New Rochelle. We could stay there for a few days." He patted her on the shoulder opposite her injury and turned to Tamera. "New Rochelle isn't that far away. Tamera, could you come to Steve's house every day, or even live-in, if necessary?"

"Yes, I'd be happy to," she assured them. "Should we take the chili?" she asked with a chuckle.

"There is a lid. It's tipped slightly off the pan, not really well sealed. But, there's glass on the stove top. I wouldn't want to risk eating glass that might have flown into it," Karl apologized. "Sorry, Tamera, I was looking forward to enjoying it."

Karen patted her husband's hand. "Would you mind making it again tomorrow, Tamera?"

"I'd be happy to," she answered as she leaned down to face Karen directly.

"We'll pack some things and pick up some southern fried chicken on the way to Steve's," Karl stated. "Tamera, I would appreciate it if you would come into the bedroom and help Karen get her things. Thanks."

That was it. Karen had suffered through the hit-and-run attack, surgery to re-set broken bones, and the violent headaches that went with the concussion. Now, her safe homecoming had been shattered—just as her drive to the office the other night had been—all for the price of helping others.

Chapter 25
Back to the City

It was late Saturday afternoon when Clisty, Jake and the others disembarked from the plane in Detroit. They would have a layover in Michigan with time for supper at the LongHorn Steakhouse at Gate A66 there in the terminal.

"We have about three hours to eat supper," Clisty reminded them. "This Steakhouse probably has a large enough menu we should all find something we like."

"Well," Jake began, "we haven't seen the menu yet. Don't know if Griff's infamous hamburger will be available."

The dining room had a massive fieldstone fireplace as its focal point. With a heavy wooden beam for a mantel, the handsome fireplace and its surround easily caught the diner's eye. It was cool enough for the faint perfume of wood smoke to hover around the hearth. However, Clisty was one who couldn't get enough of the majesty of flight, so her focus was on the runways beyond the floor-to-ceiling windows. The beauty of the day added to the joy of airplane watching.

The dining room wasn't crowded so they quickly found a table where they could watch the planes land and take off. With Jason working back in Indiana, they only needed a table for four, which they were able to maneuver into place so all could see the runways.

Everything on the menu looked good. They all agreed to order Texas Tonions to share as an appetizer, and a full pot of coffee. For the main dish, Clisty ordered a hickory salt crusted filet mignon, a side of broccoli, and a salad.

The server smiled and apologized. "I know you'll love the steak, Ma'am. But, this is an airport. You'll find it hard to cut the meat with TSA approved plastic knives. If you have a problem, the kitchen can cut it into bitesize pieces for you."

Clisty laughed and waved her hand. "I have nothing to prove. Yes … please ask the kitchen to cut my meat for me before you bring it to the table. Also, I'm afraid I don't like animal fat. Please, while they have the sharp knife in hand, have them cut off all fat. Tell them, 'Thank you.'"

"No fat at all?" Jake gasped. To the server he said, "I'll have the same thing, but swap the salad for a baked potato, with butter and sour cream." Turning to Clisty he added. "I thought it was Jack Sprat who could eat no fat, not his wife."

"Wife?" Becca asked as she sat up straight, her wide eyes shifting from Clisty to Jake.

Clisty shrugged off Becca's question and filled in the rest of the nursery rhyme. "Becca, don't be silly. You remember Mother Goose. 'Jack Sprat could eat no fat. His wife could eat no lean.' That's whose wife he was talking about, Jack's not Jake's."

"Yeah … right," she agreed and winked at Clisty when Jake looked down to pour his coffee.

Griff ordered a Steakhouse Burger. "See, hamburgers are available after all."

They all laughed and checked the menu again. Maybe they had missed other tasty dishes.

"The sandwich will be enough for now. I have to allow room for dessert," Griff said with a smile. "So go light on the mayo. The caramel apple gold rush looks good to me. If the burger tastes as good as the picture looks, I'll trust the dessert menu to deliver what they promise."

As Clisty enjoyed the rhythm and synchronized dance of the aircraft marshallers on the tarmac, her phone rang. "Clisty Sinclair here."

"Clisty, this is Nicole. We just received word from Karl Kramer that Karen came home today and—"

"Already? Wonderful!" Clisty lifted her mug in salute and took a sip.

"Clisty," Nicole was hesitant and sounded worried. "Karen was home less than an hour. Karl had gone to the drugstore, when there was gun fire from a motorboat on the lake into the rooms facing the water. I know windows were shattered in the kitchen and living room. I don't know if the master bedroom was damaged."

"What?" Clisty felt the blood drain from her face as she sat up stiffly. "Did they find out who did it? Was anyone hurt?"

"Who? What?" Becca asked.

"No, no one was hurt, thank goodness," Nicole explained. "The Kramers, and Karen's home healthcare nurse, Tamera Valdez, have moved to their son's home in New Rochelle. Steve Kramer and his family are on spring break in Florida, visiting Heather, her husband and the kids. Heather is the Kramers' daughter. The CSI team is going over everything at the Twilight Cove house before the Kramers can even replace the broken windows. Hopefully, the police will release Karen and Karl's home by the time spring vacation is over. Steve and his family will be home then."

"What is it, Babe?" Jake asked when he saw Clisty's face.

Clisty stared out the window, stunned. "The Kramers' house was attacked by gunmen, basically knocking out the windows on the water side of the house. No one was hurt but they are out of their home for a few days while CSI processes the scene. Karen had just gotten home from the hospital minutes before, and Karl was away picking up her prescription."

"Clisty, this is getting dangerous," Jake said calmly. However, the furrow in his brow couldn't hide his concern.

She looked at him intently. "What are you saying? The job is dangerous, or this story in particular is dangerous?"

Becca opened her mouth to speak and then stopped. She looked out on the airplanes as they skidded to a stop. "We have hardly gotten into the job, Clisty. I agree there are dangerous elements to this story. But, Jake, I don't think you're saying the whole job is dangerous are you?"

Clisty reached for Jake's leg under the table and ran her finger tips over his strong, lean knee. She wasn't sure if she was calming him or herself. "I'm an investigative blogger, Jake, and this is my team. You're a police sergeant. Sometimes we both run into real bad guys. You've known that all along. Besides, these new stories are about good, ordinary people doing extraordinary things."

Jake's expression softened. He seemed satisfied with Clisty's explanation, but she wondered if she was.

•••••

When they arrived in New York a network driver met them at the baggage claim carrousel. Clisty saw a man holding a sign with a handwritten message, "Welcome Clisty Sinclair." Clisty smiled and approached the man.

"Clisty," Jake snapped. "Stand back."

"Why?" she reacted, startled.

"Get behind me," he said sharply. Turning to the driver, Jake stated firmly, "May I see your I.D.?"

The driver's expression faded from welcoming to confusion. "My I.D.?" He fished in his pocket. "Sure." He glanced at Clisty. "Is there something wrong?"

Clisty immediately grasped who was in charge of security and stayed back. While Jake cleared the driver with a phone call to Nicole Bernard, Clisty smiled. Her mind flashed back to her conversation with Jake when she was in the process of deciding whether to take Bradley Funderbird's offer at BNN. Jake wasn't trying to take over the leadership of the Kramer story. He was offering his strength and expertise when needed.

Clisty remembered Jake's words. "I can't be one of those guys who are so insecure that they have to force the woman in their life to give up who she is to be with him. I want you to walk beside me, Clisty. I depend on you and you depend on me, out of love, not out of manipulation. We are each perfectly capable of depending on ourselves."

Clisty knew, Mr. Funderbird hired Jake to head up security for Clisty and her team. That's what Jake was doing, protecting them all by not allowing a strange man to lure them into his car. After all that had happened with Karen Kramer and Jerry Wintergardner, security would have to stay on constant guard.

As Clisty and the group moved toward the town car, Clisty slipped her hand into Jake's. "Thanks," she whispered.

"For what?" Jake asked, not aware that it was anything different from his daily work on the police force.

"For knowing your job and doing it boldly."

"Thank you, Clisty, for believing that I know my job and for letting me do it."

She squeezed his hand gently. "Remember, the Lord blesses couples with many talents. But, each member of the couple doesn't receive all of the strengths. Sometimes, you have a talent and I respect that. Other times, I have a talent and you respect that. We'd look silly if we always demanded to do the very thing we are least capable of doing. The problem arises when one half of the couple doesn't respect the strengths of the other. I respect you, Jake Davis. When we get to the hotel, I'll respect my job enough to bring my blog readers up to date and post it."

Crime Beat
✹
From the Heartland

10:15 PM

This blogger checked back into a New York hotel this evening. We came to film a special segment of the American News Magazine tomorrow evening. It will be a forum format for those who received the Walking Buddy, their family and friends. There will be a few seats open to the general public who may have questions or can offer information about the hacking of the Buddy.

Our new program, *Stories from the Heartland,* is an opportunity for this True Crime Blogger to switch focus. Rather than dwelling on the negative side of life, this blogger will lift up ordinary people doing extraordinary things to benefit others.

The problem that changed our focus from the good deeds of others into a research effort for *Crime Beat* is the segment you saw recently in which we lifted up the wonderful Walking Buddy. Invented by Dr. Karl Kramer and programed by his wife, Professor Karen Kramer, someone hacked into that un-hackable blessing. That leads this blogger to open another *Crime Beat* investigation as we help police solve crimes that are the result of compromising the Walking Buddy.

THE MYSTERY WITHIN THE JOY

Professor Karen Kramer arrived home from the hospital this morning. Within a half-hour of her return, a gunman pulled a speedboat into the cove and opened fire. In order to try to maintain a measure of security for her and her husband, I will identify her home as located on the water's edge in the Stamford, Connecticut area. If you live in Stamford, or were visiting there, and heard rapid gun fire from a small boat on the water earlier today, contact us if you have information about the incident. We are looking for any identifying details regarding the motorboat that floated into the dock at the Kramer residence, and then sped away after gun fire destroyed the windows on the water side of the home. Anything, regardless of how small, may help.

If you heard the boat, did it have any unusual sound, pitch, rhythm, or meter? Please, use your own words to describe it.

Did you see anything: color, size, all or part of the boat's registration numbers? Registration numbers are located on each side of the bow on the forward half of the boat. The painted or decaled numbers are clearly visible as they are at least three inches tall in bold print.

If you remember any identifiers, please contact the police and/or this blogger.

| Share |

SEE YOU AT THE BOOKSTORE

Remember, if you're in the Fort Wayne area, drop by Barnes and Noble Bookseller on South Jefferson. I will be signing copies of *The Lottery Looser*. See you there.

| Share | *Contact: clistysynclair@ebox.com*

Chapter 26
Sunday Morning

In New York City the next day, the Sunday morning was glorious for walking. As Clisty and Jake passed one of the entrances to Central Park where a wide walking path wound around benches next to a foot bridge, children laughed as they tossed a ball back and forth. It appeared they were trying to throw hard enough the next child couldn't catch it. Every part of the city was so magical to Clisty she didn't want to blink. The soothing sound of a small water fountain caressed her ears off to the left. There, birds preened their feathers to align them for flight, and fluffed their wings. A dog barked and nipped at the hooves of a mounted policeman's high stepping steed. The yapping was so loud, it sounded like a pack of wolves instead of the high pitched silky terrier it was. Spring encouraged a young couple on a park bench to pay no attention to the world around them. Clisty wondered if she would ever feel free enough to show her love in public. Maybe it wouldn't just happen. Maybe freedom like that was a decision she would have to deliberately make.

She slipped her hand through Jake's arm as they walked up the steps of a beautiful old church not far from the southern tip of the park. Clisty wasn't sure of the time of services but that would be okay this time. She just needed to be in contact with her faith among other faithful, if only for the benediction.

"I'll admit it," Clisty spoke softly as Jake pulled on the church's brass thumb latch door handle, "I'll miss celebrating our wedding in my home church with our

families and friends around us. But, I know it can't happen."
She looked around to see if anyone heard her.

"It really can be the wedding you want, Clisty," Jake
assured her, "if you're ready to tell Funderbird that you're
getting married. Children can come years later, if that's the
only concern."

"What about the wedding you want, Jake?" she asked
as they stepped inside to the music of a large pipe organ.

"I have only one thing I will demand, and trust me on
this point, I will not give in," he insisted, tapping her
shoulder. "Invite whoever you want, but I only need one
person there ... you."

When Jake first began his manifesto, Clisty was
worried. When he concluded, she wanted to jump into his
arms; but ... this was not the place. Lately, it was never the
place.

Inside, the arches of the foyer led reverently into the
vaulted ceiling of the sanctuary. The downward sweep of the
dome seemed to gather each note of the song the
congregation was singing and amplified the harmonies:
There's a sweet, sweet presence in this place, they sang. The
vibrating strings of an accompanying harp played an
interlude before the last verse. The music warmed Clisty's
soul.

They slid into a back pew where they wouldn't disturb
the service that had already begun. Running her fingers over
the back of the pew in front of them, Clisty could feel the
raised grain of the quarter sawn walnut ... just like in her
grandmother's church back home. A small boy in a
superhero red T-shirt, turned around and waved his fingers at
them while the pastor began her sermon. The boy smelled
like fruity gummy worms. Evidence of the colorful sticky
substance still clung to the one remaining tooth he had in his
smile. Clisty closed her eyes and inhaled the fragrance of the
Spirit in the room. She had grown up in the church.

The sanctuary was all of that and more, a place of
solace beyond the hubbub of the street and the noise of

Clisty's life. Now, she was planning the most important day of her life. What was she thinking? How was she going to settle for a non-church, non-family wedding? Would it be safe to step out of the usual routine?

As Clisty looked around at the worshipers she began to see that comfortable sameness may not be as necessary as she thought. Some of the congregation wore the usual dress of the day with women in sweater covered sundresses and men in business suits. But, that didn't appear to be a Sunday morning uniform. Teens and young adults wore jeans and T-shirts, while some men had on cargo shorts. Would she be able to see life differently than the rigid planning she had always expected?

As the service ended, those near them crowded around, welcoming them to the church and the city. Even her previous mental picture of unfriendly New Yorkers was debunked.

"You look so familiar to me. Have we met?" A lady sitting on the end of the pew near the center isle reached out her hand.

Clisty smiled and studied the woman's face. "I...don't thinks so. I've just been here a few days for work." Her smile broadened.

"That smile...I know I've...." The woman stopped as her eyes widened. "Clisty Sinclair! I saw you on the American News Magazine." Her cheeks turned a little red. "I'm sorry I bothered you in church." She turned to Jake. "I'm glad you and your friend came this morning." She started to slink away, apparently embarrassed.

Clisty touched her shoulder. "Thank you for welcoming us. It's good to worship with others on Sunday morning." She thought about all the familiar members of her church family who would be shaking hands and sharing hugs back at her home church, a familiar Sunday routine that made her world safe.

"You are always welcome when you're in the city, Clisty." The lady gave her a little hug and joined her family at the door.

Clisty walked out silently, thinking of how different her Sabbath worship had been, among strangers. How long would it take for her to adjust to a completely new life? How many other "normal and consistent" concepts were easier for Clisty to believe than the possibility of change? Could their wedding really be a fun secret and still a blessing?

So many details rattled around in her head, it sounded like the jazz group they listened to were warming up between her ears. Was this going to be the new pattern of her life?

Yet, her new experiences had clarified so many misperceptions. Maybe her new-normal would let her break free from the fears of the past.

Chapter 27
Dinner with Rockefeller

"This space will be perfect," Clisty and Becca agreed when Nicole Bernard showed them the area being set up for that evening's forum. The room was the studio where they telecast BNN's nine o'clock news during weeknights. It was square but the platform was set up in the round with graduating wide risers and chairs on each of the three tiers. Spotlights hung from the catwalk above. TV cameras, placed strategically on the outer ring, all pointed to the center of the room. A small platform with two comfortable chairs facing each other sat in the middle.

"You have until 5 PM. The taping is at 6—shop, rest, have a long lunch—whatever you want to do," Nicole said with her hands on her hips.

Clisty didn't look at Jake. She knew these were not the plans he originally had for the weekend. When she finally stole a glance, he winked. She blushed what felt like hot, crimson red.

"Okay … Jake and I went to church and haven't had lunch," Clisty began as she sized up the afternoon in her head. "What about you two?" she asked Becca and Griff.

"I slept in," Becca admitted. "I haven't even had coffee yet." She looked down at her clothes and spread out her flared lightweight navy skirt. "I might be presentable in most any restaurant … so your pick is fine with me."

Griff smiled sheepishly. "As long as there's plenty of food on the plate, the location makes no difference to me."

Jake laughed, slapping Griff on the shoulder. "Well said my friend."

Becca brightened. With her hand on her stomach, she stood as tall as possible. "Come to think of it, since I'm the one who is starving, I'll select the place. My cousin Connie ate at the Rock Center Café last winter. It's the restaurant at Rockefeller Center. She said she really enjoyed looking out on the ice rink and watching the skaters. Obviously there is no ice now, but the plants and outdoor tables would be fun to see."

"That sounds wonderful," Clisty said as she headed toward the elevator. "It's like a dinner theater but you don't have to pay for show tickets. Makes me almost miss winter — almost."

In the hall, Jake pushed the elevator command button. "We'll be in New York from time to time. We could eat there again during the Christmas holidays."

"Christmas season in New York?" Becca asked. "Wow, maybe we can be here for the Thanksgiving Day Parade. Check with Nicole about rooms on the parade side of the hotel. I've always wanted to relive the *Miracle on 34th Street* scene of watching the parade from the warmth of inside ... inside anywhere."

Clisty jumped into Jake's arms and clung on with joy. "Isn't this going to be fun?" She laughed a giggly laugh. "Don't think about the danger. Look forward to the magic of it all. This is like living in a movie, like Becca was describing."

They walked out of the BNN building and into a brilliant afternoon sunshine. In spite of the wind, springtime in New York City was magnificent and it was even better on Sunday. The bustle of women in business suits and Reeboks hurrying to and from their offices; couriers on bicycles; people pushing racks of clothing in the garment district; and the general life of work in the city evaporated on Sundays. Like a spring rain, Sundays in New York left the city clean and exclusively available to Clisty and the team. The wind blew through the tunneling streets. With so few people to block it, it nearly knocked Clisty over. They walked the few blocks to Rockefeller Center and easily found the Café. It was open until 9 PM so they had all afternoon to eat and prepare for the forum between relaxation and their lunch.

"Would you like a booth or table?" the hostess asked. "It's only 12:15 so you have your choice."

"A table, please." Clisty's eyes danced at the sights outside. Inside the restaurant, the tables placed in front of the huge windows commanded a spectacular view of the gilded statue of Prometheus. Everything was so real. Holiday television programs with a scene of winter ice skaters usually included a shot of the statue. Booths, lined up parallel to the tables but further from the windows, had padded benches that looked equally comfortable.

A young server with raven hair handed each of them a menu. "I'm Danielle, your server. I'll give you some time to look it over. What can I bring you to drink?"

"Coffee," was the uniform answer.

Clisty leaned on the left armrest of the pale gold chair and gazed out the window. Many flags flanked the plaza, standing proud as they waved in the breeze. Outdoor tables with their white umbrellas had traded places with winter skaters on ice. "Um, I'd better decide what I'm going to order before she comes back. I could sit here and watch the wind blow through the plaza and forget all about eating."

Griff closed his menu and slapped it down on the table. "I cannot be dissuaded," he said and smiled defiantly. "I'm ordering the Chef's Burger—it's a Black Angus short rib and chuck blend, with cheddar cheese. I'll even take the tomato and their in-house pickles. Oh, yes indeed, fries come with that."

"Why am I not surprised?" Becca asked as she shook her head in Griff's direction. "It's chicken Milanese for me."

Griff blinked his eyes in confusion. "What is that?"

Becca cocked her head and announced with fun, "I have no idea. But, doesn't it sound exotic?"

"I suppose you are going to have a steak," Clisty teased as she leaned in Jake's direction. "That seems to be your go-to order."

Jake picked up Clisty's hand and pretended to nibble her fingers. "Of course I am … with roasted fingerling potatoes … it says right here." He chuckled as he pointed to the menu item.

Becca yawned. "Ah yes, a fancy name for stubby, chubby potatoes."

"Well, have your stubby spuds if you want to," Clisty said, brushing her hair back from her shoulders. "For me … it's Atlantic salmon with a tabbouleh salad. Doesn't that sound scrumptious?"

Griff leaned back in his chair, put his hands behind his head and studied her face. "They don't usually sell Tabba-something-salad under the golden arches … unless it's a limited time offer of course. Explain please."

"Okay," Clisty agreed. "But, I'll admit I'm going to need a little help." She pulled her cell phone from her purse and asked the screen, "What is a tabbouleh salad?"

The electronic voice of the cell phone spaced out evenly, in measured tones. "Tabbouleh is a Levantine, or Middle Eastern, vegetarian dish or salad made of tomatoes, chopped parsley, mint, bulgur, and onion with an olive oil and lemon dressing."

"Oh yum," Griff moaned.

Clisty raised her nose in the air, flipped her cloth napkin open and draped it across her lap. "Well … it sounds good to me. If you're not too sassy, I'll let you taste some of it when it comes."

"That's okay," Griff said with a wink. "I'm good."

As soon as the server came and took their order, they all sat back and relaxed. Another mission accomplished. It was only lunch, but once decided, there were no misleading twists that carried them into unknown food choices or dangerously allergic reactions. Clisty felt victorious.

"Isn't this picture perfect?" Becca swooned as she stared out the window. "It would make a beautiful wedding reception venue. Our reception was in Grandma and Grandpa's back yard."

"Yes, it would be wonderful," Clisty agreed but said no more. Deep down, she knew that any wedding reception would be perfect with Jake as the groom, just as he described.

Clisty intended to put all worry behind her for the afternoon. The restaurant and the scene on the other side of the windows filled her with the magic of New York. But, she couldn't shake an uneasy feeling. A group of people entered the restaurant and quickly found seats. One man, apparently with the group and yet a straggler who couldn't keep up, followed them to their table. She thought it was odd that the man didn't remove his ball cap. Every man with any social awareness knew to take their hat off when they came indoors. Clisty felt a chill up her spine.

"Grandma and Grandpa's back yard," Clisty heard Jake say, "sounds good to me." Then he whispered, patting Clisty's knee under the table. "I've seen your grandmother's back yard, Becca. It has flower beds and a classy water fountain in the middle." He glanced at Clisty. "Not interested in backyard weddings?" he hummed a little stiffly in her ear.

"Yes, Jake," Becca agreed as her face lit up with an obvious memory. "I remember when some kids tried to steal Grandma's water feature and one of the boys broke his foot attempting to jump the fence after the security lights came on," she said as she turned to Griff.

Griff stirred his coffee vigorously. "My foot still bothers me when the barometer falls."

Clisty nearly spit coffee all over the table and gulped. "Griff! That was you?" She had listened to the others talk but, fixed by the strange fear that came over her, she turned her major attention back to the man in the cap.

"It was me and a few friends," Griff confessed as he sipped his coffee. Fiddling with his cup helped take the focus off him.

"What's wrong?" Jake whispered to Clisty.

Becca reached up and ruffled Griff's dark curly hair. "It was the best thing that ever happened to him."

"Nothing," Clisty insisted to Jake under her breath.

Jake's other ear was directed to the table conversation. "The best thing? A broken foot and a jail record are good things? I hadn't heard that one before."

Griff sat back and spread his arms on the back of the chairs beside him. "No record. When I broke my foot, Dad got me a small camera. While my foot healed, I fell in love with photography. I got pretty good at it."

"Pretty good?" Becca protested. "He's the best. The station wouldn't have hired him right out of high school if he wasn't great."

Clisty's gaze shifted back to the blue cap man. What was he doing? He wasn't really sitting with the others. He sat down at a table behind them, took out a small pad of paper, jotted something down, handed the note to the server, then got up and left.

Jake focused on what Becca just said. "I had forgotten that culprit was you, Griff," Jake admitted. "You're lucky Becca's grandparents didn't press charges. They're good people. But, Becca, I do remember the yard." He paused and wrinkled his forehead. "Maybe I should have been a gardener, rather than a police sergeant."

Clisty tried to sound relaxed and interested. "You're a great SWAT leader and your trainees think you're awesome, Jake Davis," she corrected him. "You can figure out anything. I've been around you enough I think it may be rubbing off on me."

"Oh, really?" Jake asked with raised eyebrows. "So you learned to be a Crime Blogger by osmosis? That's a new approach. I'm learning all kinds of things today. They don't teach osmosis down at the Police Academy in Plainfield."

Clisty was determined she would not be intimidated by the stranger in the ball cap, someone she didn't even know. She was going to have a nice lunch with good company. "Right," she agreed. "Jake, do you remember that story I am looking into in Brown County?" Clisty asked with a tongue-in-cheek expression.

"Brown County?" Becca asked. Her eyebrows rose in surprise. "I don't remember you talking about something in the southern part of the state. What story was that?"

"It—" Jake stopped at the exact moment the heel of Clisty's shoe stomped on his foot. He drummed his fingers on the table and sat back with a twisted smile on his face. Actually, the look of satisfaction seemed to say that he had covered the excruciating pain quite well.

"I know the network said they would channel all stories through the New York office," Clisty explained in bits and pieces. "But, I heard about a … a little lady of … eighty-three who … who has turned her living room into a … like a chapel. She performs weddings there … kinda. She's like, ah … the Vegas Wedding Chapel of Southern Indiana."

Becca stared, her mouth gaping. "Really?" she drug out unconvinced. "And, how did the new investigative talent of yours help you with that one?"

"Well …" Clisty stammered, "it seems …some people in her neighborhood don't like the … traffic."

"The traffic?" Becca asked while Jake sat grinning at the entire conversation. Becca turned to him and asked, "What do you know about all of this?"

"Oh look," Clisty exclaimed as she pointed to the server. Danielle came near the table, carrying a large tray piled with plates of food. Dangling from her arm was a folding tray table. Clisty's lunch was far more than salad and fish. Her exotic lunch was an escape route out of embarrassment that the whole Brown County fantasy created. "It looks wonderful."

Becca inhaled deeply as the exotic aroma of her entree rose from the plate. "Let me know if you need help with that Indiana/Vegas story," she said with a knife in one hand and a fork in the other. "Right now, I'm famished."

"Me too," Jake offered quietly. "If there's anything I can do to help you with that southern Indiana story ... whistle. It sounds really interesting."

"Okay," Clisty sat back when Danielle placed the salmon on the table at her place. "I think you may be just the person to help me on this one, Jake." She quickly looked over at Becca, who was completely engrossed in Chicken Milanese, her eyes closed. "I agree. It sounds very interesting. You can check into any laws the woman may be breaking."

"I hope you enjoy your meal," Danielle said with a smile. "Let me know if I can get you anything else." She started to leave then turned back. "Oh, Miss Sinclair, a gentleman handed me this note to give to you before he left."

Clisty froze in fear as she looked for the man in the baseball hat. He was gone. She hadn't even noticed when he left. As she unfolded the piece of paper, her hands shook. It read, "You just won't leave this alone. You will be next." She folded the threatening note and slipped it over to Jake.

Jake kept the paper below the table since Clisty apparently wanted to keep it quiet. His head shot up as he appeared to search the dining room for the person who sent it.

"He left," Clisty whispered hoarsely.

"Who?" Becca asked as she looked around the room.

"I'm hungry," Clisty announced. Her voice sounded strained. "We'll talk about work when we're done eating." She picked up her fork with trembling hands and ate a bite of fish, but had no idea what it tasted like.

Chapter 28
The Forum

6 PM

"Good evening," Clisty spoke into the camera as the forum taping began. "This is Clisty Sinclair at BNN in New York City," she announced. She felt professional in a black gabardine sheath dress and resisted the need to adjust the self-fabric belt. "I'd like to thank all of you for coming and those of you who are watching from home."

The cameras panned the audience of invited guests who gathered for the town-hall meeting. A man in the second row wrinkled his brow. Clisty could feel his pain as his expression distorted. One woman blotted her eyes, most gave enthusiastic applause.

"Many of you have heard the rumors surrounding the Walking Buddy, invented by Dr. Karl Kramer. Serious issues have risen regarding the Buddy's ability to be hacked, placing its wearer in possible danger. We have arranged a forum style meeting to try to determine if this was possible. We have invited several people, involved in various ways with the Buddy, to join us this evening. Our main guest is Dr. Kramer. His wife, Professor Karen Kramer is here but not on camera. As some of you are aware, Professor Kramer—"

"Karen," a voice called out from the darkened area behind Karl. "Please, call me Karen."

"Thank you, Karen," Clisty said as she smiled. "That will make it easier." Clisty waved at the professor who sat in a comfortable lift chair in the back of the space. "A week ago, Karen was stalked by a driver while out walking. Later that same night, a hit-and-run driver deliberately struck her car. We are all glad you can be here, Karen." Clisty didn't describe any details about the recent barrage of bullets on their home.

"Thank you," Karen's voice was weak but lilted up at the end of each sentence. Again, those in attendance applauded. Karen gave Clisty a thumbs-up, signaling her appreciation of their agreement that Clisty would not reveal that their home, secured only with plywood across the lake-side of the house, may be vulnerable to looters.

Clisty strode back and forth in front of those gathered. "Also in the audience, let's welcome, Dr. Jeffery Jorguson, the neurologist who provided the names for the first group of patients to receive the Buddy … the test group. Thank you for coming, Sir."

"I'm very happy to be here," he responded, adjusting himself awkwardly from the front row facing the two center chairs. "We are all interested in maintaining the positive reputation of this excellent product, the Walking Buddy, and Karl and Karen Kramer who invented it."

"Thank you, Doctor, for your comments and for being here." Clisty raised her hand in acclamation. "Sitting beside Dr. Jorguson is Jerry Wintergardner's son, Kevin. Jerry was one of the patients from Dr. Jorguson's list of volunteers given the Walking Buddy to test. Jerry was killed by another hit-and-run driver … while out walking, guided by the Buddy."

Clisty searched out and walked over to the opposite side of the front row. "Also, our researchers were able to track down a family member of a man who started stalking me in Indiana, Hiram Hubley." She touched the shoulder of a tall woman in a red dress with white sleeves who sat on the front row. The woman's face was drawn and her eyes darted around the room. "It's alright, Renée." Clisty faced the camera and added, "Renée is Hiram Hubley's daughter. Thank you so much for coming. We have agreed that we will not use her married name in order to protect her husband and children. Renée and her family are upstanding members of their community."

With an iPhone in her left hand, Clisty pointed to a middle aged woman with white hair, cut in a short textured bob. She was dressed in an exquisitely designed navy blue suit. "We are also grateful to Terry DeCamp, the CEO of Boston Technologies, manufacturer of the Walking Buddy, for joining us this evening. We know that you and your company have a stake in proving that the Buddy is un-hackable."

"Thank you for inviting me, Clisty. We, at Boston Tech, are eager to vindicate our production of the Walking Buddy." DeCamp looked into the camera, steely-eyed. "Trust me … the product we manufactured cannot be hacked. We stand by our guarantee and know that the truth of these accidents will soon be uncovered."

Dr. Kramer placed his hands together. "Thank you," he silently mouthed.

"Please, Dr. Kramer," Clisty motioned to Karl, "please, you're still standing. Take a seat." She pointed to one of the two chairs in the center of the spot light. "All of this has been very traumatic for you and your family." Clisty sat in the chair opposite him.

"Like Karen," the doctor began as he situated himself in the chair, "I prefer that you call me Karl."

"Then, Karl it is," she repeated. Addressing the audience, she added, "We also appreciate the presence of friends, family and neighbors of those involved and those interested in the outcome of this discussion." Looking around the audience with a small smile, she asked, "How many of you have used a Walking Buddy or know someone who has?"

Everyone in the room raised their hand as a hum of chatter and nodding heads spread across the room. Some people clearly had tears in their eyes.

"So, for us here, the fate of the Walking Budding is very important." Clisty glanced down at her cell phone where she had posted a list of names in the memo app along with a few words identifying their concerns. "I'll ask Breanna … where are you Breanna?" Clisty looked out into the group of those gathered, paused and smiled when she spotted a woman in a yellow dress raise her hand. "Yes … Breanna, you have a question for Dr. Kramer."

"Yes," Breanna spoke slowly with eyes on Karl, then on Terry DeCamp. "Boston Technologies tells us that the Buddy cannot be hacked. How do you explain that two people wearing the Walking Buddy were involved in traffic incidents … both struck by hit-and-run drivers? They did not know one another and their only connection was the Buddy."

Clisty studied the woman for a second. "Breanna, are you saying that the incidents are related?"

The woman in yellow sat back, her mouth gaping. "You mean you're saying they're not? How is that possible?"

Kevin Wintergardner blurted out, "What do you mean? Miss Sinclair, how can you say that the two accidents have no connection? I don't think Dad ever met the Kramers or knew anyone at Boston Technologies. The Buddy itself was his only link to any of them."

Terry DeCamp simply answered, "I am saying they cannot be related. The Buddy cannot be hacked once and certainly not twice. I know, because I tried … several times." She stood and looked back at Professor Kramer. "Karen, you did a great job of programming." She started to sit down and added, "We'd hire Karen in a second. In fact, we've already tried that."

"To clarify for our viewing audience," Clisty began, "the Walking Buddy is a wrist watch with GPS and an additional program. Karl, why don't you tell our audience about your invention?"

Karl's smile still revealed pride in the Buddy in spite of the recent problems. "As the wearer walks around his or her neighborhood, the GPS is constantly monitoring their position. If the walker makes a wrong turn, a preprogramed familiar voice, such as a spouse, son, daughter, or friend, tells them they are off their route and redirects them. The voice tells them where they are, the landmarks, and where to turn to get back home." He paused and looked at Kevin. "Your father, Jerry Wintergardner, was out walking when, according to police, his Walking Buddy began giving him incorrect information. Following the misinformation, Mr. Wintergardner was eventually off his route by many streets. He ended up on a two-lane road with no sidewalks and a fifty-five mile-an-hour speed limit. Struck and killed by a driver who did not stay at the scene, Jerry died instantly. The driver didn't call 911, or report the accident to anyone." Karl addressed Kevin with compassion in his voice. "Am I correct about your dad, Kevin?"

"Yes," he said and nodded slowly. "That's what we were told."

Ms. DeCamp straightened up, her eyes flashing. "Was the Walking Buddy taken into evidence?"

"No …" Kevin drew out hesitantly. "I don't know. You'd have to check with the police, but I don't think so."

Clisty quickly looked back at Jake who stood behind the outer ring of seats. "I believe we were told, the police did take the Buddy in. Did they return it to you?"

"No …" Kevin said, his head tilted. "No, they didn't return it to me. I can check on it for you."

"Yes," Karen interrupted. "The police took the Buddy for evidence."

"Good. I'll have to inspect it," DeCamp stated, her eyes narrowed.

Clisty addressed the two, "My researcher is monitoring this forum." Looking into the camera she stated, "Nicole, please see if you can locate Mr. Wintergardner's Walking Buddy. It may still be with the police."

Karl seemed to listen intently, then, shaking his head he asked, "How is Jerry's hit-and-run driver related to Karen's? Except for the Buddy, Karen and Jerry have no connection."

A woman dressed in a causal green T-shirt in the second tier of chairs, raised her hand but didn't wait for recognition. "Sorry to interrupt," she blurted out. "We've all heard the line, 'Follow the money.' Ms. DeCamp, what investment do you and your company have in the Walking Buddy?"

"As we stated," DeCamp sighed heavily, "we manufacture the Buddy."

The woman in green continued, undaunted. "Do you have a percentage of the profit ... above and beyond the manufacturing income? What happens to the Buddy when the Kramers are gone?"

DeCamp sniffed indignantly. "They have children who will inherit I assume. I'm not privilege to their personal wills."

Clisty shifted a little in her chair, looked back at Karen, then leaned in Karl's direction. "Thank you for your question," she began. "Did you ..."

"Sorry again," the last questioner interrupted. "You didn't answer my question. Do you or Boston Technologies own a percentage of the Walking Buddy?"

"Yes ..." DeCamp squirmed slightly. "Boston Technologies owns twenty percent of the rights to the Walking Buddy."

The woman in the T-shirt scooted to the edge of her chair. "And, if both of the Kramers die, then what?"

DeCamp's voice raised slightly in pitch and volume, "Young woman—"

The woman grabbed the back of the chair in front of her. Speaking slowly and firmly, she added, "And then what?"

"Our contract," DeCamp enunciated sharply as she adjusted the collar of her suit, "our contract reads ... in the event of the death of both Dr. and Professor Kramer in the first five years of manufacturing, in order to recoup losses due to development, Boston Technology's share of the Walking Buddy will increase to forty-five percent."

"And, how would you regain your losses?" the woman asked.

DeCamp's face grew red. Her voice was coarse. "We are a technologies company. We had a similar device designed for the same Alzheimer's population, but the Kramers developed and patented the Walking Buddy first." She straightened stiffly and added, "We would manufacture an even newer and better Walking Buddy."

The audience dissolved into low level mumbles and uneasy shifting in chairs. Clisty didn't attempt to calm their reactions. The editing department would sift through the taping and shorten it to fit the program's space as need. It was important for the entire group to vent their feelings. After all, that was the main purpose of the forum.

"Finally, my last question," the T-shirt woman continued unstopped as she sat back and crossed her arms. "Does anyone else have a percentage of the profits of the Walking Buddy?"

Karl shifted from one hip to the other, inclining his body in the woman's direction. "Yes, Ma'am, Dr. Jorguson has a ten percent share." He smiled at Jeff in support of his interest. "Jeff has a lot of personal time invested in testing the Buddy, creating a lot of expenses for his practice in time and tracking."

"I was, and I am, very happy to help my patients by choosing them to test the Walking Buddy," Jorguson offered.

The woman asked, "What if something happened to the Kramers?"

Jorguson answered, "I would hope Boston Technology's would be able to use my services in some way."

"Thank you for answering some tough questions," T-shirt woman exclaimed, sat back and flopped both arms openly across the arms of the chair.

"Thank you for your excellent inquiry," Clisty said as she glanced back at Jake. Redirecting her questions, she asked, "Dr. Jorguson, do you have any additional comments?"

"No, I don't think so," he replied, his expression relaxed. "I have been very proud to be a part of this great product. I thank both of the Kramers for their creativity and their generosity."

"Thank you, Doctor," Clisty responded as she glanced down at her notes. "To get back to the questions regarding training for the Buddy's use, Karl … did you or Karen actually meet those who were given the Buddy to test?"

"Well … yes," Karl began as he slowly steepled his fingers. "Jeff Jorguson arranged a meeting at the hospital for all of the patients he selected for participation. Jerry Wintergardner would have been there."

"No," Jorguson lifted a finger. "Jerry wasn't able to be there so I went over the directions with him and his family later in my office. His son, Kevin, recorded his own voice for his dad's Buddy. Then a set of algorithms cloned his voice, capturing the nuance of his particular inflections. Both Kevin and his sister, Jennifer, were present for the training."

"So Jennifer knew and understood the way the Buddy works?" Karl processed. "Good."

"Pardon me again," green T-shirt woman interrupted. "Mr. Wintergardner, what do you personally get out of your father using the Walking Buddy?"

"Well…" Kevin stretched out. "I'm sorry to say, I get a little freedom."

The audience whispered between each other.

"I know. Dad got some freedom, too. That was what the Buddy was invented for." Kevin lowered his eyes, embarrassed. "But, every time Dad was able to exercise some ability to come and go on his own, I was free to do something else, go to my son's Little League game or whatever."

Clisty raised her index finger indicating another question. "Kevin, what payments did you get from the Walking Buddy?"

"Payments?" Kevin asked, stunned. "None, I received nothing from the Kramers, Dr. Jorguson, or Boston Technologies."

Continuing on the "Follow the Money' thread," Clisty asked, "Dr. Kramer ... Karl, what would you and Karen get out of hacking the Walking Buddy?"

"Financially?" Karl gasped. "Financial ruin is more like it. Besides the money I invested in developing and producing the Buddy, I imagine there would be law suits from those who were injured."

"I understand," Clisty replied. Then she paused, "I'm sorry, Karl, but I have to ask. Does Karen have life insurance?"

"Some," he said as he looked back at his wife and smiled. "Karen has the same life insurance as the other professors and employees at the university. It's not a tremendous amount... but it's sufficient."

"Thank you Karl," Clisty said with an encouraging smile.

Clisty turned to the woman in the T-shirt again and asked, "Do you have any money invested in the Walking Buddy ...Miss—?"

"I have nothing invested in the Walking Buddy or its success." She paused. "My name is Maddie Highland."

"The columnist?" Clisty asked. "You write for The New York Journal? Will you gain anything from this forum or an investigation into whether the Buddy was hacked?" Clisty was shocked. Why hadn't she asked Miss T-shirt her name or where she worked when she began questioning? The woman didn't have to have any money invested in the product for the fate of the Walking Buddy to benefit her immensely. "Let me ask this," she framed her question

201

carefully. "If you write several good columns following this forum, how will your good work benefit you?"

"The paper said," Maddie began slowly, "if the articles are well received, they will syndicate my column."

"Thank you, Maddie," Clisty said with a smile. "If your column is syndicated you will become nationally known and benefit a great deal. Thanks for your openness. I believe you will be honest and report in a non-biased manner."

Changing the topic completely, Clisty pointed to the back of the room. "Karen, did you see the person who struck you? Or, their car … color, make, or model?"

"Not the driver," Karl said as Clisty checked for Karen's reaction. She nodded vigorously in agreement. "But, she said she saw the car."

"Were the police able to track it down?" Clisty hadn't intended for the forum to follow the elements of the two crimes. *We can edit it out later if necessary,* she reminded herself.

"Yes," Karl answered, "but, it was a rental car, rented under an assumed name and completely wiped clean of all fingerprints."

Jake made a gesture imitating someone putting on gloves … and nodded.

Karl leaned forward and rested his forearms on his knees. "Then there's the matter of the gunfire attack on our home. We weren't going to bring that up because I couldn't see how that's involved with the Walking Buddy. But, all of this adds up to something. I just don't know what."

A man in the back of the room spoke out. "Maybe someone blames you two, Karl and Karen, for what could happen if the Buddy were actually hacked."

Terry DeCamp closed her eyes and droned again, "The Buddy cannot be hacked."

"Well, I for one," a man in the second row began, his arms leaning on his legs, "would like to thank the Kramers for the Walking Buddy." His gaze shifted to the floor as he cleared his throat. Looking up, he squared his shoulders. "I am in the very early stages of Alzheimer's."

"You're looking good," Clisty affirmed. Her blue-green eyes were large.

"He is doing really well," the lady beside him said as she patted his arm. "I'm Stacy, his wife."

"My name is Tim," the man continued, "and I use the Walking Buddy every day. I have been very active and athletic all of my life." Tim held his head high. His voice was strong. "I will not be ashamed," he announced with a taut set to his jaw. "Every day since I retired, when I'm home, I jog slowly down to the activity complex in my neighborhood and shoot baskets. If other guys show up we have a game. If only one other person comes, we play H-O-R-S-E." He smiled proudly. "I'm pretty good. When I'm done, I jog a few blocks, and then walk to cool down. A few times in recent months, I've gotten lost on my way home. When the doctor told us about the Walking Buddy, I quickly volunteered to test one." He smiled as tears gathered in the corner of his eyes. "I have been blessed every day by wearing the Walking Buddy."

Clisty rarely teared up in an interview. Today, she could feel Tim's strength but also his fear of losing that energy. "You have found a way to continue to stay in charge of your own life. You found the Buddy helpful and have had no problems related to it? Good," Clisty summed up.

"I would like to say something if I may?" Renée brushed blond bangs out of her eyes.

"Renée," Clisty acknowledged and turned slightly in her seat to be able to look at the woman more comfortably. Renée was the only person there connected in some personal way to Clisty, her home, and her own safety. "Of course, Renée."

"Neither Daddy nor I ever heard of the Walking Buddy, until the police interviewed him after his incident at your apartment in Fort Wayne," she said determinately. "Miss Sinclair," she began, her voice shaking, "my father,

Hiram Hubley, was in an accident at work a year and a half ago. He was working on the lighting system at the high school football field when he fell from scaffolding. The resulting concussion and brain injury left him with faulty judgements, impulsivity problems, and an inability to understand the consequences of some of his actions."

"I am sorry to hear that, Renée," Clisty said, but inside, she felt conflicted. She was concerned about Hiram's stalking her, even though she was beginning to understand the cause of his behavior.

"He has never stalked anyone before he started following you," Renée explained as tears threatened to choke her voice. "I have a picture of my mother who died three years ago," she offered. She held the photo toward the camera. "This was her college graduation picture. Her name was Rachel."

The camera zoomed in for a closer view. The entire audience gasped.

Clisty could barely breathe. Rachel looked just like Clisty in her own graduation cap and gown. "Renée ..."

Renée gulped to clear her throat. "As you can see, Miss Sinclair, Mom looked just like you at the same age."

Pulling an old fashioned white linen handkerchief from her pocket, Clisty blotted tears that rolled down her cheeks. "Renée..." she began to ask but had to stop to inhale slowly. "Your father told me, 'I followed the bread crumbs?' Do you know what he meant?"

"Yes," Renée whispered. "I don't know if I should tell you. His lawyer told me I shouldn't even come this evening. But, you had to know. Number one, it might put your mind at ease. Number two, as investigators search for clues to what happened in the Walking Buddy case, my father's behavior needs to be ruled out since nothing about Daddy was related to the Buddy."

"Would your explanation help him or hurt him?" Clisty asked.

Renée stared down at her fingers for a few seconds. "I don't really know. But, I think it does explain his confused thinking. I talked to him in jail the day after the police arrested him. He told me he had hung around your apartment complex for a few days so he could see you coming and going. He first noticed you at the grocery near your place and followed your car when you came out, to see where you live."

The hair on the back of Clisty's neck stood up. She had not even been aware of Hiram's presence until he showed up at her door. "I didn't know that," she whispered.

Renée smiled a little. "Daddy said he noticed you had an oil leak under your car."

"Yes," Clisty's eyes narrowed as she tried to dredge up the memory. "Oh yes," she finally exclaimed. "I had to have a quart of oil put in the car the other day."

"Daddy said he waited in the shadows one evening when you pulled out of the strip mall's parking lot. When you parked at your apartment, he could identify your car by the oil drippings." She raised her hand to prevent interruption of the implausible story. "I know, Daddy could have checked the license plate for confirmation but that's not what he did. He looked for the oil spot. After he identified your building by your car's oil stain, he waited for you in the darkness and followed you to your door." Humiliated, Renée focused on the floor. "Daddy laughed. He said, 'Rachel had dropped bread crumbs.' I said, 'Rachel? Daddy, Mama's gone.' His eyes grew huge … then he broke down and cried for the longest time. He was inconsolable." Renée sobbed into her tissue.

"Bread crumbs … the oil drops," Clisty nodded in confirmation. "I'm sure the police will talk to him some more, but it doesn't sound like he had anything to do with the Walking Buddy." She looked at the woman and had words only for her. "Renée, we will see if there is any help for your father. Thank you for clearing that up for me."

Clisty let out a deep sigh of relief. Hiram Hubley was not sinister. He was sick.

The forum continued for another hour. Becca supervised the production of the show, and Griff manned the camera that focused mainly on Clisty. Two other camerapersons captured the comments and reactions of people at different angles of the room. Becca and the New York staff would work their magic, cutting it to a ten or fifteen minute segment for *Stories from the Heartland.*

Clisty looked down at her phone, then stood and looked into the camera. "I understand that the police are still investigating several of these points. I just received a message that they found some evidence that will explain all of these seemingly disjointed happenings. They tell me that a team of detectives is executing a search warrant at this moment. We are taping this on Sunday evening. Hopefully, by the time this airs on the American News Magazine, we will have some answers we are not able to address tonight. We don't want to spread rumors. We want only the truth. Thank all of you for coming. Your questions and comments have been valuable. I also want to thank all of you for watching. I believe we will find answers to the mystery because of all of you. If this program has jarred memories, regardless of how small, message us through the *Contact Us* link on BNN's Website; call your local police station; or post a comment on www.crimebeat.blogsmith.com. This is Clisty Sinclair with *Stories from the Heartland.*"

Chapter 29
Another Lake House

It was after 7:30 PM. As the team prepared to leave the studio, their cell phones all buzzed at the same time. Clisty still had hers in her hand so she was the first to answer. "Clisty Sinclair," she sang into the phone.

"This is Detective Esposito," a voice with hard-as-nails authority announced. "If you can, I think you and Sergeant Davis would like to come back to Twilight Cove this evening. We have some important developments."

"All right," she replied and looked at Jake who had also just finished a short call. "Thanks. Be there in a bit."

Clisty's brow furrowed as she looked at Jake. "This evening?" she mocked, looked at her watch and shrugged. "I guess I should be glad he called."

Becca interrupted with her cell in her hand. "Nicole called. There's a network van waiting for us downstairs." She motioned for Griff to wrap up his equipment quickly and started toward the elevator, then turned. "Are you guys coming?"

"Sure," Clisty fumbled as she put her phone in her pocket and gathered up her purse.

Jake slipped his hand in the crook of her arm and whispered, "Are you all right? I'm sure the forum took a lot out of you."

"I'll admit," she agreed, leaning her head on his arm, "I am tired. I guess I'll have to start an energy enrichment program if I'm going to be able to keep up with this new pace—exercise, proper diet, enough rest—the whole thing."

"That's the smartest thing I've heard since high school," Becca agreed. "Coach Clutch carefully planned our swim practices and recommended a diet so we would peak during State Finals." She grinned. "Life can be a real race. Prepare for it."

"Yes, Ma'am," Clisty saluted in fun with three fingers to her brow.

Jake chuckled and gave her a gentle squeeze. "That's the Boy Scout salute, but that's okay. We get it."

Clisty sighed. On the way down in the elevator, each stood in their own thoughts. Finally, Clisty started speaking aloud but to no one in particular. "Wonder what's going on in Twilight Cove?" She stared at where the two elevator doors met. "Wonder if they found something with the search warrant?"

"Was the warrant for someone in the Cove?" Jake asked. "Detective Esposito didn't say who. He just gave the address. It wasn't the Kramer's home."

"What's all the secrecy about?" Becca asked.

Jake put his hand on Clisty's shoulder. "Maybe the suspect was at the taping and the police didn't want anyone tipped off."

"At the taping?" Clisty felt a chill slither down her back.

• • •

Twilight Cove was as beautiful at night as it was in the daytime. Lights from coastal homes danced across the water sending golden shimmers toward shore.

As they neared the target address several squad cars dotted the narrow lane that ran behind beautiful water-kissed properties. "There," Clisty pointed toward the garage and backyard of a two story, rambling white clapboard house.

"Yep ... we're here," Griff mumbled. "But, where is *here*?"

"Well," Becca drew out, "let's get out. We won't know where we are from inside the van."

"Jake," Clisty began as she slipped off the back bucket seat, "you had better lead the way. We don't know what we're getting into."

"My thoughts exactly," he agreed and led the team to the flagstone pathway inside the fence.

Griff pulled the smaller camera from the back of the van and followed the three as they cautiously walked through the back gate and toward the house. When they neared the home, he positioned the lens for filming. The green light flashed on as Jake knocked on the door.

Becca kept up with Clisty who walked directly behind Jake. "Griff, film whatever you can. We can sort out the details later. Here's the rub. Try to be as inconspicuous with that big camera as possible."

"Sergeant Davis," a tall muscular man stood at the back door of an expansive home. "I'm Detective Esposito. Glad all of you could come. Come in."

"What have you found?" Jake asked, getting right to the point.

"This is the DeCamp house," Esposito waved an open hand at the large white kitchen when they entered.

"Boston Technologies?" Clisty asked. "I thought Terry DeCamp, the CEO, would live in Boston."

"She does," Esposito agreed. "This is where she lived before her company began to grow and burst at the seams. This house is where her ex-husband and teen-age son live."

"The son didn't move to Boston with her?" Clisty asked.

Esposito smoothed the narrow brim of his charcoal grey fedora around in his fingertips. "The boy wanted to stay and finish school with his friends. He visits his mom all summer. He'll be leaving in a few weeks, or before."

"Before?" Jake asked.

"The search warrant uncovered some incriminating evidence against his father, Bruce DeCamp. Alex may have to move in with his mom, depending on the outcome of this investigation."

Clisty looked past the detective and as far into the open concept home as she could see. "Terry DeCamp was in New York for taping of the forum. Was she notified?"

"Yes, she just got here. She's in the living room with Bruce." Esposito led the way through the house to where the others were gathered. "You remember Clisty Sinclair?" he gestured to the DeCamps.

"Of course," Terry said smiling weakly, as the sass and starch that stiffened her demeanor at the forum dissolved with the police search. She stood and reached out for Clisty in a hug. "Thank you for coming. I know you will report this honestly, without spin, exploitation or sensationalism."

Clisty sat on a side chair and patted Terry's hand where it gripped the arm of the couch. "Can you fill us in, Terry?"

Terry focused on Bruce sitting beside her and squeezed his hand. "Detective Esposito called and told me to come right away, to be here for Alex's sake. He said they found some evidence in Bruce's house, implicating him in the tampering of the Walking Buddy." She wiped tears from her cheeks with the back of her hand.

Esposito pulled a straight back chair in from the dining room, sat down and pointed to the other chairs for Jake, Becca and Griff. Becca and Griff waved him off with a smile.

Jake leaned forward, resting his hands on his knees. "Bruce, tell us what the police discovered in your home."

Bruce DeCamp, a ruggedly strong man in his mid-fifties, sat on the couch with his arm around Terry. One would not have guessed they were divorced. "They came in a while ago with a warrant to search my basement." He shook his head in disbelief.

"Why specifically … the basement?" Clisty asked. "Why not the whole house … unless they knew what they were looking for and where to find it?"

At that moment, the front door opened and a lanky teenage boy casually walked in. He looked like Bruce

DeCamp and had the confident swagger of his mother, Terry. He searched his father's face, then his mother's. "What's going on?" he asked.

"You're late, Alex," Bruce said as he reached out for the boy's hand to bring Alex onto the couch between him and Terry. "A lot is going on, and I worried about you. Where have you been?"

"I took the boat over to Madison's house. Her mom wanted me to help her hang some new drapes. She's ..." he looked around as his voice faded ... "not very tall." With his gaze darting about the room, he finally added, "Then, we were watching TV and lost track of time." He looked intently at the camera, all the strangers in his home, and tightness on each face. "Dad?"

"Alex," the Stamford police began, "I'm Detective Esposito. I have some questions to ask you."

"Okay ..." Alex had a confused tone in his voice.

"When was the last time you were in the basement here in your dad's home?"

"The basement?" Alex questioned. "I don't know ... a long time ago. Dad and I were talking one time about making a rec room down there. Right now, it's not usable. There's just too much junk down there."

"And, your Dad's workbench," Esposito added. "Do you ever tinker around, making things ... whatever?"

Alex blinked and nodded. "Yeah ... of course I've been down there, but haven't been for a long time." Then he looked up. "Why? It's our basement. What's that old workbench got to do with anything?"

Terry patted her son on the knee. "The police received an anonymous tip saying they would find some evidence linking Dad to the hit-and-run accidents that have happened recently."

"Anonymous?" Alex sneered. "Why do the police pay attention to cowards who won't even admit who they are?" Alex looked at his father with eyes full of questions. "What does an old workbench have to do with it? Was the hit-and-run guy driving Dad's workbench when the accidents happened?"

"Good question, Alex," Clisty agreed. "I was asking myself the same thing."

Esposito held his hat in both hands and continued to twirl it slowly by the brim. "Mr. DeCamp, I understand you worked at Boston Technologies when it was still located here in Connecticut ... right?"

"Right," Bruce confirmed. "The name Boston is not named for the city. It was actually Terry's maiden name."

Esposito attempted to pull together the findings of the search. "Then the Walking Buddy Case and small tools we found on your workbench are from your attempts to hack the device."

"What? Of course not. Detective," Terry explained as she leaned forward. "Bruce was the accountant for the company. He doesn't know anything about the actual creation of an electronic device, or an attempt at hacking one for that matter." Then she reached for the so-called evidence. "May I see that, please?"

"Sure," Esposito said. "Be careful of any fingerprints." He handed her some latex gloves to protect any evidence that may still be there. Then, he gave her the piece that the CSI team discovered in the basement.

Clisty watched as Terry held it in her hand, lifting it up and down gently. "What do you think?"

Terry turned the piece over in her hand. A small, crooked smile began at the corner of her mouth. "First, there's no BT, Boston Technologies, logo on the bottom. And, there wouldn't be, because, this isn't a Walking Buddy case." She removed a decorative pin from her jacket and used the point to pry the back off. Looking at the insides, she handed it back to Esposito. "This is a cheap watch, a ten-dollar time piece. There are no other electronics inside."

Griff zoomed in on the fake watch case, and then panned out to get the reactions of everyone gathered in the room.

Clisty smiled and finally sat back in the chair. "If this isn't even a Walking Buddy, who could have planted the evidence in Bruce's home?" she asked.

Alex gasped and covered his mouth with his hand. "You mean someone was in the house? Gag ... that makes my stomach flip."

"Me, too," Terry agreed.

Bruce shook his head slowly. "I'm away at work all day. I have an accounting business and office in town. Alex is at school. No one is here, so I lock the house. Anyone could have broken in I suppose."

Jake jumped in, "Do you have any kind of security system? Alarm? Cameras? Anything?"

"No ..." Bruce said slowly. "I feel like a fool. I should have installed a whole system, especially when Terry's company took off. Alex could be vulnerable."

"Oh, Bruce," Terry gasped. "You're right." She grabbed her son and hugged him close. "It always seemed like Stamford was this quiet, safe town, away from the city and its dangers."

"Dad," Alex interrupted, "did you forget the security doorbell? It has a camera."

Bruce jumped up and started toward the door. Esposito was after him immediately. "Wait, Bruce," Esposito barked. "Don't touch it. We'll have to have our forensic team dust it for prints and check any pictures that might be there."

"Right," Bruce agreed, stopped and sat back down beside Alex.

Clisty turned to the detective. "What about it then? Do we actually have any evidence?"

"Well, yes ... and no," Esposito said as his eyes searched the ceiling for the correct explanation. "No, there is no evidence that makes Bruce DeCamp a suspect in the Walking Buddy tampering and the hit-and-run cases." He turned to Terry and Bruce. "But, what we did find is evidence that someone tried to frame him, which only lends proof to his innocence."

"Then, Bruce is okay now?" Terry asked as she put her arm around him and held on.

"I hope we'll know more after forensics goes over the doorbell," Detective Esposito agreed. "But, we have nothing to hold him on now, or even keep him on a short list."

"Oh, thank God," Terry sighed as she held Bruce's hand to her chest. She reached up and kissed him tenderly, then blushed. "I'd better go."

"Terry," Bruce whispered with a tremor in his voice. "You can stay if you want to."

"Please, Mom," Alex agreed.

Clisty looked over at Jake and smiled. He too seemed to watch as a family reunited. Clisty wondered how a couple who apparently loved each other could dissolve a marriage. Searching Jake's eyes, Clisty thought of another couple who obviously loved each other, and wondered why they hadn't even begun a marriage.

Chapter 30
Late Supper

It was late when they all got back to New York. Clisty was exhausted physically and mentally. Her grandmother would have said, "I'm weary." Now, she knew what Grandma meant. Clisty was too tired to say anything. She merely clung to Jake's hand as all four of the news team walked through the hotel lobby.

"I am so hungry," Griff moaned, holding his stomach as they walked past the main floor bar and grill. He gawked at every plate he could see—those freshly placed on the table, some half eaten, and a few leftovers.

Becca noticed a hamburger on a diner's plate. "It's not my preferred entrée but it's filling. Do you guys want to eat something?" She stopped by an empty table and waited. "Please, I may not wake up in the morning if I don't get some nourishment tonight."

Jake squeezed Clisty's hand and slowed his steps. "Eating something light would be good for you. You might actually sleep better, Babe, if starvation didn't keep you awake half the night."

"I doubt anything could keep me from sleep tonight," she whispered. Her eyes rolled as she visually followed a server who placed a BLT in front of a patron at a nearby table. "Well, that might tempt me," she admitted. "Bacon on toast could be called breakfast. I could tell them I'd like to order a BLT, but please hold the tomato, lettuce and mayo and add a fried egg instead. Perfect."

Jake pulled out a chair for Clisty as she and the others sat down. The quartet was amazingly quiet, partly because of the hour, partly because of all that had happened that they had no time to process.

"Was the forum earlier this evening?" Griff asked as he rubbed both hands over his eyes.

"Yep," Becca agreed while twisting a tissue in her hand.

When the server came up to the table, all four said in unison, "No coffee."

Clisty didn't hesitate. She chose hot chocolate and the others nodded in agreement.

"Hot milk is good for sleep," Griff agreed. "And, I'll have a hamburger, catsup and cheese, no onion."

Clisty ordered the toasted breakfast sandwich she had just created out of a modified BLT … on whole wheat bread. Becca and Jake dittoed that item and waited for their cocoa. They all sat in silence for a few minutes, seeing dimly through foggy eyes. Each appeared lost in their own first level of sleep, drifting in and out with their eyes wide open, or nearly so.

A woman wearing a T-shirt with *I Love NY* on the front paused beside their table. "I liked your broadcast last Tuesday, Clisty."

"Thank you." Clisty replied automatically with surprise. People in Fort Wayne sometimes approached her table while dining out, to encourage her. She assumed New York City was too large for anyone to notice a single newscaster among the millions of people. "I appreciate your comments. Watch next week. We've been working really hard. We have an additional segment for you. It's more about the Walking Buddy."

"Wouldn't miss it." The woman smiled and patted Clisty's shoulder before she walked on.

"That was nice," Becca said as she watched the woman walk away. "I haven't seen the statistics yet. At least we know that one person watched the show."

"One?" Jake quipped. "It was in the millions, Becca."

"I know. It's amazing." Becca continued to watch the woman walk out into the night. "Out there on the street, the bright lights are dazzling. It's almost beyond my ability to take it all in. It's like the lights are shining on you, Clisty. For me, this whole thing is only real when a viewer is standing there in flesh and bone."

Clisty, worn out, nodded in agreement, aware of her own inability to wrap her mind around the instant national celebrity. "From Indiana to New York in a matter of weeks—it's going to take some time for me to catch up to it all."

Jake's eyes, not focused on the conversation, followed a man from the middle of the lobby to the bank of elevators on the other side of the concierge's desk. He wore a light blue oxford cloth shirt with rolled up sleeves, and a dark blue Yankees ball cap. He carried a large shopping bag from *Men's Wearhouse*. Jake finally looked away. The man Jake tracked with his eyes, laughed and high-fived a guy beside him, appearing to be part of that group.

"Who are you watching?" Clisty asked when she saw Jake's brows knit together. She tried to follow his gaze but only saw a group of people laughing and enjoying the evening.

"I don't actually know," he said as he rejoined the table talk. "But, I thought he looked familiar."

Clisty reached over and took Jake's hand where it rested on his knee. "I suspect everyone, too." To Clisty, the whole world couldn't be trusted. Since none of the DeCamps were the hit-and-run driver, that made everyone a suspect again. She picked up the cup of cocoa as soon as the server removed her finger from the thumb ring, blew across the surface and sipped. "The scary thing is the killer is still out there."

Becca took her mug and held it close to her face with both hands. "I'm warming my cheeks," she said. "Clisty, at least you know your stalker in Fort Wayne wasn't the same guy who killed Jerry Wintergardner. Maybe Indiana will feel a little safer."

Clisty smiled faintly. "And, he isn't really a stalker. He is a grieving, damaged man who thought he had seen his beloved wife again."

Griff picked up his spoon and stirred his cocoa around and around. The sweet fragrance filled the air. "For being one of our segments for *Stories from the Heartland*, this Walking Buddy bit has been all over the eastern half of the country, from Indiana to Connecticut."

"Heartland stories," Clisty explained as the waitress placed her bacon and egg sandwich in front of her, "are about folks who don't live in the big cities of New York or L.A. They are everyday people, but they use their gifts to help others. Those are stories with heart … from the Heartland."

Each fell silent as they dug into their late night supper. They were too tired to talk and eat at the same time, and had been too busy earlier to eat and work at the same time. Clisty didn't even check her watch. She knew what time it felt like and that was enough … it felt like exhausted-o'clock. She stopped, studied her sandwich, and smiled. The whole wheat bread reminded her of the wholesome people in the heartland. The egg, the new beginnings they provided for others, and the lean center cut bacon, the backbone of the country. *Oh please*, she cautioned herself. *You're so tired you're even finding poetry in a pig sandwich.*

"Are you ready, Babe?" Jake asked as he stacked his cup on top of his plate and folded his napkin.

"More than ready. I've been ready for hours," Clisty said, smiling with her eyes closed.

Jake put his arm around her shoulder and drew her close.

"Lead me upstairs, please, Sir," she joked. "I'll get started sleeping on the way, as long as you don't let me run into a wall."

Becca looked at Griff's plate, polished clean of every crumb of bread. "Actually, I think we're all ready."

They each signed their own room number on their bill and placed some green folding money on the table for a tip. Since all four rooms were on the twelfth floor, they marched silently onto the elevator. Jake wrapped his arm around Clisty's waste and balanced her under his arm. She felt safe and supported. Her thoughts were no longer on the events of the long night. They were already dancing through tomorrow.

"Good night," Becca said as she swiped her room card.

"Uh-huh," Griff groaned and disappeared into his room.

"Night," Clisty echoed back. Reaching behind her, she pulled on Jake's hand. He said nothing but followed her into her room.

The lights from the city lit up the room with neon colors that flashed across the walls in rainbows of fuchsia and citrine. Jake pulled Clisty to him and surrounded her with his love. "Oh, Babe … when are we getting married?"

"I'll let you know tomorrow," she answered breathlessly, her eyes flashing with love.

"Tomorrow?" His arms dropped to his sides as he wilted into a slump. "Why can't you tell me tonight?"

"It's a good thing, Jake." Clisty reached up and kissed his cheek. "Tomorrow, you'll see. It'll be a good day."

"If you say so," he agreed as he started backing toward the connecting door to the adjacent room. The lock clicked as he released it. "I can stay if you need me," he whispered.

"I will always need you, Jake." Clisty didn't move from her spot half-way across the room while her eyes locked on his. If she had taken one step, the new distance would mark a drastic change in their relationship. She couldn't wait to be with him … but … she would.

Chapter 31
Darkness Crept In

After Jake left, Clisty was so tired she tossed her purse onto the opposite side of the bed where she wouldn't roll onto it during the night ... if she moved at all once she fell asleep. Her cell phone fell out of the pocket on the side of her purse but she didn't care. Laughing to herself she marveled. She saw the cell phone there, out of its assigned niche, but it was okay ... life was still safe. Kicking her shoes to the side of her bed, she padded over to the windows and partially darkened the room by pulling the drapes nearly closed. Clisty enjoyed the lights of the city that shone all night too much to entirely blacken the space. In the bathroom, she quickly slipped into her night clothes, washed her face and brushed her teeth. Her shower would have to wait until morning. Falling into bed, she was awake only long enough to pull up the covers.

The last time she looked at the clock, it was 2:24 AM. At 2:46 she had already been asleep for twenty minutes.

• • •

Sometime around 3 AM, as Clisty was deep in sleep, what seemed like a dream began to sneak across her brain. The closet door silently slid open. The squeak caused by the brass finger pull on the door was barely audible. Clisty didn't rouse or hear anything. Her body was motionless except for her rapidly moving eyes beneath closed lids. Exhaustion had taken her deeper into sleep than she had slid for many nights. With each exhale of her breath, she drifted deeper and deeper into a wonderful relaxed state. It was almost hypnotic.

Suddenly ... silently ... within the fog of her dream, with only the remaining glint of light that filtered in, a shadow crossed the room and blocked the prisms of color that bounced off the wall. The dark figure stopped in the middle of the room seeming to study Clisty's position. Trapped within the nightmare, the silhouette of dark-on-black crept over to her as she slept. The shadowy presence inched close enough to lean over her and match the rise and fall of her breathing, as if he were mocking her.

Clisty roused a little and whispered into the night, "Jake?"

In her seeming dream, the darkened form did not respond but stood unflinching in his spot. When Clisty settled again, the darkness reached for the spare pillow at the foot of the bed. His heavy breath was near. In evil silence, he raised the pillow high over Clisty's sleeping body. In an instant, the phantom from her most terrifying nightmare slammed the pillow down on her face with might and force, panting. The horrible image in her dream revealed arm muscles that strained under the ridged exertion of his shoulders.

Clisty floundered as she awakened, disoriented and groggy. Struggling violently, she gasped for air. It wasn't a dream. The darkness was real. Clisty's arms flailed; her legs kicked and jerked as she wrestled with her assailant. Finally, she doubled up her fists, pounding the monster with all her might, trying to land serious blows to the man's head and tender ears. *Oh, dear Lord*, she cried out, buried beneath the pillow, where no one could hear her but God. The pillow muffled her screams.

The man, dressed completely in black, climbed onto the bed and positioned his two-hundred pounds over Clisty with even more weight and power, grunting and growling. Her arms were shorter than his, making landing a serious blow impossible. With one large hand on the pillow, he reached in his belt. Instantly ... a lethal blade flashed in a tiny beam of window light.

Gasping beneath the pillow, Clisty caught a glimpse of the shinning steel and knew her life was flashing by. Instantly, she remembered the near stiletto heels on the shoes she dropped on the floor beside the bed. She struggled and groped but couldn't reach one of them. Her purse ... it had to be inches away. She grabbed the over-stuffed bag by its soft leather covering and dashed it at the dark figure again and again. When the attacker flung it behind him, its contents crashing into the wall and door. Flailing and fighting, Clisty's hand touched the coolness of her cell phone. She snatched it up and, using all the strength she could muster, she threw it, slamming it against the interior door that separated her room from Jake's. It shattered against the wood. Under the muffled insulation of the pillow, she screamed out in high pitched trills, using all the deep breathing she could remember. "Kevin, no! Kevin, stop. Jake ... Jake!"

Her hand reached out again, grappling with a shape that had fallen out of her purse. When her hand felt the hard smoothness of her ball point pen, she wrapped her fingers around it, brought the dagger-like pen up and pounded the man on the head, his face, his eyes, wherever the pointed end could land.

Instantly, Jake burst through the door, grabbed the man under his left arm and leg and flung him across the room. The attacker crashed into a chair, slid down the opposite wall, and slithered to the floor where he lay motionless. Jake snatched the knife from beside the bed and tossed it onto the desk.

"Babe," he desperately gathered her in his arms and rocked her back and forth. "Are you okay?"

"I think so," she choked as she threw her hands to her throat. The ghastly image of dying alone in the dark terrorized her. "Oh Jake, you heard me. You got here just in time."

Jake turned on the light and reached for the house phone on the table beside the bed. "This is room 1226.

There's been a break in. Call 911 for police and medical treatment."

"Yes, sir," the operator's voice quickly snapped to attention.

"Does he have a gun?" Clisty asked as she swung her legs around and sat on the edge of the bed. "Can you see who it is?"

Jake knelt on one knee and checked the man's pockets and waist band. Except for the knife already secured, there was no other weapon. Jake jerked Clisty's cell phone charger from the pile of stuff that had landed on the floor and used the chord as a rope to tie the man's hands behind him while he was still unconscious. "Did you pack any pantyhose?" he asked.

"It's sandals weather but, yes, I brought a pair."

"Get them," he ordered crisply.

She jumped off the bed, her short nightie swaying as she moved to her suitcase. With the carry-on jerked open, she grabbed out the pair and tossed them to Jake.

Barefoot and barelegged, Jake caught his foot in the pillow that had fallen on the floor when he grabbed the attacker, and stumbled over Clisty's high heeled shoes. "Ouch," he moaned.

"Jake, I am so sorry," she apologized as she jumped up on the bed and drew her feet back up under the covers.

"Oh, Babe," he began as he tied the pantyhose around the man's ankles, brought the attacker's legs up behind him, and tied his feet to his hands. The phantom in black was hogtied cowboy style. "Don't apologize. Your shoes would have been the next great torpedo."

Clisty strained to see the masked man. "When you remove his disguise, Jake, you'll find Kevin Wintergardner, all tied up with panty hose and a cell phone cord. I suspected him earlier but then I knew for sure." Now, she was certain as she leaned toward Jake and the man she believed to be Wintergardner.

Jake pulled the ski mask from the attacker's face just as the man began to rouse. "Kevin Wintergardner," Jake drew out in amazement. "You were right, Babe."

"You attacked me!" Kevin screamed, shaking his head and struggling with the make-shift bindings.

"I attacked you?" Clisty raised herself up on her knees.

"No ... he did!" Kevin motioned with his shoulder toward Jake.

Clisty startled when someone banged on the door. She jumped up and looked out the security peep hole. A man holding up a badge stood in the hall.

Clisty put her hand to her chest, still panicked as she opened the door. "Thank you for coming so quickly." She grabbed the pillow off the floor and clutched it in front of her, in an attempt at modesty.

"What's going on?" the man with the badge asked when he saw the unique bindings.

"That man is Kevin Wintergardner," Clisty pointed. "I woke up choking with someone on top of me, trying to smother me with a pillow. I knew it had to be Kevin. I don't know how he got in here. I guess he came in before I got back, and waited for me to go to sleep."

Jake kept one eye on Wintergardner and offered the security officer his hand. "I'm Sergeant Jake Davis from the Fort Wayne, Indiana police department. The Network hired me as security for Clisty Sinclair, her producer and cameraman. I heard the struggle from next door and came in to find this guy in black attacking Clisty with a pillow. He clutched a knife in his other hand and held it over her. I subdued him and tied him up until backup came."

"My name is Williams, the head of hotel security. I notified the police. They should be here shortly. In the meantime," he turned to Clisty, "Miss Sinclair is there any place you can stay for the night so the forensic team can process your room?"

"I can stay with my producer," she stuttered as she looked around the room. "Will I be able to get my clothes back? What will I wear tomorrow?"

"I think the police can go through the room pretty fast. It's obvious what happened here," Williams agreed with a note of recognition on his face.

Clisty breathed out a deep sigh. "Oh, thank you! I hope they're done by morning."

Williams smiled. "I saw your show the other night, Clisty. It was great."

"Thank you," she said. "This attacker is connected to the story we aired." Her eyes glared at Wintergardner as she shook her head. "Kevin, you're the one. You ran over your own father. Why?"

Williams unknotted the pantyhose and charging cord and replaced them with handcuffs. "Sit right there, on the floor," he ordered Wintergardner.

Kevin eyed Clisty unbelievingly. "How did you know it was me?"

Clisty shook her head in disgust. "At the forum, no one asked you the other question. Not, 'How would you benefit from the Walking Buddy, hacked or not?' The question to you should have been, 'What would you gain from your father's death?'"

Kevin hung his head, now avoiding eye contact. "My father's Alzheimer's Disease had advanced really fast in the last six months."

"Wintergardner, stop," Jake cautioned. "You have the right to remain silent." Jake looked at Clisty.

"I know, I know," Wintergardner insisted. "I don't care. That old man was dumping his whole family. He told me he was changing his will. He was going to sell his business and donate the money to Alzheimer's research." Kevin's face grew hard and his jaw flexed tight in anger. "I have worked hard building that company for thirty years with the promise that I would inherit it one day. I get nothing. Dad didn't even come to the office. I ran the company which I built. Now… this!"

"How did you hack your dad's Walking Buddy?" Clisty's eyes grew large.

"I didn't. I took an old watch that looked a little like the Buddy, inserted some simple electronics, and recorded directions to the highway. Dad was so far gone, he didn't notice the difference." Kevin gagged, fighting back a flood of tears.

"You entered the DeCamp home on Twilight Cove with a lock picking kit of some sort." Jake shook his head in disgust. "I saw the scratches on the lock. You went down the basement steps, deposited the phony Buddy, and slipped out of there in minutes."

Kevin remained silent.

"And, Karen Kramer?" Clisty asked. "You attacked Karen Kramer for no reason except misdirection. You wanted the whole thing to look like the Buddy itself was being hacked, not that you were looking for a cover-up for the murder of your father."

"Kevin, don't talk. Remain silent," Jake warned.

"No! You have to understand. I had to hit her, too. Can't you see? I had to make it look like the Walking Buddy was at fault. On Dad's watch, I overrode the verbal commands," he stumbled through the explanation. "When I hit Professor Kramer, it had to look like the inventor's watch was hacked, to draw the police off Dad's Buddy. I didn't really do anything to Karen's."

"Then, there was gunfire at the Kramer home, Kevin." Clisty spit out, demanding an explanation. "You did that as another distraction, to make it look like someone was after them."

"No one got hurt," Kevin started to cry, and then choked. "My God, what have I done?" With his hands cuffed behind his back, he couldn't blow his nose and began to sniff deeply.

"Shooting at a house is illegal, regardless if anyone is hit!" Jake ground out through gritted teeth.

"The whole thing, Kevin, the threatening notes, everything was all done to hide the truth of the murder of your own father," Clisty summed up. "Tonight, you tried to kill me," she insisted as she rubbed her hands over her cold arms, "because you knew I was on to you."

Wintergardner sniffed again as tears ran down his cheeks. "You wouldn't stop!" he demanded, with his teeth grinding bitterly. "I hoped some crazy person would be accused and steer the police away from any possible thought it was me."

"I think a crazy person was just apprehended," Jake growled as he put his arms around Clisty and held her close.

When two uniform policemen came to the door, Clisty let go of Jake, grabbed the pillow more tightly, hugging it in front of her to hide her nightie.

"Police," one of the officers announced. "I saw CSI on their way up, too," he added.

Williams gestured for the two men to come in. "I'm head of security here at the hotel. I called CSI when I called for the police. I'll fill you in."

"Crime Scene Investigator," a woman announced at the door.

"In here." Williams stepped out of the way and made room for the investigator and her partner.

"We are supposed to fly back to Indiana tomorrow," Clisty began. "And, I'll have to get dressed. Will I be able to get my purse, clothes and bags by morning? My cell phone may be dead."

"You can take your purse and room card now," the CSI officer said as she looked around. "We will be here about an hour, take pictures, dust for fingerprints, and take notes. The room will be released by morning unless you get up before 5 AM."

"No, I seriously doubt that." Clisty yawned. "Thanks," she sighed as tears began to gather in her eyes. "I'm sorry, I feel really tired."

"You should be checked out at the hospital," Williams stated clearly. "The police will also need to take your statement."

"No hospital," she refused emphatically. "I'm exhausted and I want to go to sleep."

"You can check in with the police in the morning for your statement. For now, you said you'll stay with your producer tonight?" Williams asked. "Which room is she in?"

"No," Jake ordered with a firm grip on Clisty's arm. "She'll stay next door with me. I can't protect her in another room."

"Okay," Williams agreed.

"If you don't need Clisty any more tonight, I'm putting her to bed." Jake put his arm around Clisty's shoulder and directed her to the adjoining door.

"Good night," the crime scene investigator said. "We shouldn't be too loud."

"You wouldn't be able to be too loud considering how tired I am." Clisty saw the uniformed police lead Wintergardner away just as Jake closed the door to the adjoining room and threw the deadbolt.

Clisty couldn't talk through the fog of fatigue. Their silence spoke volumes. As she began to feel the exhaustion take over her mind and body, she began to chill, shaking painfully. Jake picked up the long sleeved shirt he had thrown on the back of the desk chair hours before and slipped her into it. Clisty felt him scoop her off her feet, place her on his bed and pull the covers over her trembling body. When the bed moved again she knew he had gotten in with her and waited for his body to warm hers. Gathering her in his strong angular arms, he pulled her close, one body warming two as they both drifted off to sleep.

Chapter 32
Safe with Jake

Clisty awakened to warmth as the sun burned off all the icy fear from the night before. She heard the shower water turn off and knew Jake would be coming back into the room. Under the covers, she checked to make sure Jake's shirt still covered her skimpy nightgown. Smiling, she wondered what she had been thinking when she packed such shear sleep wear. Long pajamas were her usual choice.

Her grandmother told her about the time she had awakened on the sixth floor of a hotel with the fire alarm blaring. "Always be prepared to meet unknown neighbors in a hotel hallway," Grandma had cautioned her.

When Jake walked out of the bathroom, he was barefoot and dressed in slacks. His muscles rippled under a sleeveless undershirt Clisty wasn't aware men wore anymore but was glad this one did. To her, it looked romantic. He looked like Clark Gable in an old black and white movie.

"Well …," Jake paused in midstride, rubbing a small hand towel through his wet hair, "you're awake early."

"It may turn out to be a busy day," she said as she yawned, stretching her arms above her head. "First, we have to eat breakfast. I don't want to forget meals again today," she cautioned with a roll of her eyes. "I have to give my statement to the police and … I want to do some special sightseeing."

"Sounds interesting." He pulled the towel from his head. Running his fingers through his hair, he smoothed the front that was wonderfully falling into his face. "Where?" he asked as he sat on the edge of the bed beside her.

"For now, it's a secret," she whispered as she leaned up to kiss him, paused, and then backed up. "But, I guarantee you'll like it."

"Good." He stood up and went to the dresser to retrieve a comb. "What about the film crew? Do you want to see if Becca and Griff are awake?"

"No," she swung herself to the edge of the bed, her legs hanging over. "My official police statement can't be filmed ... or shouldn't be. I'm sure they would be bored waiting around at the police station."

"Hope news of your attack isn't on TV," he winced. "What if Becca wakes up to last night's nightmare?"

"The news," Clisty gulped. "I'd better call Mr. Funderbird. It would be a major blunder if another network scooped him. The network can send out a camera team to the police station and I can make a general statement out front before going in."

"Why not Griff? He's our man with a camera." Jake turned with his hand in his pocket and studied her for a moment.

"Oh ..." Clisty brushed off the idea, "I don't want to wake them." She jumped off the bed and started for the door that led to her room. "Cross your fingers. Hopefully, I can get into my room now. I'll take my shower and be ready in a half an hour. I'll see if I can hurry enough to be back in here at 7:30."

"Let me check your room first, Babe." Jake put out his hand to stop her, then opened the connecting door. With a quick sweep of the room, under the bed, inside the closet and bathroom, he finally relaxed his shoulders. "All looks clear."

"Thanks Gunny." In her room, her first task was to call the network. Her cell phone was on the end table beside the bed. She was glad the CSI officer had replaced the protective case that had popped off when she used it as a battering ram. It was hard lugging the cell around with the extra strong case but the heavy duty shell had saved the phone. It appeared to have all of its pieces. With the phone to her ear, she was relieved to hear a dial tone.

When she called, Bradley Funderbird was already in his office. Clisty explained all that had happened in her room just hours before.

Funderbird sighed deeply. His tone was low and dire. "Thank goodness you had security with you, Clisty. For positive stories of good people, it sounds like the darkness in this world demands that you continue with security."

"Yes, Sir," she agreed, secretly thankful that Jake would be able to stay with them. What would have happened last night if he hadn't been next door? "Mr. Funderbird," she began professionally, "I would like a fresh camera team to meet me at the police station. I can give the viewers a brief explanation of all that happened, before or after I give my statement to Detective Rodriguez."

"A fresh team?" He paused. "Generally, we like to continue with the team that's learned to work together. That's why we hired your Fort Wayne crew. Is your team all right?"

"Indeed they are," she puffed them up. "Becca and Griff are wonderful. But, I thought they may need to rest after the long day yesterday."

"Sometimes, every day is a long day, Clisty. The guy last night attacked you. Take care of yourself a little. Your team will be fine."

"Yes, Sir, I agree." She knew she needed to fill in the chinks. "Mr. Funderbird, the man who tried to kill me, was Kevin Wintergardner, the son of the walking Buddy tester who was killed. Kevin murdered his father for personal reasons, having nothing to do with the Walking Buddy or the Kramers."

"So ..." Funderbird summed up, "his arrest closes the Heartland story? Wonderful!"

"Yes, the conclusion is clean. I'll film a warp-up when I get back home. We're ready for a new one." She gathered her thoughts and added, "I'm wondering if I could borrow an unmarked sedan from the network for a few hours today, if that is possible. Or, perhaps Nicole could rent a car for me. I'll repay the network. I need some time to reknit my interior."

"Nonsense, I'm sure one of the network cars will be available. I know you must need some relaxing diversion. As long as you take security with you," he demanded. "I want you to stay safe. Around home, it may be different, but when you're away, in cities with unfamiliar faces, you'll need Jake to go along. And, yes, I'll have a car waiting for you at the police station. We'll leave a key with the police. Return it to Nicole when you get back."

"Yes, Sir. Thank you."

"What time do you want the car there?"

"I hope to be at police headquarters at 8:30," she said as coffee, a bagel and cream cheese popped into her mind. "The car could arrive anytime around 9 AM."

"Sounds good," Funderbird said. "If I don't see you when you drop off the key, have a safe trip back to Indiana. And, Clisty, I'm really pleased with the town hall segment you did. We'll be able to wrap it up tomorrow night." Then he hung up.

Clisty wondered if Becca would stop speaking to her when she woke her up earlier than planned. "Becca," she spoke quickly into the phone, "call Griff, please. Meet Jake and me at the breakfast bar downstairs in ..." she glanced at the clock on the side table, "in twenty-five minutes, ready for a quick taping."

"What? Why?" Becca asked ... her voice groggy.

"Breakfast bar at 7:30 ... ready for taping."

"AM?" Becca raised her voice in a slight panic.

"AM," Clisty repeated. "Gotta run and get ready."

Clisty quickly pushed the end-call icon on her phone screen, closed her eyes and held her breath a few seconds. If she and Jake were going to be able to have a little alone-time together, she would have to rehearse a good story for Becca and Griff as she showered.

Chapter 33
Regrouping

Clisty and Jake were already sitting in the breakfast bar when Becca and Griff nearly slid into the area on a run. Clisty patted the seat beside her for Becca to sit down.

"Better get a cup of coffee," Clisty suggested. "You're going to need it."

"For what?" Becca's sleepy face woke up with wide eyes.

"Get it quickly," Clisty urged as she motioned toward the coffee bar. "We don't have much time."

"For what?"

Jake smiled and raised one eyebrow. "Didn't you just ask that? Coffee or not, we have something serious to talk with you two about."

Becca weaved her way over to the coffee bar, poured a cup and selected a pecan twist roll from the tray. "I see you chose some coffee cake. Wish I had seen that first," she eyed the cake wishfully.

"Take a bite of mine," Clisty offered.

Becca took her clean spoon and broke off a small bite. "It is wonderful," she swooned.

"I love sour cream coffee cake," Clisty admitted. "Aunt Donna didn't want a normal, sugar-flower topped birthday cake. She always wanted to celebrate with a sour cream coffee cake. And, not just any recipe, she wanted our friend Essey's version. It melts in your mouth." She took another bite of cake, closed her eyes and smiled. "This tastes just like Essey's cake."

Griff quickly joined them. Since hamburgers were not a breakfast menu item, Griff chose a glazed doughnut large enough to use as a chair cushion. Clisty thought that should hold him for an hour or two.

"Okay, what's so serious?" Becca asked as she sat down. "You're really dressed up for a Monday morning. I like the great jacket you bought in the network gift shop. It looks really good on you."

"Thanks," was Clisty's simple reply.

Jake took Clisty's hand and kissed her fingertips. "Clisty was attacked last night."

Becca and Griff nearly choked. "What?"

Clisty drank some coffee and slowly broke off another bite of coffee cake. "And, the attack solved the mystery of Jerry Wintergardner's death at the same time." She put the bite in her mouth, and then added through the crumbs, "In fact, it solved the entire mystery."

"What?" Becca yelped, grabbing her chest. "Clisty … what?" She shook her head in disbelief.

"Kevin Wintergardner, Jerry' son, must have snuck into my room before we got back to the hotel last night. He was hiding in the closet. And, unlike my usual habit, I didn't open the closet because I didn't hang anything up."

"Kevin hiding in the room is something I've been thinking about," Jake interrupted. "When we were eating our bacon and egg sandwiches last night, I saw a man in a ball cap follow a group of people into the elevator. He looked familiar. When he talked to the people he was standing with, I dismissed the thought of danger, assuming he was with the others." Jake turned to Clisty and added, "I am so sorry."

"Jake," Clisty soothed, "don't blame yourself." She looked from Jake to Becca, "I saw a man in a blue ball cap follow a group of friends into the Rock Center Café when we were there. Only, he didn't sit with those people. He sat at another table, wrote a note, and then left."

"Probably the same guy," Jake agreed. "We're going to have to learn to be more 'city' than 'small town.' We can't trust everyone."

"I finally understand that," Clisty agreed. "Because, sometime between 2:46 and 3 AM, after I went to sleep, that dangerous man came out of my closet and tried to smother me with a pillow. When that took too long, he pulled a knife. I couldn't yell because he had my face covered. Finally, I threw my cell phone at the door, making noise." She gulped down her coffee. "Jake came in, yanked him off me, and tied him up until the authorities came."

"Good grief," Becca stammered. "What did you have along to tie him with, Jake?"

"Me? Nothing," Jake blustered. "Clisty, do you want to tell her?"

"He used my cell phone recharger cord on Kevin's hands and my pantyhose were used to hogtie him." Clisty covered her smile with her hand. "Kevin said he killed his father to keep him from changing his will." She took a deep breath. "I have to go down to the police station to give my statement. I want Griff to film my wrap-up to this case in front of police headquarters. It will have to be general information. When we get to Indiana, we'll put in the details with a voice over or an off-site video clip."

"Wow! I don't know if I can keep up with all of this," Becca said as she shook her head. "Are you all right, Clisty?" She patted Clisty's arm. "You must be exhausted."

"I am worn out, really frazzled," Clisty agreed. "That's why I won't go with you two after the taping at the police station. While I go in and give the police my statement, I want you and Griff to get some background pictures so we can cut some flavor into the wrap-up of the story. I'll rest some before we fly back."

"I'm sure the network will have tons of New York background photos on file," Griff said as he brushed large sugar flakes from his shirt.

"I imagine they do," Clisty agreed. "But, I want to make sure we have common-man type images in the foreground … young people in jeans and shirts walking in the park … absolutely no one on roller skates. I'm tired of seeing that cliché depicting young energetic people. Not just the Statue of Liberty and the Empire State Building either, but mid-western tourists at those locations. You may recognize them." Clisty bubbled with ideas.

"After all you've been through you have more energy than I do." Becca looked at her with squinted eyes. "How do you do it?"

"Adrenalin," Clisty offered as she looked into her coffee cup. "Pure adrenalin. I would have slept in after all that happened last night. But, Williams, the head of hotel security, said I have to give my statement. I'll have to do that this morning."

• • •

They finished their breakfast and hurried over to the police station closest to the hotel. Before going in, Becca staged the angle she wanted for Clisty's shot. Since neither Becca nor Clisty had time to write a proper script, it would be short.

Jake watched passersby with a more cautious eye. "Clisty, as a trained policeman, I see a conmen behind every request for a charitable donation, and child abductors on every park bench at neighborhood playgrounds." His eyes followed a man with a shopping bag until he was long past. "Last night upped the need for vigilance. Now, I'll watch every nice middle-aged man, loving husband, and pillar of the community with a warry eye."

Clisty paced back and forth a few minutes as Jake fixed his gaze on the people as they passed. Finally, she looked up and held the microphone in position. "I'll do a close-up of my final remarks regarding the entire Walking Buddy matter, the death of Jerry Wintergardner and the attacks on Karen Kramer when we get back home and link it to the network. I just need some statements here in front of the police precinct to lend authenticity to the project."

"That makes sense," Becca agreed.

"Jake and I will go in as soon as we're done here," Clisty looked intently at Jake and smiled. "Becca and Griff, you can then go collect the background flavor."

"Sounds fine," Griff agreed. "We may have time for a nap, too."

Clisty held the mic close and made her few explanatory remarks. "The Walking Buddy is a time piece and an opportunity. A real chance for many to walk safely in their own neighborhoods," she began. Continuing, she added, "I've come here today to tell how, last night Sergeant Jake Davis was just in time to save my life."

Griff panned the front of the precinct. He managed to get an angle that included Clisty and the lettering on the front of the building all in the same shot.

"That's great," Becca said as she concluded the tape and reviewed the piece on her iPad. "We'll see you guys at the airport," she said with a wave as she latched on to Griff's arm and hailed a cab.

Inside the station, Detective Rodriguez met Clisty and Jake and ushered them into a room where someone was operating a digital recording machine. "Here are the keys the network dropped off for you," he said as he handed them to Clisty.

"What keys?" Jake asked sitting down beside her.

"I asked Mr. Funderbird for an unmarked sedan so we could get a little R&R," she answered with a small smile.

"Oh," was Jake's only comment. Then he added, "I thought you wanted to rest."

"It will be very relaxing," she agreed. "We'll drop the car off at BNN when we get back, and give the key to Nicole."

"Okay," he said as he leaned his hand on his thigh and looked at her carefully.

"Trust me, you and I both need to get rid of a lot of tension," Clisty smiled sweetly.

Rodriguez nodded at the technician and began. "We are interviewing Clisty Sinclair regarding Kevin

Wintergardner's attack on Miss Sinclair in her hotel room late last night. Please state your complete name, where you live, and work."

"I'm Clisty Alverta Sinclair. I live in Fort Wayne, Indiana and travel to New York sometimes for my job as one of the hosts on the American News Magazine. My segment is called, *Stories from the Heartland.*"

"What is the nature of your report this morning?" Detective Rodrigues asked methodically.

Clisty pulled her chair a little closer to the table and directed her testimony to the recorder. "Our group had been staying in New York a few days to film a special for BNN. Two tangential stories to our report on the Walking Buddy were the mysterious death of one of the patients who tested the Buddy, and the attacks on Karen Kramer, one of the inventors. Then, last night, after returning from a long night of taping, someone slithered out of my closet in my hotel room and attacked me."

Rodrigues asked, "Did you see your attacker? Do you know who it was?"

Clisty straightened up rigidly, confident in her statement. The hair on the back of her neck stood up. "Oh yes, indeed I did see who attacked me."

Chapter 34
A Special Road Trip

Clisty handed the car keys to Jake as they went out a side door of the police station to a small parking lot. "You drive and I'll rest like I said I was going to do."

"I'll be happy to drive. Just one problem … I don't know where you want to go. And … I don't know which car belongs to BNN." He looked around the lot and shielded his eyes from the sun that was now clearing some of the lower buildings of the city. It was still morning, 9:45.

"Well …" Clisty mused, "Rodriguez said it's a dark blue Subaru Outback." She looked up and down the front row of cars and stopped at the third vehicle from the left. "That might be it. Click the remote door opener. If it works, that's it."

"Yup," Jake said with satisfaction when the car responded back to the click command. They approached the car and got in. When pressing the button to start the engine, they just sat for a minute. "Okay, Babe, at a minimum, I need to know which way to turn when I pull out of the parking lot."

"Okay," she agreed. "We need to go north, whichever way that is. I'm afraid I'm directionally challenged."

"North?" he smiled as he started the car.

Clisty was hesitant to explain the next part. She knew she had taken her relationship with Jake into her own hands without talking to him about it. "I did some research the night before we left Fort Wayne. We're going to follow NY-9A N and I-95 N to Arch Street in Greenwich, Connecticut. We'll take exit 3 from I-95 N." She winced as she wondered if Jake would be as enthusiastic about her plan as she was.

"We can do that," Jake said as he raised his eyebrows and chuckled. "Is this a mystery trip of some kind?"

"Sort of," Clisty admitted as she shifted around uncomfortably in her seat. As the sun streamed through her side window and warmed her face, she began to relax. "Okay …" she sighed deeply, "we're going to 101 Field Point Road in Greenwich, Connecticut."

Jake threw his head back and laughed, then lowered it again, leading in a mockingly serious posture. "Is that the home of your first husband?"

"No," she teased as she glanced at the passing street signs. "He lives in Kansas City with his other family."

"Oh, right. I forgot," he pretended.

Clisty fumbled in her purse for a tissue and used it to blot her eyes. Turning away, she watched the city pass by outside the window.

"Babe," he reached for her and patted her knee. "What's wrong? Do you want to go back to the hotel and sleep? Are you too tired?"

"Yes, I admit I'm tired. But, no, I don't want to go back," she whispered.

"Honey, you're crying. I feel like I'm pushing you."

"You can't push me when you don't know where we're going. No, Gunny … I'm afraid," she admitted as she blew her nose.

"Of course you are. You were attacked less than ten hours ago, Sweetheart." He rubbed her knee and lowered his voice. "Maybe we should go back so you can still be checked out at the E.R."

"No," she stated emphatically. "I'm not afraid of Kevin Wintergardner. He's in jail. I'm afraid of what you will think."

"What!" he gasped. "That's not you, Clisty. First of all, you don't care what anyone thinks about you. You are your own person. But … you're worried about me? The man who saved you last night? I'm the man who loves you." He slammed on the brakes as the car in front of him slowed to a stop while Jake was absorbed in Clisty's emotions.

"I'm making a mess of this," she stammered, shaking her head. "And, I wanted this to be so beautiful."

"Wait, I don't know what's going on, but … let's begin again," Jake said softly, his eyes gleaming with the adventure of it all. "Good morning, Babe. We fly out at 4 PM. Do you have anything planned for the day?"

"Yes," she squealed, laughing and crying at the same time. She held her breath and blurted out, "We're getting married today!"

"What? How?" he nearly giggled. "Where?" he spluttered.

"In Greenwich, Jake. In the state of New York there is a twenty-four hour waiting period after you obtain your license. But, in Connecticut there is no waiting period at all. We would get our license immediately after we apply for it. There is no residence requirement, and no blood tests are necessary. So … if you still want to marry me, we can do it … today." She was embarrassed and threw both hands to her face, spitting out rapidly. "Or … the license is good in Connecticut for sixth-five days."

"Oh, you foolish woman!" Jake exclaimed with gusto. "Sixty-five minutes is too long to wait." Jake was nearly bouncing up and down in the car as he drove.

Clisty put both hands to her chest. "Oh, thank goodness!"

"We get the license on Field Point Road … right?" Jake guessed. "I've got it, 101 Field Point Road."

"Oh, you are a great investigator, Sergeant Davis," she said as she laughed.

"Where do we have the marriage performed?" Jake asked, his voice pitched nearly a half octave higher.

"Most ministers want to counsel a couple for several weeks before marriage. I'd like to get married in a church but I'm afraid that won't be possible." She sighed deeply. "We could get married by a Justice of the Peace and éw our

243

vows in Indiana with a clergy person when we're ready to go public with the marriage."

"You have really thought this through." Jake's pitch rose, with a generous amount of admiration in his voice. "Even your dress is perfect."

"I hope so," she sighed deeply. "Somehow, I want to get some pictures." With shaking fingers, she smoothed the gorgeous Chantilly white lace over-laying a champagne satin dress. Street length and capped sleeve, to others it might have looked like an attempt to rush summer, rather than an informal wedding dress. She had slipped the cropped mauve leather jacket on top for the taping at the precinct and left it on when she went into the police station to give her deposition.

"I wondered why you had on such great perfume," Jake whispered. "I'm glad it wasn't the thought of seeing Rodriguez again that made you think that woody, earthy smelling perfume would be the perfect scent to wear today," Jake teased as he put his hand on her knee.

"Rodriguez?" she over dramatized a denial. "Who's he?"

They laughed and settled in for the remainder of their tip. It was early enough in the day and late enough in the morning for them to get through city traffic in good time. Clisty had calculated it would take less than an hour to get there, specifically fifty-seven minutes. On her computer, Greenwich appeared to be less than five miles inside the Connecticut line. She clung to Jake's hand most of the way.

Chapter 35
Promises Made

"Uh ... 97, 99, 101—here it is Jake, 101 Field Point Road," she pointed. Clisty vacillated between blocking giddy laughter and holding back hysterical tears to the point the mixed emotions made her rattle inside. After she and Jake arrived, she didn't know whether to laugh or cry or scream at the top of her voice. She chose a peaceful silence. The sky was robin-egg blue, the grass was spring-green, and sunny yellow tulips were flowering in the beds near the large building. It couldn't have been more perfect.

Jake parked the car in the lot to the side of the building. Walking in, Clisty held Jake's hand tightly until she lost a little of the feeling in her fingers. Was there anyone who would recognize her and spoil her day? Hoping not, she wore sunglasses. Before getting out of the car, she added a white lace-covered baseball style cap with scattered sequins to her outfit.

Once inside the building, they got in line behind a young couple who appeared to be from farther south than Indiana.

"Howdy," the prospective groom began. "We just blew into town and want to get hitched."

"You drove all the way from ... where?" the clerk asked with a little smile on her face.

"Well now, today, we drove from New York City. We're here on a senior class trip," the soon-to-be-bride bubbled over.

"Your age?"

"We're both eighteen," they giggled in harmony. "We each have our driver's license to prove it."

"Take the form over to that table and fill it out," the clerk droned as she pointed to the blond colored, high-gloss wooden table behind them. "You'll need a pen."

Jake turned his head away from the high schoolers. "Not a crayon," he whispered. Then he added again in hushed tones, "Take the form over to where you see the stack of coloring books."

Clisty laughed and jabbed Jake lightly in the ribs. "Be good, Gunny. Don't you remember being that age?"

"Yes, I do," Jake said with a wink. "Yesterday, I think."

Now it was Clisty and Jake's turn as they stepped up to the clerk. "We'd like a marriage license," he told the woman.

"Fill out the form over there," the clerk motioned toward the table. "Bring it back here with your thirty dollars." Luckily, she didn't seem to recognize Clisty.

The form had the standard items: name, address, birthplace, mother's and father's names, number of marriages, Social Security Number, and a signature line at the bottom. Once completed, Clisty and Jake took the form back up to the clerk and paid their fee.

It all seemed so business-like to Clisty. To her, it was more like the company contract she recently signed with the network than a plan to get married.

All was done and filed when Clisty bounced down the City Hall steps, nearly skipping, as she and Jake moved toward the car. With their license in hand, they set out to find someone to perform the service.

"The clerk said there's a retired judge who still performs marriages two streets over," Jake twisted back and forth along the sidewalk, walking with Clisty, then walking backwards for a few steps.

"Okay ... but first, drive down a few of these streets for two or three blocks. Let's look for a church," Clisty said as she waved the license in the air. "I know it's a long shot, but I'm willing to take it if you are."

"Whatever you want," Jake offered. "No, I take that back. I guess I'll have to practice the standard phrase … *yes, dear.*" He looked at his watch and frowned. "It's almost noon and our plane leaves at 4 PM. An hour back to New York, grab our bags, time to get to the airport in order to be there an hour or two before our flight leaves. It'll be close."

They hopped in the car and buckled up. As they drove down a side street, overhanging leafy tree branches enhanced their path, like a wedding arch in a cathedral. A few blocks down, Clisty saw a sign at the side of the road. Both of them held their breaths as they wound along a narrow street past Victorian-style two-story homes. There, on the left side of the street was a small white frame church that couldn't have included more than a sanctuary on the first floor. A man in his late sixties locked the door and started down the steps.

"Is the pastor still in there?" Jake asked.

"No," the man responded with a wry smile. "He's standing here on the steps." He laughed and then mellowed. "What can I do for you?"

Clisty thought her heart would catch in her throat and choke her. The pastor looked like a nice man but she didn't think he looked young enough to step out of his life-time protocol. How could he be flexible enough to go against the habits of his ministry and marry a couple he just met? "We want to get married … now."

"My, my, you're in a hurry." He put the key back in the lock and turned it. "Well, come on in … let's talk about it."

Clisty slipped her arm through Jake's as they entered the sweet pre-sesquicentennial church. Royal blue carpet stretched from the entrance up to the altar. Crown moldings that looked like cherry wood to Clisty, anchored the walls to the ceiling. The craftsman who trimmed out the room had repeated the same hardwood in the elegantly crafted pulpit and lectern. To Clisty, it was a perfect setting, on a perfect day.

"I'm Pastor John Albertson," he began as he motioned for Clisty and Jake to sit down on the front pew. "And, you want to get married ... today. Why today, Clisty?"

"You recognize me?" she asked as her steely posture wilted. "We didn't want anyone to know we're getting married. It's just for us."

"Why just you two?" the pastor asked, his voice mellow. "Don't you have family and friends? How will you keep this a secret?"

"We won't have to keep it quiet for too long. Just for a while, Pastor," Jake explained. "Clisty's new boss expressed pleasure that she isn't married with the possibility of time off right away to start a family, just as the new show is starting. He certainly didn't say she couldn't get married. Legally, he couldn't do that."

Clisty added, "But, I reminded him I wasn't married and probably wouldn't marry in the near future."

"We're here in New York to wrap up the first segment of Clisty's Heartland stories," Jake explained.

"The Walking Buddy," Pastor John confirmed. "I can't wait to get one for my father."

"You know the story?" Clisty asked. "I'll talk to Karl Kramer about one for your dad."

Pastor John smiled and listened intently.

Clisty leaned toward Jake. "I am so sorry we are rushing you, Pastor. We're not rushing this marriage at all ... just the ceremony." She looked down at her fingernails. "I was attacked in my hotel room last night."

Jake frowned, his face drawn. "I can't protect her from the next room, or down the hall," Jake said as he put his arm around her. "Besides, I love this woman."

"I can't just live with someone, Pastor, not even Jake," she spoke with certainty. "I had a traumatic experience when I was nine-years-old. Someone kidnapped my best friend ..."

"Faith Sterling," the minister joined in. "I read that in your blog." He blushed, "I'm a Crime Beat fan."

Clisty gasped, "Yes! He snatched me too, but I got away. I didn't trust men for a very long time. I know Jake is worthy of my trust. I want us to make promises to each other before God. It's important to me."

"Then, I think you should get married," Pastor John concluded. "Do you have a license?"

"Right here," Clisty said as she waved the document in her hand.

"Well, if I have questions later, I certainly know where to find you … every Tuesday evening," John said as he brushed his hands on his jeans. "I should wash my hands first. I've been installing light bulbs."

"You're perfect," Clisty protested lightly. "Just make sure we have your contact information. I want to always know who married us. Plus, I want to make sure your father gets a Walking Buddy."

Pastor John pulled his billfold from his hip pocket and fished out a business card. "Here you are, in case you want a do-over."

Clisty put the card in her purse and put the bag on the front pew. Taking off her jacket, she folded it carefully and placed it on top of her purse along with her hat. When she looked down at her dress and early summer white sandals, she felt like a real bride. That thrilled her all the way down to the polish on her toenails.

The three of them laughed as Pastor John positioned them in front of the altar. "If you have your cell phone with you, we can get a couple of selfies." Then he smiled. "What am I saying? Of course you have your cell phones. You're under forty-five years old."

"Will your denomination object if you perform a quick wedding?" Clisty asked.

"This is a confidential service, remember. I'm very willing to keep your private business private." He straightened a necktie that dangled around his neck. "Do you have rings?"

"Oh, Jake," Clisty sighed. "He can't bless the rings."

"Yes, he can," Jake corrected with a loving smile. He dug deep into his pocket and pulled out something wrapped in white tissue paper. "Remember, we talked about picking out gold bands to use in the ceremony. If you want to use it, I have my grandmother's plain gold band … and Grandpa's for me. I was going to have yours fitted with a bail and a small cross inside so you can wear it as a necklace. Then, I thought, how would you get the ring on during the ceremony? So, I bought the gold bail from which I'll hang the band and this small cross." He turned the small gold and silver cross with a heart at the center over in his hand. "When I can get some tools, I'll secure the bail. It will be a unique piece of jewelry to wear on this gold chain." He stroked her cheek. "The cross swings free and isn't soldered to the ring. The whole thing represents eternal love, free to be the person God created you to be."

"Oh Jake," Clisty sighed with tears in her eyes. "It is beautiful. What an honor to wear your grandmother's ring. And … your ring?" she asked. "You said you have your grandfather's ring, too?"

"Right here." With his hand deep in his pocket, he pulled out another small package. "I've been carrying these rings around for more than a week, since we started talking about getting married."

Jake folded back the piece of tissue that covered it and revealed a similar gold ring and a money clip. "When we get back home, I'll have it attached to the clip and carry it in my pocket. I'll see it every time I get money out to pay for something," he said as he hugged her.

"You two are amazing," Pastor John marveled. "I've only known you a few minutes and already see that you want to honor each other as much or more than others I've done pre-marital counseling with for six weeks. And … since I have been working here in the sanctuary," he smiled triumphantly, "I happen to have some tools that will close the bail and Clisty can wear it right away."

"That's great," Jake said as he patted the pastor on the shoulder. "In Fort Wayne, we'll take it in and have the bail gold soldered to make sure it's safe."

"It couldn't be more perfect," she whispered. "I wonder though, Jake, if you put your ring on a bail and attached it to that little loop on the top of the money clip—" Clisty pointed to the small loop in the deer stag emblem on the clip. "You can wear your grandpa's ring as your own when we announce our marriage, rather than having it permanently attached to the clip."

"Clisty, that's perfect," Jake agreed as he reached over and kissed her cheek.

Pastor John smiled and asked, "Have you by chance written your own vows already, too?"

Jake spoke up immediately. "Not written, but I've thought about them every day for weeks."

"Great, then let's begin," the Pastor said. "Dearly beloved of God, we are gathered here because this couple loves you enough to want you to be part of their lives and home from the very beginning." He turned his eyes to Jake and glanced down at the marriage license. "Jackson Allen Davis, do you take Clisty Alverta Sinclair as your wife?"

"I certainly do take Clisty as my wife. I promise to be loyal to you, to love you, even when times are tough or your job takes you away for a while. I promise never to ask you to choose between me and who God has called you to be. I know you may walk into danger at times; and, I will not stop you. I will stand between you and any threat that may come your way. You are your own person, not mine. I am just privileged to walk beside you through life, not steps ahead or trailing behind." He looked at the pastor and nodded.

"Clisty Alverta Sinclair, do you take Jackson Allen Davis as your husband?"

"Indeed I do, Pastor," she grinned broadly. "Jake, I promise to be only yours, to hold you in my heart and mind, even when we're apart. I know your job can be dangerous sometimes, but I trust you to always stay within the outstretched hand of God. You too are your own person, not mine to possess. I am thrilled to have you walk beside me, not make me run to keep up or to lag behind. I have loved you since the first day I saw you and am thrilled to be your wife, even if I didn't know your first name is Jackson," she chuckled. "No one else need know we are married. It is more than enough that we know for now and that God knows."

"Beautiful," John spoke reverently. "May I have the rings, Jake?" the pastor nearly whispered.

Jake placed the soon-to-be-modified gold wedding bands in John's hand and smiled lovingly at Clisty.

"Father, God," John began, "I ask that these symbols of their marriage be blessed." He handed the ring to Jake. "Repeat after me, 'With this ring I thee wed.'" As Jake slipped the ring on Clisty's finger, the pastor paused for a moment and added, "I hope the use of *thee* fits with your modern notions."

"I love it," Clisty's shoulders rose in joy.

"Okay, Clisty, repeat after me. 'With this ring, I thee wed.'"

Clisty looked at Jake then at the old warn ring as she said the words that made her Mrs. Jake Davis.

"I now pronounce you Mr. and Mrs. Jackson ... Jake Davis. You may kiss the bride," Pastor John concluded as he beamed.

Jake folded Clisty in his arms, kissing her tenderly. Two cell phones flew into the air above the couple, then click, click and pictures became stored in private files. Jake pulled some money from his billfold and offered it to John.

"I will not take a dime for this wedding," Pastor John refused with empty palms thrust up in determination. "This has been the highlight of my day, actually many days. May the Lord bless you two as you start this secret life together." He patted them both on the back. "Send me a message when you decide to let the rest of the world in on it. I have bragging rights you know. I want a picture when you take them out of the vault." Then he paused and walked over to the open tool box. "I have some needle-nose pliers in here for that necklace bale."

"Oh, wonderful," Clisty said as her joy bubbled over.

Jake pulled the silver cross from his pocket, the thin gold chain, and small gold bale. He smiled at Clisty and removed the wedding ring he had just placed on her finger. Next, he looped the bale around the gold band and through the tiny hole at the top of the cross, and closed the link with the needle-nose pliers John offered. The slim chain slipped easily through the bale. Jake fastened the "wedding necklace" behind her neck and kissed her cheek. "It is beautiful," he whispered.

"It is lovely, my dear," Pastor John said as he smiled.

"Don't know why, but I bought two bails. I guess I figured I'd lose one. I usually do."

Clisty nodded, "Daddy always says, 'One to use; one to lose.'"

Jake quickly looped the other bail around the deer's neck where the head stood proud of the body on the top of the money clip. After he slipped his ring onto the loop, he pinched the bail tightly and completed the job. Handing the pliers back to Pastor John, Jake slipped the money clip into his pocket.

"If you have a secure phone, take a picture with us. Then, post it later," Clisty offered as she repositioned the pendant on the chain, making sure it hung perfectly straight. With her hand slipped around Jake's back, she stood in the middle with John Albertson beside her and Jake on the other side, snapping a selfie.

They used the lectern to fill out the papers. John signed them and put them in the provided envelope. "Mail them here in town or in New York. It doesn't matter. Just don't forget."

Clisty whispered as her voice cracked. "I'll not forget any of this. We are blessed by your kindness and generous spirit." She reached up and kissed Pastor John's cheek. With that, the newly married couple hurried back out into the same beautiful day, with an entirely new way of encountering life, as two made one.

Chapter 36
Going Home Together Alone

Later that afternoon, when Clisty and Jake hurried into the hotel, she found a note from Becca left at the hotel's front desk.

> "Clisty — I haven't seen you this afternoon.
> Knocked on your door. No answer. Hope
> you're okay. It's 2 PM. Griff and I will meet
> you in the concourse at the airport. Don't
> want to miss the flight. Jason is ready for me
> to come home, and I am more than ready to be
> there."

Clisty smiled and held the note to her chest. Now, she too had someone who would be waiting for her to come home.

Neither she nor Jake had packed before they left the hotel that morning. Clisty did remember to request permission to bump their check-out time back to 6 PM given the events of the night before. After all, Kevin had attacked her just twelve hours ago, in their hotel. They had to accept some responsibility.

"Hurry," Jake said as they each opened their hotel room doors. He kissed her on the forehead and laughed. "Funny, the term *wedding day* has never conjured up images of going to separate hotel rooms to pack, hurrying off to the airport, and flying for several hours."

"Believe me, it wasn't my fantasy either," she said as she blew him a kiss. "Not in my wildest dreams. Thank goodness we already dropped the car off to Nicole. It's almost 2:30. We'll have to hurry. Check out of the hotel on your TV screen."

255

"Right on all of the above," he grinned.

They darted into their respective rooms and began a rough imitation of folding clothes for packing. In a few minutes, Jake popped his head in Clisty's room through the adjoining door.

"Ready?" Clisty asked. "I have just a few more things."

"I am," he said as he looked at himself in the mirror. Jake had changed into Levis and a light-weight knit, V-neck sweater, and athletic shoes.

"Ready," she dittoed, then re-checked Jake's travel attire. "Fiddle, you changed your clothes and chose such a good idea." She grabbed jeans from her open suitcase and slipped them on under her dress. "Guess I don't have to be so modest," she said with a coy smile. Pulling the dress over her head, she replaced it with a pink long-sleeved T-shirt and her new jacket, and then slipped on her white crew socks and Skechers. "Did we have lunch today?" she asked as she gazed toward the ceiling.

"No, we didn't," he announced with certainty. "My stomach will testify to that."

Clisty folded the special Champaign colored dress and pressed it into the suitcase. "Food? There is a meal on the flight but I don't know how big that will be. It may be a small pack of crackers."

Jake shook his head. "Wow ... maybe there will be enough time to get a sandwich or something in the airport after we check in."

"Maybe, but I need protein not sugar," Clisty moaned. "Every doughnut and candy bar will scream at me from the hallway kiosks as we pass."

"And, I need sugar," Jake winked as they pulled their luggage and carry-on cases out the door. "Jack and Mrs. Sprat again. This time, the Sprats have reversed their eating preferences."

To their amazement, there was an airport shuttle waiting just outside the huge revolving doors past the lobby.

After their bags were stowed, they jumped on the mini-bus and slumped down into a puddle-couple in the first available bench seat. Jake put his arm around Clisty, ever aware of appearances and who might see and recognize his bride with a new and unique pendant hanging from a chain.

At the airport, they checked in, went through TSA screening and nearly ran down the hall to their gate. It was 3:10 PM when they got to the waiting area.

"Thank goodness," Becca said as she threw her arms open to Clisty. "I was so worried. Where have you two been?"

"Thanks for caring, but I'm fine," Clisty gasped as she sat down and tried to catch her breath. "I rested and then we did a little sightseeing. We didn't eat lunch. I am so hungry, I'm wobbly."

"There's juice at the kiosk right out there in the hall," Becca stated as she patted Griff on the back. "Run and get her some orange juice." To Clisty she clarified, "Orange okay?"

"Yes," Clisty called after him as Griff jumped up. "Get one for Jake too, please. We'll pay you later."

Becca waved her hand as Griff dashed off. "Don't worry about it. If you don't stay healthy, we won't have jobs."

Clisty threw her head back and laughed. "Well, there's that. So, the orange juice is really an insurance policy for job security."

"We're going to be close on time, Clisty," Becca reminded her. "The broadcast of the forum is tomorrow night. I can splice in the New York images but you'll still have to record your wrap up at the end. I know you'll want to sleep in. I'll write the closing. You can film it about 9 tomorrow morning and I'll send it to the network." She watched Clisty and asked. "Is 9 AM okay? Griff and I can come over to your place and you can film it there."

"Nine is awful early," Clisty spoke up, trying hard not to look at Jake. She was afraid she would burst out laughing. "Let's make it at least 10 AM." In her mind she ran over whether Jake would be out of her apartment and at his desk at the police station by 10 AM.

"I have to have time to slip over and see Mom and Dad's studio. I promised her before we went to New York." Clisty looked out at the incoming planes. When her cell rang, she paused.

"Hi, Mom," she said as she looked around the group and nodded. "I was just talking about your studio." She listened and added, "I'm going to put you on speaker."

"Hi, everyone," Carol spoke excitedly to the whole group."

"You sound excited," Clisty noticed. "What's up?"

"Dad and I have been doing some planning."

"Hi, Clisty," Al chimed in. "Mom put her phone on speaker, too."

"Great. Good to hear your voice, Dad."

"We've been talking about having an *Arts Workshop* before school starts, for ages six to whatever. I know how busy you all are, but I hope you will have time to teach writing skills. We won't throw pottery this time, but Jake, if you're free you can supervise the painting of bisque pieces and then I'd bring them home to pop them in the kiln so the pieces can be fired."

"That is something I can do," Jake added. "You know what … I would have fun painting a piece, too."

"Great," Carol agreed. "Griff, are you there?" she asked.

"Yep," he spoke fluently as he returned with the juice in hand.

"Would you teach photography?"

"Oh, wow, yes," he confirmed. "I would love to teach it. Will everyone have their own camera?" He handed a bottle to Clisty, then Jake.

"We would have to require that they supply their own. We can't supply cameras. Any type of model we could suggest?"

"We can talk about that when we get back," Griff bubbled. "Even cell phones have pretty good cameras these days."

"Who are you, Griff?" Becca asked. "Oh man of few words."

"Good to hear your voice, Becca," Carol said with a smile in her voice. "You and Clisty took ballet for years. I was wondering if you could teach interpretive dance."

"Carol, that sounds like fun."

"Great." Jake rubbed his hands together as if he couldn't wait to get his hands on a sandwich or T-bone steak.

"I'll let you go for now. Drop by if you can, Clisty. Or, we can talk on the phone."

"I'll talk to Nicole to see if there is any way our schedule can be adjusted so we can set a date for the *Arts Workshop.* These interviews aren't emergencies." Clisty looked at the team and cringed. "Well, not usually." Then, she realized she hadn't called her parents following last night's attack. "When I get home, we also need to talk about a little dust-up I had last evening. Don't let the news scare you. They need fresh meat for their 24/7 news programs every day. I am fine. Catch my blog post."

"Are you sure?" Carol asked. "No, never mind. I've started a new plan. I won't pay any attention to what the newscasters have to say … sorry Becca. I'm just going to trust God and wait to get the truth from you. Okay, bye, Honey," Carol sang out and disconnected.

Clisty put her phone in her purse and smiled at the group. "I like it. Besides, the workshop will make a great vacation at home."

Becca smiled. "I like the way Carol's going to handle the media." Back on topic, she added, "The Arts Workshop sounds like my kind of fun. Jason can help, too." Then, she turned back to Clisty. "Ten AM tomorrow," Becca agreed. "Okay, that'll work. It'll be close but at the pace of this show, I have a feeling we'll have to get used to tight deadlines." She studied Clisty up and down, and then looked at Jake with squinted eyes. "What sites did you two see?"

Jake looked over at Clisty and grinned. "Oh, it didn't matter to us. After last night, it was just good to be able to see *any* sites."

Griff gestured toward the orange juice he had retrieved. "Drink up. We'll board soon."

With the juice in her hand she was glad to take the focus off where she and Jake had been. She was too tired to come up with a plausible story. She shuddered as she thought of how she might slip up.

"What a beautiful necklace," Becca admired as she picked up the ring and cross that hung around Clisty's neck. "It's so unusual."

"Thank you," Clisty paused. "That was one of the stores we popped into. I don't even remember what street it was on. But, the salesman was so convincing," she said as she smiled at Jake. "I couldn't resist him ... but then I didn't try."

"Wow," Becca fanned herself with her airplane ticket. "Weren't you jealous?" she asked Jake.

"No," he said as he finished his juice. "I loved the design and wanted her to have it."

"So, you bought it for her?" Becca asked, seeming to try to put all the pieces together.

"I sure did," he agreed.

Breaking the secret moment, the announcer called over the speaker, "First class to Fort Wayne, Indiana will board now."

Clisty's cell rang at the same time she heard the boarding call. "Clisty Sinclair here," she answered. "Yes, okay ... already? Great."

"Already what?" Becca asked as she gathered up her things.

"It was Nicole. She has a new assignment for us. We'll be going to our next location very soon. She'll share the details tomorrow."

"That was fast," Jake offered.

"It is a weekly show," Clisty reminded them. "There will be thirty-one shows between September and May. We'll not be on every weekly show but we'll be working on a new show production every week for those that require more time. Then, we get to rest during part of the summer. The shows that take more visits and investigation, like the Kramers' story, we will work on through the summer. We'll get four weeks off for actual vacation."

"That sounds good to me," Becca added. "Part of that work will be done at home." Then her eyes brightened. "I still think you should consider a house with a studio in it. Everything could be organized just the way you like it."

Clisty smiled. "That sounds good to me. I'll look into it."

Jake took the empty juice bottle from Clisty as soon as she finished the last swallow and threw them in the trash. "Come on Babe," he said as he squeezed her hand. "It's time to go home."

"With our layover, it will be after nine when we get to Fort Wayne," Becca yawned and stretched. "This has been some weekend. Clisty, you were even up half the night. I'll bet you'll get home just in time to fall into bed."

"I'll bet you're right," Clisty answered as she took Jake's arm and flipped it over her shoulder, snuggling up as close to him as she could. "I'll write my blog during the layover this evening. It may not be a long post, but my readers need to know what's happening. Then, I can get to bed when I get home. Right Jake?" she asked with a secret smile.

Jake smiled.

Crime Beat

✸

From the Heartland

4:30 PM

Good late afternoon, my friends. So much has happened in such a short length of time. Hold on, we're going to run through it all. This blogger doesn't want anything left out, but I'll have to mask a few facts for safety and legal reasons. Here we go.

OUT OF THE DARKNESS

BNN has informed everyone of last night's terrifying experience for this blogger. In order to protect the prosecution's case, full discussion cannot happen at this time. Last evening, this blogger taped a town-hall forum with the inventors of the Walking Buddy and other interested parties. The hour ran late after another necessary interview kept us on the road. Before we returned, someone entered my hotel room in New York and hid in the closet. During the night, the assailant slipped out of the closet and attacked this blogger with intent to kill. The security personnel assigned to our team heard the fight and threw off the attacker. Be sure to let others know that this blogger is fine, just exhausted.

Share

THE MYSTERY WITHIN THE JOY

This blogger would like to thank those of you who posted comments on the blog, placed phone calls, and wrote emails with evidence in the Walking Buddy case. Your involvement pressured the perpetrator to reveal his hand. Caught attacking this blogger, he is in jail. Together, we brought a swift end to this case. My friends, there is nothing wrong with the Walking Buddy. It was the deeds of the one who tried to cover his own evil motives, by sabotaging the integrity of the Buddy and attacking those who created it, that was the problem. None of what he did had anything to do with the Buddy.

Be sure to tune in to the segment on the Walking Buddy when it airs, to see the truth of this case. It is early in the prosecution. At this time, his capture last evening is stage one. Again, thank you.

Share

Other Joys

This blogger has not vacationed in a long time. Thank you to those who commented on all of the exciting sites of New York and the beautiful connecting state of Connecticut. Believe me, all of the things I have experienced have checked off many items on my to-do list. Loved it all.

SEE YOU AT THE BOOKSTORE

The book signing is coming up. Come in and get your copy of *The Lottery Looser*. I'll be happy to sign your copy. This is the beginning of a completely new way of life for this blogger, both professionally and personally. I will be excited to continue to see you all at book signings and around Fort Wayne. We will also connect most evenings on this site as we sort out mysteries from the heartland. I look forward to your feedback as we launch into this new reporting of positive news, about ordinary people, doing extraordinary things, to benefit others. Many blessings to all of you.

Share   *Contact: clistysynclair@ebox.com*

Recipe:
Essey's Sour Cream Coffee Cake

Cream together:　　1 cup butter or margarine with
　　　　　　　　　　2 cups sugar
Add:　　　　　　　 2 eggs, one at a time – beating well
　　　　　　　　　　after each
Turn mixer to lowest speed:
Add:　　　　　　　 1 small container of sour cream
　　　　　　　　　　½ teaspoon vanilla
Mix together and fold in on low speed:
　　　　　　　　　　2 cups flour
　　　　　　　　　　1 teaspoon baking powder
　　　　　　　　　　¼ teaspoon salt
Grease and flour Bundt or tube pan, (or use baking spray):
　　　　　　　　　　Spoon half of the batter into the pan
Mix well and sprinkle with largest part of this:
　　　　　　　　　　½ cup chopped pecans
　　　　　　　　　　½ teaspoon cinnamon
　　　　　　　　　　2 teaspoons sugar
Spoon remaining batter on top and sprinkle remainder of
cinnamon topping over all.
Bake at 350⁰　　　 55 to 60 minutes or until brown and
　　　　　　　　　　firm to touch
Cool in pan before removing
Keeps well

About the Author

Doris Gaines Rapp — Novelist, Psychologist, Catalyst

After moving nineteen times, Doris Gaines Rapp now writes from home. Relocating frequently left her feeling uprooted and homesick for many years. She now visits the people and places she loves in the characters and scenes within her novels. She relives the experiences in her life through the images in her mind, then transfers those sights and sounds into words on paper. As a psychologist, she understands people, their motives and dreams, and therefore is able to delve more deeply into the characters in her books. As a motivational speaker, she is a catalyst for change.

Doris' love of writing began as a child. Since retiring as a psychologist, she reclaimed her joy of creating word pictures by writing ten novels.

Dr. Rapp recently received the Marquis Who's Who Lifetime Achievement Award. She and her husband, Pastor Bill, hope to travel when he retires … someday … for the fourth time.

Rapp and her husband, live in Indiana.

Other Books by Doris Gaines Rapp

<u>Novels</u>:
Tucker McBride
Escape from the Belfry
Escape from the Shadows
News at Eleven – A Novel (Prequel to Just in Time)
Length of Days – The Age of Silence (1st in the trilogy)
Length of Days – Beyond the Valley of the Keepers (2nd in
        the trilogy)
Length of Days – Search for Freedom (3rd in the trilogy)
Hiawassee – Child of the Meadow
Smoke from Distant Fires

<u>Children's Picture Book:</u>
Shyloe and the Mayor
Lincoln's Christmas Mouse

<u>Collection:</u>
Christmas Feathers, one of eight short stories by eight
        authors in a collection titled, Christmases Past

<u>Non-Fiction:</u>
Prayer Therapy of Jesus
Promote Yourself
Waiting for Jesus in a Can't Wait World – Advent 2014

<u>Watch for:</u>
Tucker McBride's Many Lives – available in late 2020

<u>Internet Presence</u>
Facebook: Doris Gaines Rapp – Author Page

Website:	www.dorisgainesrapp.com
Blog:	https://www.dorisgainesrappphd.blogspot.com
Blog - old:	http://prayertherapyrapp.blogspot.com
Blog – new:	http://prayertherapyofjesus.blogspot.com
Blog:	www.tuckermcbrideintheclassroom.com

www.ingramcontent.com/pod-product-compliance
Lightning Source LLC
Chambersburg PA
CBHW061024120726
47910CB00006B/2094